The Care

and

Feeding

of

Exotic Pets

THE CARE
AND
FEEDING
OF
EXOTIC PETS

DIANA WAGMAN

PUBLISHING

BROOKLYN, NEW YORK

Printed in the United States of America
10 9 8 7 6 5 4 3 2 1

Ig Publishing
392 Clinton Avenue
Brooklyn, NY 11238
www.igpub.com

Library of Congress Cataloging-in-Publication Data

Wagman, Diana.
 The care & feeding of exotic pets / Diana Wagman.
   p. cm.
 ISBN 978-1-935439-64-6
 1. Divorced women--Fiction. 2. Mothers and daughters--Fiction.
3. Abduction--Fiction. 4. Iguanas as pets--Fiction. 5. Victims of
violent crimes--Fiction. 6. Los Angeles (Calif.)--Fiction. 7. Psycho-
logical fiction. I. Title. II. Title: Care and feeding of exotic pets.
 PS3573.A359C37 2012
 813'.54--dc22
                                            2012025277

For Tod,
always

"We strongly oppose keeping wild animals as pets. This principle applies to both native and nonnative species, whether caught in the wild or bred in captivity."

—The Humane Society of the United States

1.

The same old sun was shining. The same old sky was blue and cloudless, vacant as a starlet's smile. Los Angeles in November was the same as Los Angeles in April or August, was the same as Los Angeles whenever Winnie Parker happened to look out her window. The palm trees were always green. The temperature was always moderate. The cars were always driving by.

Same old dog scratching to go out. Winnie stood in front of her washer and dryer and contemplated the laundry. Dirty clothes were so elemental, so primal. A red stain on that T-shirt; something crusty on the front of those jeans. Simple scientific testing could reveal sexual partners, dinner choices, lapses in personal hygiene. If you really wanted to know a person, Winnie thought, just look at his or her laundry. If she ever had a date again, if she ever went home with a man, she would sneak a look in his laundry basket. She sighed at her own undone heap. She could throw in a load right now and then come home after her tennis lesson and put it in the dryer, but her arms felt heavy, her bare feet fused with the floor. In the kitchen, NPR reported the latest disaster. She wanted another cup of coffee. She had to wake Lacy. Dress for tennis. Make Lacy's lunch and take her to school. Drop the car off at the shop, get the rental car, go to her tennis lesson, then the grocery store and the drug store and the dry cleaners and stop by work to get that folder she forgot. Pick up Lacy at five-thirty after orchestra.

The dog whined. Winnie let him out the back door and

watched as he went immediately to the wicker chair on the patio and lifted his leg.

"Stop it!"

He finished his business before trotting away.

"Stupid dog."

She knew she shouldn't complain. She was a reasonably attractive thirty-eight-year-old divorced woman. She had a job and she paid her mortgage and she loved her pain in the ass sixteen-year-old daughter. She had a couple of good friends. She read and went to the movies and flossed most nights before bed. There was just no air in her lungs anymore. She was deflated, like an old balloon caught on a fencepost.

She left the laundry undone and went upstairs to wake Lacy. Her room smelled as always of vanilla oil, fruity hair products, and the pungent gunk of teenaged girl. Her favorite stuffed bunny slumped against the wall underneath a taped-up scrap of paper, "Just Say Fuck Off!"

"Time to get up, Sweetpea."

Lacy slept on her stomach on top of the sheet in boxers and T-shirt, legs splayed, one hand flung over the edge of the bed. As if she had been thrown there and abandoned. The multiple piercings in her left ear made Winnie wince. She bent down to smooth a blond curl off her daughter's cheek. Instead she smacked her butt.

"You smell like smoke."

Lacy groaned.

"Have you been smoking again? Cancer. Emphysema. A hole in your throat. Do those words mean anything to you?"

"Mom, for Christ's sake."

"Nobody wants to kiss an ashtray."

"I don't kiss anybody. And I don't smoke. I told you that. Everybody else smokes."

"Secondhand smoke kills too. Tell them that."

Lacy rolled over. "Five more minutes."

"Now!"

"M-o-m."

The teenage whine was worse than the toddler's.

They fought on the way to school. As usual. About nothing; about everything; the same old everything. Lacy wanted to move in with her father. This morning she shouted that she wanted to be as far from her mother as possible. Winnie felt her heart contract as if Lacy had squeezed it until it couldn't beat anymore. Lacy slammed the car door shut. She sashayed into her whitewashed cinderblock public school, her button-covered backpack bouncing against her back.

Wait, Winnie wanted to call out. Wait! That was the chant going through her head these days: Wait. Not yet. Wait. But it was impossible to tell a child not to grow.

She looked through her windshield. There was new graffiti on the wooden fence, the initials of the local gang. Trash lined the gutter. Winnie watched a gust of wind animate a red foil chip bag. It swelled and collapsed, swelled and collapsed, taking two deep breaths before it spun away and died.

Her cell phone rang. Her ex-husband.

She answered it, "Jonathan."

"Winifred."

Winnie heard Jonathan's young wife, Jessica, in the background. She said something unintelligible, but high pitched and feminine. Winnie could picture the long legs and tiny silk nightie. Lacy said Jessica's boobs were fake, but Winnie thought they were just fresh and unused.

"So, have you decided?" Jonathan said.

"I don't know."

"I have to tell them soon. She can start second semester,

after the holidays, but I have to let them know." When Winnie didn't answer, he continued, "Any new piercings?"

"Not that I've noticed. Of course she could have done her labia."

He grunted. "Don't even joke about it."

Maybe it would be better for Lacy to live with Jonathan. Probably it would be. A large, well-appointed house with two adults in residence and a TV in every room. An expensive private school with a lacrosse field and a ceramics studio and no graffiti or broken toilets or missing textbooks. Next year Lacy would start looking at colleges. She needed to do better, concentrate on her schoolwork. Lately she seemed to be giving up. Winnie had tried so hard to be a good mom, to listen, to pay attention, to be everything her own mother was not, but still Lacy couldn't wait to leave her.

"He's really a great therapist. All the kids see him."

Jonathan was still talking. "Who? Listen, I'm on my way to the car place."

"I said I'd get you a new car."

"I like this one." It was an old battle. It was Jonathan's guilt about leaving her versus her need for him to feel as guilty as possible. They'd bought the Peugeot station wagon when they were still married. He had loved it. Now she loved the wistful expression on his face when she drove it over to his house to drop off Lacy. "You know how I feel about this car."

"Can we do lunch today?" he asked. "Early, 11:30?"

She looked at herself in the rear view mirror. "Not today," she said. "I can't." Not sweaty from tennis, without makeup or a better bra.

"Someplace near you would be fine."

He wasn't listening. She said again, "I'm busy. I can't have lunch today."

Jonathan had also offered to buy her a new house closer to his. Two years ago he found her a condo, Beverly Hills adjacent and much more appropriate for the ex-wife of the host of television's most popular game show. She had said no. She loved her two-bedroom, one bath bungalow in the low-rent part of town. They had lived there together; Lacy had always lived there. None of the windows closed tightly, the living room floor sloped to one corner, but she could afford it all by herself. It was home.

"You'll love this guy—this psychologist. Very hip. Very chill."

"Hey," Winnie said. "I'm losing you." And sighed. Lost so long ago.

"Call me at eleven."

"Okay." She hung up. Same old Jonathan. Same old very chill Jonathan.

The station wagon barely made it into the mechanic's driveway. Thick gray smoke poured from the exhaust. The car shuddered, gave a final kick, and died. She tried, but it would not start again.

"I'm surprised you got here," her mechanic said.

"It's my lucky day."

Moments later she was standing on the sidewalk with her tennis racket, waiting for the van from the car rental agency. A breeze had come up, but in Southern California her thin nylon jacket kept her warm enough. She remembered Novembers growing up in New York City, her wet breath turning to ice in her wool scarf and her toes so cold it made her stomach hurt. A gust lifted her pleated tennis skirt; she got a whiff of old sweat. She had not washed her outfit after last week's lesson. Her legs needed shaving. She pictured stretching out to return a groundstroke and jumping up for an overhead, all with her skirt fluttering. She flexed one foot, then the other and shook her head, feeling her ponytail swish against her neck. She had sworn she would never play tennis again after Jonathan left her, but four years had passed and there was nothing he wouldn't do without her. At least her same old outfit still fit.

She looked down the street hoping to see the van. A black Toyota sedan turned the corner, headed her way. It slowed, went past her, stopped, and reversed to right in front of her. The car was so clean and shiny the passenger door was like a curved funhouse mirror. In its reflection Winnie's legs looked short and wide and her forehead like a billboard. She bent down as the window sunk into the door. The driver had to be Irish, young and skinny with bright red hair and pale eyes, wearing blue jeans and a black leather jacket, a white button down shirt and a tie.

"Are you from Enterprise?" Winnie asked.

"Have you been waiting long?"

"I expected the van."

"It's a very busy day."

He leaned across the seat and opened the door. Winnie saw a penny in the street, almost under the car. It was heads up, a wishing penny. Jonathan had always hated her wishing. She wished on pennies and dandelions, the first star at night, white horses, and the turned up hem of her pants or shirt.

"They never come true," he had said.

"How do you know?" she had joked so long ago. "Maybe I wished for you to be an asshole."

"Get in." The Enterprise driver sounded anxious.

It bothered her, but she left the penny on the road, got in the car and adjusted her tennis bag between her legs.

"Tennis game?"

"Just a lesson. I'm not ready for a game yet."

"Put your racket in back."

She did. He nodded. His thighs were long and thin. His jaw was well defined, his face covered with freckles. His ears were oddly small and paler than the rest of him, like tiny snails curled beneath his almost orange hair. Winnie wondered about the color of the hair on his chest and his legs and other places, then blushed and looked out her window.

"What else do you have to do today?" the driver asked.

"Errands. Nothing. It's my day off."

He turned right and got on the freeway. It was not the usual route.

"Do you have a cell phone?" he asked. "Can I borrow it?"

"Did you forget yours?"

He shrugged.

"Guess it has been a busy day for you." She dug her phone out of her purse and handed it to him. "It's on."

He held it in his hand, playing with the smooth cover. They exited the freeway and headed into a residential neighborhood. The houses were small and unremarkable, the one story stucco boxes common to every Los Angeles suburb, with neat lawns, closed doors, empty driveways. The Halloween decorations had all been put away. One zealot had already put up his Christmas lights. A friend could live here.

She looked up at the flat, no color sky. A cold front was moving in. The palm trees bent in the wind and waved at her. "What is this neighborhood? Is there an Enterprise near here?"

He shook his head. He rolled down his window.

"How long have you been with Enterprise?"

"I'm not with Enterprise."

"You just drive for them?"

There was a sparkle of sweat on his temple as he turned and looked at her. His eyes were the bleached green of dead grass.

"Do I look like I drive for Enterprise?"

He threw her cell phone out the window. The car bounced over a speed bump. Confusion rattled in Winnie's head.

"I need a rental car."

"That's not my department."

"Thank you. Thank you so much. I'll just get out here."

She pulled on the handle, but the door was locked. She tried to lift the button, but it was hiding inside the door, impossible to grip. She searched frantically for some other control.

"Child safety," he said. "You can't get out."

"I have a child."

"Okay, Mom." From his lips it was a curse, as if he had called her bitch or whore or cunt. "Mommy."

Winnie could not breathe. Her hands began to shake. She could not grasp the door handle. He turned right again onto another tree-lined street of small houses, but instead of friendly, these felt haunted by the ghosts of this man's prey. She was only minutes from the mechanic, barely more than a half hour from home, but she could have been in another country.

"I have to go," she said. "They're waiting for me."

"The other tennis moms?"

"My husband."

He snorted. "Where's your ring?"

"I don't wear it for tennis."

"Women like you always wear a ring."

"I… I don't…" She was a terrible liar.

He lifted a hand to the visor and Winnie waited for the knife, gun, rubber hose, but it was a remote control. He hit the button and a garage door opened. He turned into the driveway, coasted into the empty garage. The door dropped shut behind them.

"Mom, I'm home," he said.

He released the door locks. She leapt from the car, ran to the garage door and banged on it with her fists. She screamed.

He got out of the car. "That's enough," he said. "Stop it now."

She yelled, kicked, pummeled the door. Someone had to hear her. He grabbed one flailing arm and pulled her close. Winnie could smell coffee on his breath. She kept on screaming, right in his face.

"HELP!"

He slapped her hard. "I said stop it."

"I want to go home." She began to cry. "Please. Please."

"Think of this as your home." He paused. "For as long as it lasts."

Her knees collapsed and she sank to the cement floor. He tugged her up by her arms, but she let her legs buckle. She wanted to be a dead weight in his hands. He stumbled forward, almost fell and caught himself.

"Stand up," he commanded.

She did not move. He squeezed her upper arms, tighter, harder. She would have bruises, she realized, but would anyone ever see them? Stop it, she told herself. Find the remote for the door. Find it.

"Stand up." He shook her as he spoke through his teeth. "I said, get the fuck up."

"Let go of me and I will."

He dropped her arms and she got up slowly. She pretended to sway as if dizzy and put out one hand to steady herself on the car. She took a step forward. Then suddenly she leapt for the driver's door, opened it and reached somewhere, up toward the visor, anywhere for the remote. He pulled her back and tossed her against the wall.

"Forget it. Whatever you're thinking, forget it."

He grabbed one of her arms and dragged her to the door leading into the house. Winnie struggled. She began to scream again. Let him kill her now. Better than whatever he had in mind for inside. She refused to walk. He was slight; she was stronger than she seemed.

"Help me!"

He dropped her and she fell on her ass on the cement floor and her neck cracked. A hot needle of pain shot up her spine into her head. But she shook her head, rolled to her hands and knees and tried to crawl under the car. Anywhere, anything to get away from him. He grabbed her feet and tugged. She grasped for the tires, the axle, but it was slippery with grease. He pinched her bare calf and she yelped and he slid her out from under the car, rolled her over, and pulled her to sitting.

"We're going inside. Now."

"Why?"

"You'll see."

"I don't want to." She could not stop her tears.

"I'm not going to kill you." He reached in his pocket and pulled out a flat folded knife. It opened with a press of his thumb. The blade was long and partially serrated. "But I will hurt you if I have to. I will."

He did not look at her as he said it. He seemed to be staring at his knife, at his hand holding the dark handle, and then at his other hand circling her wrist.

"I will," he said again.

He was young, younger than Winnie first thought. His skin was as smooth and flawless as Lacy's. Had he grown up setting cats on fire, ripping the wings off butterflies, beating up kids for their lunch money? His fingernails were gnawed to the quick. His cuticles were raw.

"Why are you doing this?" she asked. "Why me?"

"Why did you get in the car?" He pushed the knife toward her belly. "Stand up."

Slowly, she got to her feet. She would go inside. There had to be a phone, window, a front door that did not need a remote to open. He took her arm and pulled her to the door that opened into the house. Hot air whooshed out and engulfed them, so intense Winnie coughed to get her breath. The heat was shocking. The house was on fire. She tried to stop on the threshold, but he dragged her inside.

"It's too hot. I can't breathe."

"Shut up."

He kicked the door shut behind them.

2.

As soon as Lacy stepped into her first period class her cell phone went off, blaring the obscure heavy metal music she chose because it was the most annoying in class, in restaurants, in the movies. Her chemistry teacher, Mr. Bronson, sighed. He put his hands on his funny, womanly hips.

"It's my mom," Lacy lied. "I forgot my homework and she's bringing it."

She ducked out into the hall and answered her phone, breathless, laughing, "What do you want?"

It was the guy, her twenty-five-year-old guy. Again. He would not leave her alone; he called all the time. She had never before been pursued.

"Yes, yes. I just got to school," she said into the phone. "My mother's taking her car to the shop. She dropped me off on the way."

She smiled as he flirted with her. His voice was deep. She had told him she was eighteen—and a senior. She liked older men, or imagined she would.

He asked her about her mother's car—typical man—and she rolled her eyes. She didn't care. "She has a really, really ancient Peugeot. Weird French car." Then she remembered the lies she had told him. "It's very rare—and expensive. One of two in the world." Such bullshit and he bought it every time.

"Are you okay?" he said. "Was last night horrible? Are you bruised?"

She had also told him her mother had hit her with a hairbrush and locked her in her room. Some story about a sexy dress Winnie forbid her to wear, a dress Lacy did not really have and would probably never really wear. "It was okay. Listen, I have to go to class."

"I'll call you right after school. Before orchestra."

"Okay."

She snapped the phone shut and slipped back into the classroom.

"Turn your cell phone off, Ms. Parker." Mr. Bronson did not turn from the board as he spoke.

"I did."

Ten minutes later when her phone started screaming again—this time it was her stupid father—she was the only one who laughed. The rest of the class had seen it before. Mr. Bronson had seen it too many times.

"That's it."

"It must've turned on in my pocket."

"Get out," Mr. Bronson said. "Go to the office."

"You're kidding. C'mon, Mr. B, it was an accident." She appealed to her classmates, but they offered no support. Not a smile, not a nod. She felt her face flush, the sweat blossoming on her forehead. She knew her carefully blown dry hair was beginning to frizz. "Okay. Fine. I turned it off. See? It's off."

"Go."

Lacy waited for Mr. Bronson to change his mind. "This seems like a really important lecture," she said. "I hate to miss it."

"Too bad."

"Yesterday, when Eric's cell went off, you didn't ask him to leave. I mean, just because mine happens to go off more often is no reason to punish me. Either there should be a policy of no cell phones at all—which I personally do not support—or you need to treat us all the same."

"Not again," a kid in the back groaned.

"I agree," Mr. Bronson said, "Not again. Lacy, get out of here."

She gathered her books and her backpack and headed for the door. Even her classmates were rejecting her. She paused at Marissa's desk and made a face. She wanted Marissa to be her friend; she thought Marissa would commiserate with her about the cell phone, but Marissa just turned away. Her long dark Latina hair rippled and gleamed. A hot pink bra strap peeked from her tank top and graced one cappuccino-colored shoulder. Even Marissa's underwear was perfect.

"Close the door behind you, please."

Lacy left and closed the classroom door. The hallway was empty and that was a relief. Why had she been born so damn white? She was white, white, white with almost white hair that wasn't even WASP-y straight, but curly, like some Aryan Afro. Which her mother refused to let her chemically straighten. Her stupid actress grandmother had the same white hair and skin, but her hair was shiny straight and on her the pallor was stunning. Lacy also had her father's ridiculous curls, adorable ringlets when she was little that had gone nuts with puberty. Lacy hated her hair and her skin. Her translucent thighs and inner arms revealed every blue vein. Her areolas were the palest pink, barely visible on her breasts. In the dim light of a man's bedroom, she would look nipple-less. Not that any man had seen her yet, but she had tried various lighting conditions at home as she posed in front of her mirror. She thought candlelight was the worst; her skin looked healthier, but her breasts became two round undefined orbs like the tits on a Barbie doll. Her mother said she spent too much time obsessing, but what did she know? She had straight dark hair and dark eyes. That great olive skin.

Just thinking about Winnie gave Lacy a scruffy feeling in her stomach. Dry, as if she had swallowed dirt. Her mother was just so boring. She had that stupid job which she hated. She had that one friend who was always busy. She never went anywhere. When Lacy got home from visiting her dad, Winnie would be sitting on the couch reading, exactly the same as when she left. It wasn't Lacy's job to entertain her, was it? And since she had found that cigarette butt in her backpack (and she had been so damn careful!) she wouldn't let up on her about smoking. Then it was the piercings. And her grades. Even when Winnie didn't say anything it was there in her face; the disappointment absolutely obvious every time she looked at her.

And now this. Principal Dickhead would call Mom for sure. Lacy could not go to the office. Her mother was at her stupid tennis lesson anyway. She dawdled in the hallway. Her next class was in fifteen minutes, but Marissa was in that class too. That was too much. She could just imagine Marissa looking at her, then whispering to her friends and all of them laughing. Then she had stupid English and horrible lunch and then European History and she had not done her homework and there was going to be a test. So she just bent her head and walked past the office toward the doors. Who the fuck needed school anyway? She could read. She could write. Wasn't that enough?

No one stopped her as she pushed open one side of the double glass doors. She paused briefly, waiting for a hand on her shoulder, the voice of Mrs. Lopez, the secretary, saying "Young lady? Where do you think you're going?" but no one noticed as she went out and down the front steps. Or if they saw her they didn't care.

She straightened her shoulders and walked purposefully away from school until she turned the corner. Then she stopped. Where should she go? What would happen when she got there? What would Marissa think when she missed the next class? Lacy's head was filled with questions—as usual. Nothing ever seemed solid or definite to her. She was easily convinced of whatever anyone said, found herself agreeing completely and fervently. But then she would walk away and change her mind. Or forget what she had decided. The answer to anything might be yes. It could just as likely be no. She sighed. Marissa and her friends obviously knew the right answer to everything.

Lacy fingered her cell phone. Her guy would be at work. That was the disadvantage to an older man. He had a job. He paid rent. Still, if she got stuck somewhere he would leave work and come get her. If she called him, she knew he would come right away. Her hair was curling; she could feel it frizzing up around her face as the wind blew. There was moisture in the air, possible rain. The winds were picking up. She watched a leaf skitter across the sidewalk. She walked and drifted into her fantasy.

Her hair was long and straight. She stood on a street corner—no—in a parking lot by a 7-11 in a sketchy part of town. A red car filled with boys, maybe a pick-up truck, maybe a low black car with tinted windows, circled her. The boys taunted her, wanted her, called out things about her legs and her ass and what they would do to her. He came squealing into the lot in his silver Audi. Or his hipster classic car. Or his outdoorsy Subaru wagon. He fishtailed to a stop beside her and she leapt into the passenger seat.

"Thank you," she breathed. A single tear on her cheek.

"I want to kill those guys," he said. "If anything happened to you…"

They would lean together for a kiss. The first kiss. Her first kiss ever.

Next time they spoke she would ask him what kind of car he

had. She imagined a nice car, a good car, but she wouldn't care if he drove an old beater. He was a person to whom exterior, material things did not matter.

She had never actually seen him—not live and in person—only a photo he had emailed to her. That's all he had seen of her too, the one picture of herself she liked that she posted on her page. And the photo of the tattoo she wanted. That silly photo had brought them together. He'd thought it was really her leg—that she already had that tattoo. He left a comment, then she replied and they started to chat. She sent him a quotation Mr. Bronson had put on the board by some dead guy named William Durant, "Forget past mistakes. Forget failures. Forget everything except what you're going to do now and do it."

He wrote back, "Yes! Today is the first day of the rest of your life!"

She had never heard that before and it struck her as amazing. It was so, so true. That was it. They were obviously connected. She wrote him that he had inspired her. He replied she had lifted his spirits, made him glad to be alive.

"Hey. Hey, Lacy."

She was startled out of her daydream. Buster, a skinny loser she had known since elementary school, hung out his car window. His brown hair fell in his eyes. She could see the green T-shirt he always wore.

"Hey," she replied.

"What're you doing?"

She shrugged.

"C'mere."

She walked over to his car. His eyes were red.

"Wanna get high?"

She shook her head no.

"Wanna ride someplace?"

She couldn't go home, but she had to go somewhere. "Sure," she said.

She went around and opened the passenger side door. Buster threw sandwich wrappers and magazines and earphones and clothes and a dilapidated notebook into the back seat.

"Sorry. This car is like my office."

It smelled of old food and unwashed clothes. There was a shriveled apple core covered in dust and lint on the floor mat. Lacy cracked her window.

"Where to? Your chariot awaits." He tapped his fingers on the wheel in time to music obviously playing only in his head.

Would Buster take her to Rose Tattoo? She wanted to get her nose pierced. Or she thought she did. The ring in her belly-button had hurt so much, but Roger at the place said noses were just cartilage. She had been thinking about it for a while, but she didn't really want Buster to come along. What if she cried?

"Got a cigarette?" she asked.

"Are you kidding? My body is a fucking temple." Buster opened the ashtray and pulled out a joint. "I smoke only the purest, finest, organically grown weed."

Lacy laughed. You had to laugh at Buster. He grinned happily. He pulled out into traffic without looking and a car coming up behind honked.

"Bless you, neighbor!" Buster waved his hand out the window. He lit his joint. "I know just where to go. I will take you to an amazing place."

The SUV behind them pulled around and the driver flipped Buster off. Buster just shook his head. "Negative energy will get you nowhere, my friend." Then he looked at Lacy. "What're you doing out of school? You're not a deviant."

"My cell phone went off and Mr. Bronson kicked me out of class."

"Those cell phones will give you brain cancer."

"I usually just text."

"It is a fucking gorgeous day."

Lacy frowned at the gathering clouds, the palm trees bending in the wind.

Buster continued. "Life experience on a day like today is as important as anything you could learn in a classroom."

Lacy leaned forward to look up through the windshield. "Maybe it'll rain."

"Fuck no. Warm. Sunny. So Cal, man. So Cal living!"

Almost every day was warm and sunny in LA. The relentless sunshine depressed her. She was so easily sunburned. Her hair preferred air conditioning. And the weather was boring. She and her mother agreed on that one point. Her mother. Why was she such a bitch lately?

"Stop over there." Lacy pointed at a bodega on the corner. " I need a pack of cigs."

3.

Jonathan let himself in. He still had his key on the same ring Winnie had given him seventeen years ago on their honeymoon. If Jessica knew he carried the keys to their house and his Porsche and her SUV on the old ring, she'd run right out and buy him a new one, but she thought the sterling silver seashell was a souvenir from way back, before Winnie, from his surfer days. Even though it said Tiffany's right on it, like he would have been able to afford anything from Tiffany's back then. She wasn't the sharpest crayon in the deck—or whatever that expression was. She was cute and she was fun. Of course, if she found out he was hanging out at his ex-wife's house she would not be fun. No. That would not be any fun at all.

He took a deep breath. He could smell coffee, Winnie's good coffee. He went into the kitchen. He stood by the counter in front of the window, in the very spot he remembered Winnie standing when he told her he was leaving. There was her blue mug. There was Lacy's cereal bowl. There was the cutting board covered in scraps from Lacy's cut up apple and her peanut butter and honey sandwich—she never took anything else for lunch. He licked his finger and pressed down to capture a single tiny crumb. He put it on his tongue, swallowing the morsel of his ex-wife and only child.

The dog scratched to come in. Jonathan opened the back door.

"Hey, Buddy."

He bent down to pet the black and white mutt. He and Jessica had a hypoallergenic designer labradoodle. Very sweet, but nothing but fluff between its apricot-colored, curly hair-not-fur ears. She was two-years-old and barely knew her name. Buddy sat down and thumped his tail on the floor.

"You waiting, huh?"

He took a dog biscuit from his pocket, hid it behind his back and switched it from hand to hand, back and forth. Then he put both hands out in front of him.

"Which one, Buddy? Which one is it?'

Buddy nosed his left hand. The dog got it right every time. Jonathan gave him the treat, also hypoallergenic and apricot-colored, plus organic, but Buddy seemed to like it just fine.

Jonathan made his rounds. He went upstairs, straightened a kindergarten photo of Lacy on the wall outside the bathroom, and then checked to make sure the faucet in the sink wasn't dripping anymore. He had fixed it last time he came; he was pleased he had done a successful job. He was a handy guy when he got the opportunity. He stepped into Lacy's room and shook his head at the mess. When she moved in with him, this would have to change. She needed responsibility. He was going to give her driving lessons, but he would not buy her a car until she proved she was ready for it. He walked past the master bedroom, but he couldn't go in. Today he even averted his eyes. He didn't want to see the unmade bed, the book on her nightstand, the dust on his.

He went back downstairs to his special chair. He had taken nothing when he moved out; Jessica didn't want any reminders of his old life. Except Lacy, of course. The give of the cushion, the scratch of the worn upholstery, the faint smell of dog, was all as it should be. He picked a piece of lint off his expensive long shorts. They weren't particularly comfortable, but Jessica had bought them for him. They were what everybody was wearing and they made him look young. His shirt had the logo of a skateboard company across the back, even though these days the only wheels he rode were on his car and the stationary bike at the gym. Nobody would know that looking at him. He weighed almost the same as when he'd first met Winnie. Of course, his hair was a little thinner, and he had help keeping it this shade of blonde, but he had his fans. Plenty of them.

She was at tennis. She said she couldn't have lunch, so she was probably out for most of the day. He leaned his head back, closed his eyes and then opened them again. He wanted to see. There was the piano they had inherited from a friend who moved away. The dent in the coffee table where seven-year-old Lacy had dropped her roller skate. The ugly painting on the wall, a thrift store find she loved so much. Her old twenty-seven inch TV. His eyes caressed each. It was as if he had never seen them before and as if he always saw them, as if he carried these items in his pocket wherever he went.

And he was here too. He was still here. He had painted the ceiling and missed those spots around the light fixture. He had bought that silver candlestick for Winnie the day he got the beer commercial. He stood on this rug and stared out that window as he practiced his lines for his first movie. It was all here. If there was anything new or out of place, he always noticed it immediately: even if it was just Lacy's socks and sneakers kicked off under the couch, or an empty glass on the end table, or those ugly bright colored pillows Winnie had bought for some unknown reason. What was different today? Nothing. Winnie had straightened up a little. The pillows were now in Lacy's room. It looked exactly as it did when he lived in this house, as if he was still here. And he was.

He breathed out, sucking in his stomach as he relaxed his shoulders. Jessica was a yoga teacher; she had taught him proper breathing for relaxation and rejuvenation. He started to look at his watch, then forced himself not to. He was here now. There was no rush to get over to his office. His show was on hiatus until after Christmas, but he still liked to make an appearance, to remind the producers he was the reason the audience kept coming back. He exhaled loudly and Buddy thumped his tail, once, twice.

"Good dog."

Sometimes Jonathan craved this old house. Sometimes he ached for it even as he sat in the living room of his new, creamy mansion. Jessica had chosen the furniture, wallpaper, carpets, art, everything in the color of nonfat honey-sweetened organic yogurt. This house, the first house he had bought, was messy and mismatched, but it was so quiet. As if the shabby things had absorbed the noise and the troubles all around. He had begun here and in this room he heard his young self moving, going forward. Only in this silence. He was here. His best self was still here. This had to be the quietest house in America. In the world. In the universe.

4.

The heat was astonishing. Winnie expected it to shimmer off the wall-to-wall carpeting like a highway in the desert. The house was empty. There were no pictures or decoration, only a brown plaid couch and matching chair and an oak coffee table with nothing on it. It was all like rental furniture, ugly and sturdy. There was no television, not even a lamp, just the unbelievable heat. The tears evaporated on her cheeks, but the perspiration collected under her arms, slid down the back of her neck, pooled between her breasts.

He let her go. "Sit down."

She did not want to sit on the couch or the chair. She would fuse with the fabric; her skin would melt into the fibers. He poked her in the back with the handle of the knife. She obeyed and sat in the chair. She caught the faintest chemical odor. It reminded her of a pet store, then of Lacy's first grade classroom. Cedar chips. Guinea pig cages. Despite the heat, her legs were trembling.

"Why is it so hot?"

He said nothing. He opened the little closet by the front door, took out the single hanger and hung up his leather jacket. His white shirt was small on him, the shoulders were tight, the sleeves too short. He closed the closet door. He took off his tie and looped it over the doorknob. He did it with such practice, like a ritual, like what he always did before he mutilated his victims.

"What are we doing here?" Winnie had to keep talking, to tell him she was human, she was real; she was just like him. "It's a lovely house. Really. I love this fabric. And everything is so clean and tidy. Not like my house. My daughter. What a mess she can make. Boy, oh boy." She stood up. "What's the kitchen like?" She tried to sound friendly, to be his friend.

There was an open archway into the empty dining room. The swinging door to the kitchen was closed.

"Sit down."

She did.

He unbuttoned his shirt. Underneath he wore a white sleeveless undershirt. She had wondered about the hair on his chest so long ago, in the car, before. It was as orange as the hair on his head and sparse; a hair or two curled above the scooped neckline. His shoulders were dusted with freckles, like cinnamon on vanilla ice cream. He hung his shirt on the doorknob and turned to her. The muscular beauty of his arms stunned her; the way his skin stretched over his biceps. She had thought he was skinny, now she could see how strong he was.

"What do you want?" she whispered.

"I wouldn't know where to begin."

He sat down on the couch across from her. He stretched his arms wide. The orange hair in his armpits was damp with sweat. The hallway on the far side of the room was flanked with doors—to bedrooms, bathrooms, cozy dens—all closed. There were two locks and a chain on the front door. The large window behind his head was concealed under Venetian blinds closed tight.

She would be locked for days in this hot house, raped repeatedly and finally murdered and thrown from the trunk of his black car into a ravine off the Angeles Crest.

He put his head back. He closed his eyes. This has to be a

dream, Winnie begged the universe. I am still sleeping. I am home in bed. My blue comforter is tucked up under my chin, my pillow soft against my cheek. It seems so real, and then for some reason you realize it is just a dream. And you wake up. You wake up. Wake up!

But she was still there.

Something scratched and scraped behind the kitchen door. An accomplice? Two men at once? Her stomach lurched, her teeth chattered and in the incredible heat she felt a feverish chill.

"Just a minute!" His voice startled her.

Another scrape, the sound of someone digging into the wooden kitchen door with a spoon or dull knife.

"Stop it!" he yelled again.

The sweat spilled from every pore. She was drenched between her breasts, along the bottom of her sport bra, between her legs. The salt stung her eyes. Her ponytail wrapped around her neck in tentacles.

He stood. She shrunk into the chair, but he stepped past her, around the coffee table, through the dining room, to the kitchen door. He went inside and the door swung shut behind him.

"What's the matter with you?" She heard him complain. "Jesus Christ."

It sounded like paper ripping. Not an accomplice, it was his previous victim, or his insane mother, someone without legs lying on the kitchen floor, scratching at the walls, peeing on newspaper.

She stood and walked quickly, quietly to the front door. Her hand was shaking as she slipped the chain out of its slot and let it down gently against the doorjamb. She slid the bolt back. She turned the doorknob silently.

He grabbed her shoulder, turned her around and shoved her back against the door. Her head thumped against the peephole.

There were beads of perspiration on his nose and forehead. His eyelashes were as pale and long as millipede legs. She closed her eyes.

"Where you going, Mom?"

He cursed her with it again. She should never have told him she had a child.

"Nowhere."

"That's right."

Winnie felt his fingers brush her breastbone. He slowly, gently slid down the zipper of her warm-up jacket. She kept her eyes closed. He used both hands to open her jacket. Underneath, she wore a sleeveless tennis shirt with a logo over her breast.

"Hey," he said softly.

Maybe it was just sex. That would not be the end of the world. She would grit her teeth, get through it, and kick him in the head the minute she had the chance.

"I said, hey. Look at me."

She had lived through bad sex before, sex with men who wanted it when she did not, sex when it was easier to say yes than otherwise, sex when she felt sorry for the guy or grateful to him or obligated. On her first date after the divorce she had forced herself into bed with Phil the pharmacist. He was short and pot-bellied with thick fingers he insisted on sticking into her mouth again and again. He did not kiss her, but rubbed his chest and belly against hers in circles, squishing her into the mattress and leaving drool on her cheek. Afterwards he wanted her to tell him how wonderful he was. He had asked her for a play-by-play critique. She had cried when she was finally home, and then, two days later, laughed about it with her friend, Sara.

Why was she thinking about Phil now?

"Hey," he said again. His hands relaxed on her arms.

Her eyes opened and she kicked him as hard as she could

between his legs. He screeched like a girl and tripped over his own feet as he backed away. She spun around and opened the door. She fumbled with the lock on the screen. She yelled and kept yelling.

"Help! Help! Help me!"

The street was empty. The houses looked unlived in, as if everyone had locked up and left for vacation. Or as if every house held a solitary victim. She scratched and clawed at the rusty lock. The screen door had not been opened in a hundred years.

"Help me!"

He twisted her ponytail hard and she fell backwards onto the carpet. He slammed the door shut and leaned down and slapped her. She was too frightened to cry. Her cheek burned. Her skirt was up around her waist. She tried to straighten it without his noticing, but she saw him glance at her thighs, exposed and shaking. She blushed, embarrassed by her tennis panties with the upside down pockets for the balls. She rolled to her side to get up, but he pushed her down flat on her back. He threw a leg over her waist and straddled her. He took the knife out of his pocket again.

Now she would die.

A drop of his sweat slid from his temple, down his chin, and onto her face. Scratch, scratch, scratch from the kitchen. Scratch, scratch, scratch. A curl of his hair fell across his forehead and he used his knife hand to smooth it back. She clearly saw his watch: 9:23. She had been at the mechanic's shop before nine. Lacy was in Biology. Jonathan was at work. A car drove down the street outside. Where was that person going? What did they see when they looked over at this house, these closed blinds, this locked door? Nothing. No one saw or knew anything. They never would. Her body might never be found. Then Lacy would think her mother had left her, dropped her off at school and never come back. Winnie couldn't even remember what they had been fighting about.

Scratch, scratch, scratch. It had become rhythmic and constant.

"Cookie!" he shouted. "Shut up!"

Scratch, scratch, scratch.

He climbed off her and got to his feet. "Cookie!" he said again.

She rolled to her hands and knees and scrambled toward the kitchen. Whoever Cookie was, he or she had to help her. She crawled like a dog toward the kitchen door.

"Goddamn it!" he shouted. "Don't!"

She pushed the door open. "Help me, please," she cried and looked into the face of an enormous lizard. Gigantic. Its head was bigger than hers. It hissed. She screamed and clambered away, right into her kidnapper's legs where he stood behind her.

Cookie blinked slowly, the bottom lid coming up to meet the top.

"Get up."

She stayed where she was.

"Get up or Cookie will bite you."

She stood and backed up against the kitchen wall. The lizard turned away from her to watch its master as he went to the refrigerator. Inside it was like a small produce market, green, leafy, bright splotches of orange and red. She took a deep breath, grateful for the puff of cool refrigerated air. He grabbed a bag of spinach and three carrots. The entire kitchen had been turned into Cookie's home. There was a cave built in one corner, a real boulder, and a climbing log nailed into the wood beneath the counter. And scattered on the linoleum floor were the cedar chips she had smelled.

"No wonder it's so hot in here," she said. "It's for Cookie."

"You're a fucking genius." He threw the vegetables into a purple dog bowl. Cookie waddled in that direction. "He's beautiful, isn't he?"

Winnie heard the pride in his voice. She knew to agree. "He is. Okay? Yes. He's beautiful."

Cookie was a rusty orange, not green as she would have expected. There were olive patches here and there and his belly was whitish, but his body and forelegs were definitely orange. He had a row of spikes down his back and a large, floppy piece of skin under his neck. His eyes were small and rimmed in red. He had weird large circles of skin or scale just behind his mouth where the hinge of his jaw might be. And his legs. There was something horribly humanoid about them, the muscles so apparent under the scales, and the hands with five long jointed fingers and wicked, sharp nails. Each finger could articulate on its own.

She couldn't help it, she shuddered, but then she tried to smile. "Beautiful."

"Glad you think so."

"Is he vegetarian? You know, I'm vegetarian."

"So what."

He pushed her back into the dining room, letting the kitchen door swing closed. She was relieved to be away from the creature even as her kidnapper pushed her again with both hands, and she stumbled against the wall. He leaned over her, one hand on either side of her head.

"You're one of those women who like to talk, aren't you? You're a chatterbox. Yak, yak, yak."

"No. Actually I'm quiet. Everyone says I'm quiet. I can be quiet."

He squinted at her. She stopped talking. He was sizing her

up, trying to figure something out.

"How old are you?" he asked.

"Thirty-eight."

"Really?"

"Don't I look it?"

He shrugged.

She wanted to keep him talking. "Do you live here alone?"

"No." He looked at her as if she were stupid. It was a look she recognized from her daughter.

"Who with?"

"Duh. Cookie. I live here with Cookie."

"The lizard."

"I hate it when people call him a lizard. He's an iguana."

"What's the difference?" Keep him talking, she thought. If he was talking he couldn't hurt her.

"There are three thousand different types of lizards, from those little geckoes you see on your patio to Komodo Dragons. But Cookie is from the family *Iguanidae*. There are only thirteen kinds of iguana. He's the largest: a Great Green Iguana. And even for his breed, he's enormous. Most of them are much smaller than he is, but I know how to take care of him. He's so healthy, he'll probably keep growing. Did you see the way his scales shine?"

He grinned. His face opened, the line between his eyebrows went away.

"Shiny," she agreed. "How long have you had him?"

"All his life."

"I didn't know they got so big."

"Most don't. Cookie started out less than six inches. Now he's eight feet from his nose to the tip of his tail. Bigger than most and weighs more too. A champion."

"There are competitions?"

"Of course. There are Reptile Expos twice a year and smaller contests in between. Cookie will win every prize."

"He certainly is big."

His face clouded over again. The furrow on his forehead returned. He stepped back, out of reach of her feet. He looked her up and down.

"You're hot," he said quietly. "Take off your jacket."

"I'm fine." She did not want to take anything off; she wanted every possible layer between them.

"I asked you to take off your jacket."

"Do you need money? Is that it? My ex-husband has lots of money. I'll call him. Or better yet, take me to the bank. I'll get you money."

He shook his head.

"My ex-husband is Jonathan Parker. The actor," Winnie continued. "I'm sure you would know him if you saw him. He has a game show, *Tie the Knot*. He's the host. He's on every day. It's the most popular game show on television. Maybe you could be a contestant. Would you like that? I'll call him. Do you have a phone? You could be on TV. Wouldn't that be great? You have such a good look. You're so handsome. You could be a star. Really."

"I want you to be quiet."

"I just want to help –"

"Don't talk. Stop talking. And take off your jacket."

"Okay, okay. I'm really fine in my jacket, but—"

"Shut up and do it."

She had to peel her jacket like skin; the sleeves clung to her sweaty arms. He watched her, stared at her breasts and stomach revealed in her damp nylon shirt.

"You're short," he said, "but you have a pretty good body."

Winnie cringed and kept talking. "My mother is an actress

too. Famous. Daisy Juniper. She's won two Academy Awards. She has money. She'll pay you to let me go. She will. Is it money you want?"

"Money. Money and fame. Fame and fortune. You think being rich and famous makes you special. Every idiot with a cat on Youtube is famous."

"I'm not famous. I'm nothing. Really. Nothing. I work as a secretary in an office. I'm nobody."

"Didn't I tell you to Shut The Fuck Up!"

Winnie pressed herself against the wall, tried to be as small and flat as possible. Cookie scratched against the kitchen door.

"What does it want?"

"He. Not it. He. Cookie needs attention."

"Go ahead. I'll wait right here."

"Sure you will." He sighed again. "I think Cookie's tired of the kitchen. He'd like the run of the house, but I can't have iguana shit all over the carpet."

"He's not paper-trained?"

"He's not a pet. He's a wild animal."

He emphasized "wild."

"Like you," she nodded at him. "You seem wild, to me."

He smiled. She had said the right thing.

"It's cooler in the back." He took her arm. "Come on."

She wanted to stay near the front door, but she didn't want to make him angry again. Maybe there was a phone in the back. Maybe in the cooler air she could think more clearly. Maybe he would get her back there and slice her into pieces with his little knife. He couldn't have Winnie shit all over the carpet.

He led her toward the hallway. Her skin was slick with sweat and she easily pulled her arm out of his grasp. She looked at the front door.

"Don't," he said. "Just don't."

He took his knife out of his pocket and clicked it open. The blade was long, partially serrated. It would hurt. She offered her arm. He gripped it tightly.

"Thank you."

Two steps down the hallway she stopped again.

He exhaled, exasperated. "What now?"

"What's your name?"

"Why?"

Winnie was sure it was a good thing to exchange names with a kidnapper. She had read it somewhere. He had to see her as a person then. "My name's Winnie," she said. "Short for Winifred. Isn't that awful? What's yours?"

"Bob."

"Really?"

"No. It's Rob."

"Are you Irish?"

"Bingo. My name is Patrick."

"Do they call you Pat? Or Rick?"

"Right. Do I sound Irish?"

"So what is it?"

"Bill. Jim. No, John."

"Why don't you want me to know?" Winnie was exasperated.

"Call me whatever the fuck you want."

"How about Shithead?"

His eyes widened, then he frowned. "You will learn to appreciate me."

Winnie's stomach churned. Would she be here that long? He jerked her down the hallway.

"Can I use the bathroom?"

"Now?"

"I have to use the bathroom. Whenever I get nervous."

He looked surprised. He had obviously not thought of this eventuality. Winnie gave him a shy little smile.

"I'm so embarrassed. I'm going to—you know—I had a big breakfast," she lied, "and lots of coffee. It'll be awful. Actually, I feel kind of sick."

He didn't like mess, and she worried she had made herself sound so disgusting he would kill her just so she wouldn't use his bathroom. He grimaced, but he backed her up and opened the first door. The bathroom was as clean as the rest of the house. One threadbare towel was folded neatly over the rack. His toiletries were put away out of sight. And there was a small frosted glass window behind the toilet.

"Thank you." She smiled gratefully. "Thank you for being so understanding."

"For a shithead, right?"

He stepped back against the wall. "I'll be waiting, if you need anything."

"You might want to check on Cookie." She pretended to duck her face and blush. "This could take a while." She rubbed her stomach and tried to look queasy.

The image of her distressed bodily functions had the desired effect. He fled down the hallway back to Cookie.

Winnie went into the bathroom, closed the door and discovered she could even lock it. It was not much of a lock, but it would deter him. She could be out the window and running across the backyard before he broke the door open. For the first time, she felt a twinge of hope. She would get out of this. She gave a couple of groans for his benefit as she unlocked the window. The cheap pre-fab metal frame was tight and hard to move. She reached across the toilet and lifted, but it was the wrong angle. Finally, she stood on the toilet seat, bent her knees and pushed with all her strength. The window lifted slowly, but silently. She flushed the toilet and turned on the faucet all the way. She climbed up onto the toilet seat and punched the screen with both hands. It popped the track and flew into the grass six feet way.

Winnie hoped he was too busy with his lizard to look out the kitchen window and notice a flying screen. The window was small; she would have to go out headfirst. She pulled herself up onto her stomach on the ledge. The metal was sharp and dug into her stomach, but the air was cool and fresh. She wiggled forward. She braced herself with her hands against the stucco wall. She would fall on her face in the scratchy cactus beneath the window, but she would be free.

The door broke open. He grabbed her legs. She screamed. He dragged her back into the bathroom. The window frame gouged and scraped her stomach. He fell backwards and her chin hit the toilet as she fell on top of him.

"Fucking bitch!"

Her jaw throbbed. She scrambled to her feet and saw streaks of blood soaking through her shirt. He had his knife out. He swiped at her.

"I hate you!" he cried.

"I hate you too!" she screamed back.

She pulled the roll of toilet paper from its holder and threw it in his face. She kicked him, connecting with his shin, his knee, whatever was there. He yelled and lunged at her with his knife. She jumped out of the way and tripped over the edge of the bathtub and fell. She grabbed the shower curtain to stop her descent and pulled it down with her. Her head hit the porcelain hard and for one instant she knew she was going. Then she was gone.

5.

Storm clouds filled his head. Rain collected under his eyelids. He had the flat, small features of a Midwestern farm boy, and he could feel them swelling, growing heavy with the coming thunder.

"Why me?" he thought. His refrain throughout his life. "Why me?"

Her fucking husband game show host. Her stupid famous mother. Her easy easy life. The people who had it all never appreciated it. This was going to be harder than he thought. He had planned everything, but he had not expected her to fight. He looked down at her passed out. She was half in the bathtub and half out. He gnawed at his fingernail. He sucked and pulled at the tiny crescent, finally ripping it off. His cuticle bled, his finger pulsed. He started on the next nail—what was left of it. He was going to stop this habit. He was. He tucked his fingers into a fist and slammed it into his thigh.

He forced himself to grab her and pick her up, slick with sweat, smelly and half-dressed, but she weighed less than a rolled up 5 x 7 rug. He carried her into the back bedroom he had prepared and put her on the single bed. He got the rope and tied her down. He was prepared to do it, but he had not believed he would have to. She would not listen to him and then she fell in the bathroom. It was not his fault. He shifted her to tie the rope and her head flopped to one side and made her neck all wrinkled and pulled. The skin was almost purple under her eyes. Her mouth hung open and her teeth were not very white. Be done with her, he told himself. Three Rorschach tests of blood striped her shirt. There was a dark bruise on her chin. He knew she had bumped her head hard. Now would be the time to load her into the backseat, take her somewhere and dump her and forget the whole thing. But she had seen him; she would know him and he could not have that. He would have to make this work, or he would have to kill her.

He hoped she appreciated the bed and the clean sheets. He could have left her lying in the bathtub. That was what anyone else would have done. He stared down at her. She looked dead. It would be better if she were. If she were dead already, no one could say it was his fault. She fell in the bathroom. And if she were dead, she would never recognize him. Then she moaned. Damn it.

Why me, he thought again. It was a song in his head. Why me? Why did she do this to me?

His cell phone vibrated. He recognized the number. It was Jamie from work. He ran out into the hall and shut the door.

"This is Oren," he answered softly.

"Where are you?"

"I'm sick."

"You better call in or you're gonna get fired. Pete was screaming for you."

It was so damn nice of Jamie to call. Jamie was cool, everybody liked Jamie, and Jamie had called him. Tears came suddenly. Oren brushed them away with his bleeding finger. The saltwater stung his open cut and he gritted his teeth. "I will. Okay? I will."

"Jesus, man, I'm just trying to help."

"Sorry, sorry. I just—I feel like shit."

"Yeah. Well."

"I'll call right now."

"Yeah. Good. So." Jamie paused. "Like, feel better."

"Thanks. Thanks so much."

Oren gulped down a sob. He hoped Jamie had not heard it as he hung up. He dialed the boss.

"Pete? It's Oren. I'm sick, really sick."

"Huh. What do you have?"

Oren could hear the doubt, thick and slimy as mayonnaise. He closed his eyes. He saw Pete standing behind his desk in his office. His good ol' boy gut hung over his pants. His buttons strained, threatened to erupt every time he took a deep breath. His hand made a damp spot on the phone.

"I guess I've got food poisoning. Something I ate." It wasn't hard to sound weak. "Or the stomach flu. I hope I'm back tomorrow."

"Maybe you got some kind of jungle rot from that lizard— 'scuse me—iguana."

They all liked to give him shit about Cookie. He was used to it.

Pete sighed and continued, "Just call me later and let me know about tomorrow. We're busy. We need you."

"Okay."

"My mom always gave me Coca-Cola and saltines for an upset stomach. Try it."

"Okay."

"Take care of yourself. Feel better."

"Thanks. Bye."

Oren put his fists in his eyes to block the tears. Pete wanted him back at work, that was all, he wasn't being nice. Jamie was just overworked and needed him to help out. No goddamn crying. No crying. He looked at his watch. 10:18. He had to make the first phone call at 3:45. There was a lot to do between now and then and he had no idea how long it took to wake up from a thump on the head. He looked back into the room. She was tied up tight, not going anywhere.

He pushed open the kitchen door. Cookie looked at him— accusingly he thought.

"Stop it. This'll be good for both of us."

He sat down on the floor. Cookie's nails scraped the linoleum as he turned away from Oren. Like a child sulking.

"Don't worry," Oren said. "It'll work out. It will."

Cookie bumped his snout into the cabinet. Again. And again.

"Aw, don't do that. Don't. Cookie."

Cookie lifted his head to look at the ceiling. His nose was bleeding. Oren knew he was going into mating season; his beautiful green skin had turned a dark burnt orange. He was more aggressive and antsy. His legs pumped. He bobbed his head up and down. His tongue flicked out and in, looking for love. Oren was waiting for the call from his supplier, he'd picked out a sweet little lady iguana to keep Cookie company.

"Come here."

The iguana backed up one step toward Oren. His tail swished back and forth against the floor. Oren chewed on what was left of his nail and cuticle. He ran his other hand down the spiked ridge on Cookie's tail. Cookie stood tall, puffed out his chest, let his beautiful Asian fan of a dewlap swell. Cookie was anxious.

"Me too."

Oren was proud to call Cookie his best friend. It was obvious Cookie loved him. He woke up when Oren got home and scrambled to the door. He knew his name, and Oren could swear Cookie knew the difference between cabbage and kale, carrots and zucchini, just by the word. Do you want carrots?

Oren would ask, or zuchs? And Cookie would bob his head up and down for whichever one he preferred. And he was sweet and gentle, even though he was the biggest iguana anybody had seen. Oren took him once to the Iguana Keepers Club meeting. Even the seasoned lizard lovers had stayed back and then watched in awe as Oren let Cookie climb all over him. No wonder everyone called him the Iguana Man.

"Come here," he said again.

Cookie dropped his head, but did not turn, so Oren crawled over to him. He stroked the sides his head and scratched the scales under his chin. Cookie nuzzled into his hand. The scales weren't rough or dry, but smooth like a waxed floor. Cookie relaxed, bent his knees and sunk lower to the floor.

"That's it. That's what you like, isn't it?"

Oren stretched out beside his friend and continued petting and rubbing, massaging the muscles underneath the slick hide. He breathed deeply the reptile odor, dry and tangy like the kale that was Cookie's favorite food. He was not a fuck-up. His mother was dead and his dad had taken off, he had lost track of his older sister, but he had a house and a car and a job and Cookie. He had a woman he loved. And he had made a plan and achieved it, at least the first step. Damn it, he had done it. Now for step number two.

"That's enough."

He stood. He got a glass and filled it with water. He opened a cupboard and found the aspirin bottle. He carried both out of the kitchen and down the hallway to her room.

He pushed open her door. She had not moved. He set the glass and pills on a box he had arranged beside the bed as a little table. Would she notice the bedside table? The blanket he had hung as a curtain over the window? She should. The bitch should notice all the good he had done for her, the care he was taking. He had tied her to the bed frame with a thick, nylon rope around her ankles. He was good at knots and he felt proud again at the good job he had done, tight but not cutting off her circulation and fastening it beneath the bed where she could not possibly reach it. He had bought the rope especially for this, and paid for the more expensive nylon so the fibers wouldn't scratch her. The skin on her legs had been prickly, in need of a shave. He was surprised she was so uncared for. Her skirt was tucked up under her, exposing her thighs and her strange underwear with the pockets. Nothing seemed very clean. Her shirt was covered in blood, but at least it was dry. He did not think she had bled on the sheets. He had not expected her to try to escape. She was not supposed to be such a fighter. He had been led to believe she was a Beverly Hills pampered type who would surrender right away. This was not his fault. Really not his fault.

He had a blanket in the closet. He shook it out. He covered her completely, but then she looked dead and that was more terrifying than her slack sweaty face. As if the single mattress had become a burial plot; at any moment her hand would shoot up through the ground and grab his wrist. He bumped the bed as he backed away from it. She moaned and moved a little, the blanket trembling over her. It was just a blanket. She was still alive. He folded the blanket off her face gingerly, unwilling to touch her. He left the room and shut the door.

He paced in the hallway. He could smell her sweat on his hands, metallic and thick with blood. Women were so bloody. She smelled like the trashcan did in the bathroom at home every month.

He decided to search head injuries and fainting online. Then he had to check in with the chat room. It was 10:30 in the morning. He had been away from his computer for too long. Three hours without putting a word into cyberspace was definitely not normal for him. His reptile buddies would be wondering where he was. He was waiting to hear about a female with a clutch of eggs that was possibly available. Plus, he needed to see his girlfriend's picture again. He needed to revel again in what she looked like. She could always calm him down. She made this all worthwhile.

He hurried to his bedroom and got his laptop. He carried it back to the floor outside her door. If she woke, if she even moved, he would hear her. He opened his computer and smiled at the picture of the most beautiful woman in the world. The woman he loved. He had downloaded her photo as his screensaver.

"Hey babe," he hummed. "See you soon."

Before he went to the reptile forums, he searched head injuries. He clicked on the first website that came up. Fracture. Paralysis. Trouble breathing. His heart was shrinking in his chest. "If the victim is unconscious, do not move them in case of severe neck or spine injury. Immediately call 911." Too late, he thought. Too late. He should never have let her go to the bathroom. He should have made her shit her pants. He slammed his fist into his thigh. He punched himself in the face. He was an idiot, stupid, a buttwipe!

"Gimme a hot dog, buttwipe."

It was raining. The canvas roof of the hot dog stand billowed in the wind collecting the water and then releasing it. The intermittent stream drenched ten-year-old Oren's left shoulder as he fished in the cooker. He had forgotten his jacket. His T-shirt was already half soaked. He handed over the hot dog and bun on a flimsy red and white paper tray. The meat had been rolling in the hot water since three o'clock that afternoon. The skin was blistered and glistening with fat.

"That'll be two seventy-five," he said, but the teenager just laughed.

"In the fucking rain? Are you kidding?"

"Two seventy-five," Oren said again, his young voice getting softer. "Please?" His dad would kill him if he gave anything away for free.

"Fuck you," the boy said. He was long and skinny with a mountain range of white-capped pimples across his forehead. He took a big bite and stuck out his food-covered tongue at Oren as his friends walked up.

"Hey," he said to them, "This kid is giving away free hot dogs."

"No," Oren declared. "No, I'm not."

The teenagers swarmed the booth, like monkeys, climbing on the wheels, swinging from the corner struts. One of them opened the door and came inside. Oren waved his hot dog fork.

"Are you trying to poke me?" The boy was indignant. "Me? The customer?"

"Get away!" Oren wailed.

"Hot dogs!" the boy cried. He grabbed the fork from Oren and began spearing dogs and tossing them to the others. Some of them landed in the wet dirt. The boys laughed.

"Stop it," Oren tried. He wondered where all the carnies had gone. The midway was empty. The cotton candy girl had gone back to her trailer an hour ago. The Tilt-A-Whirl was closed. Even the Haunted House was shuttered for the night, but Oren couldn't leave until his father said so. He tried to push the boy who was throwing the hot dogs. The boy just snickered, high and mean, his derision as sharp as a stick.

"Oren!"

His father was coming. Marcus strode through the rain, his boots kicking up the mud. He wasn't tall, but he was pumped, more pit bull than man. The boys scattered. Oren slid out of the stand and began frantically picking up the hot dogs.

"Oren!"

"I'm sorry, daddy," he said. He stood up to face him. "I couldn't stop—"

Before he could finish his father's hand swung and knocked him down into the mud. Oren scrambled to his feet and his father belted him again. He stumbled, but he did not fall. "I'm sorry," he said. "I'm sorry."

"Pick up those dogs and wash 'em off good. That's your breakfast, lunch, and dinner for tomorrow."

"I tried to stop them. It's not my fault."

Marcus lifted his hand. "Do you want another one?"

Oren bent to get the dirty hot dogs. His father spread his legs, disgust washing his face, dripping with the rain on his broad shoulders, his muscular arms, those dangerous hands. Oren recognized his own freckled skin, the burnish of red hair in the dim light. He didn't want to share anything with his father.

He gathered the hot dogs and wrapped them in a soggy napkin. Marcus would not forget to make him eat them. He turned off the cooker, put the lid on it, and handed his father the cash box. Then he stood on his tiptoes on the milk crate to close the shutters as his father watched.

"Fucking idiot," his father said as he turned away. "Tell your mother I'm going out."

His father went one way, toward the exit, and Oren took off toward the RV that was home. His ear was ringing where Marcus had hit him. He always hit him on the same side. Oren wondered, why did he never give this ear a break?

Oren ran until he reached their motor home. "Mama?" he asked at the door. "Mama?"

The door opened just a crack releasing a strip of harsh light that hit him right in the eyes. He squinted at the person in silhouette peeking out at him.

"Something the matter?"

It was Jimmy, the agent for the Ferris wheel. Jimmy had a secret tattoo on his thigh of a naked woman being burned at the stake. It was a picture of his wife, he told Oren once. She hadn't been tied to a stake, but she was passed out in bed and Jimmy said he hoped she woke up long enough for it to hurt like hell.

"Can I come in?" It was his home. "Dad said he was going out."

"You cold? Take my sweatshirt." Jimmy took it off. He wasn't wearing a shirt underneath.

"Is my mother in there?"

"Just take it." Jimmy threw the sweatshirt at him and the zipper hit his face. "Leave your mother alone," he hissed. "Leave the bitch alone."

Oren tasted blood on his lip. He let the sweatshirt fall as he called again. "Mama! Open up."

"Oren?" his mother called to him, "Baby, is that you?" Her voice was way up in the top of the trees somewhere, high and thin as the whistle from a plastic toy. "Baby? Go away now. Give your mama some time alone."

"You heard her," Jimmy said.

Oren took a step forward and Jimmy shoved him hard enough to send him back on his ass. Jimmy was chuckling as he shut the door.

Oren got up and started running again. The rain didn't bother him. He knew the exact number of steps to the place he was going. The only place he could go. It didn't matter if the carnival was set up in Kentucky or Wisconsin. Each ride always sat in its same place, the popcorn wagon smelled of chemicals and rancid oil, the merry-go-round calliope slid off-key in the same measure. There were always discarded tickets under his feet, and fat people in shorts and tank tops, and mothers yelling at their children. Oren was never sure the carnival really went anywhere at all. Maybe they just pretended to drive all night. When he woke up, they were always in the same K-Mart parking lot or the same field just outside town.

He ran until he reached The Amazing Amazon, threw open the door and collapsed inside the warm stink and recorded monkey cries. The educational attraction where his fifteen-year-old sister, Fiona, worked was a forty-five-foot semi trailer transformed into a jungle habitat with fake foliage and a broken waterfall. It housed an ancient parrot, a nine foot red tailed boa constrictor, two corn snakes, some water turtles and an ever-dying collection of tree frogs. The star attraction was a pair of great green iguanas, male and female, who had just given birth to a small clutch.

Oren's arrival triggered the automatic voice. "Welcome to the amazing Amazon, the largest tropical rainforest in the world. As you walk the path, look up and watch for—"

"Done already?" Fiona cut off the recording.

"Dad." He didn't need to say anymore.

"Yeah. I'm in the shit too. The last stupid tree frog died."

"Maybe you can get another one in Kansas."

"What'd you do this time?"

"Some boys stole the hot dogs. I tried to stop them."

"You're a fucking fuck-up. Do you know that?" She shook her head at him. "Loser. Capital 'L'."

Even as bitchy as she was, she was a kind of comfort. "How's Cookie?"

"You and that lizard."

"Iguana."

"At least I haven't killed him yet."

Oren crawled through the plastic bushes and behind the exhibits. In a special tank under three incubator lights, two tiny great green iguana eyes blinked. Oren reached in and carefully lifted baby Cookie out of his cage. He was only seven inches long and Oren cradled him against his chest, smiling at how the iguana calmed his thumping heart. He stroked Cookie's dewlap, and the round scales on either side of his head. Cookie let his legs fold and settled on Oren's palm. They were friends. Best friends. Oren carried Cookie out and together they watched Fiona feed baby mice to the corn snakes. She had to poke the hairless blind infants into the snakes' mouths with a chopstick and then massage the snakes' throats until they got them down. They were old snakes, far from wild anymore. As he watched, Oren made a plan. One day soon, he would kill his father. He would chop him into small pieces and feed him to the snakes. Slowly. One spoonful of flesh would look just like those hairless pinkies. If he kept his father tied up and alive, the meat would be fresher, the snakes would eat more, and his father could watch as he was eaten alive day by day.

Oren pushed the computer off his lap. The websites about head injuries were all bad news. She had to be coherent. She had to feel pretty good if his plan was going to work. He stood up filled with heat, with frustration, with his own incredible stupidity. He jumped up and down. Fucking idiot! He bumped his nose against the wall but it didn't give him the satisfaction it obviously gave Cookie. He threw himself from one side of the hall to the other, colliding into the walls, slamming his shoulder, then his hip, then his other shoulder. He grunted with every blow. This was it. The pain, always the pain helped him forget. Forget the mother lying in the bed. Forget the plan. Forget he was an idiot, fucking idiot, idiot. He swung his head down between his knees and then back up. Up and down. He gritted his teeth and kept himself from screaming.

Stop it. His good voice told him. Stop. Look at the carpet. Look at this superior carpet.

It glittered in the overhead light. He crouched and dug his fingers into the wool and plastic-treated fibers. He had put this carpet in. He had gotten a very good employee discount. He had a good job at Carpet Barn and Uncle Nolan had been so pleased. Uncle Nolan said Oren was the best tenant he'd ever had. It was a very high quality carpet. He took deep breaths and he thought about the carpet and his happy uncle and his breath came in gulps. It was a woven carpet, not the cheaper tufted. It was a deep plush pile. Perfect for a house without children or dogs. It was spotless and would stay that way until he left. He would make her take off her shoes before she walked on it again. He took a deep breath. Yes, that's what he would do. And with her shoes off, she would not be as ready to run away. Good idea, he told himself. Damn good thinking. It was going to be fine. She was hurt, but she was not dead. Hurt badly maybe, but—

Why me, he began. Then he stopped himself.

Because I deserve it," he said out loud. He rubbed his shoulder where he had banged the wall. It was sore, probably bruised, but it would be a reminder that he was who he was. "Because I am a special person."

He had a plan. He only needed Winnie to wake up to begin step two.

6.

Jonathan heard a noise from outside. He stood up. The neighborhood was changing. When they moved in, it had been mostly Latino. Back then it didn't look so nice, some of the houses were rundown or had junk in the front yards, but families had lived here. People waved when you went out to get the mail. When he and Winnie brought Lacy home from the hospital, the El Salvadorian woman next door had brought so many pupusas Winnie had joked Lacy would be taking them in her lunchbox to kindergarten. But then, during the housing boom, a lot of their neighbors had cashed out and bought bigger homes in the far suburbs like Palmdale and Lancaster. The yuppies and hipsters had moved in, or developers who had renovated and rented. Instead of being a neighborhood, it felt like a way station, starter homes for young people who wanted to move out as quickly as possible. In the past year, with the economy in the tank, there was more graffiti and many more break-ins and muggings. Jonathan knew it. Everyday he checked the LAPD Northeast Division website and read the crime blotter. It was his job to watch out for Lacy of course and even Winnie. She wouldn't take his money, but he was still the man. He felt responsible, not like some dead-head or dead-beat ex-husbands. Look at what a good job he did coming over here, fixing things, making sure the windows were closed, the back door locked. He was indispensable.

Buddy stood and bristled. He gave a single short bark.

"Good boy," Jonathan said. "Good dog."

He tiptoed to the side window in the dining room. The table was littered with old mail and newspapers, various articles of clothing Winnie had dropped as she went past. When he lived with her he had hated her mess. Her casual attitude about where things belonged had driven him crazy. She didn't know how to take care of her stuff, herself, or when he met her, even how to boil water. She had grown up with servants, staff to cook and clean and stay with her for the long months her mother was away making films. Her mother. He snorted. Daisy Juniper was a piece of art—or work—or both—whatever that expression was. She was crazy and she cultivated her insanity. She had called from her New York penthouse in the middle of the night more than once.

Winnie would roll over him to answer. "It's her," she always said even before checking the caller i.d. or picking up the receiver. Then, "Daisy," into the phone, not hi Mom, or hello or what the fuck are you calling me for this time.

"Don't cry," seemed to be the next thing Winnie always said. Daisy had problems with men. She brought out the worst in them, and Jonathan could almost understand it.

"Did you call a cop?" Winnie would ask, but Daisy never had.

Usually Daisy stayed on the phone for an hour or more and she stayed in Manhattan. One time she had actually gotten on the plane and arrived the next day, sunglasses not really covering her beaten face. She hid in their house, this house, until her face returned to normal. One afternoon as he had made her lunch, the famous Daisy Juniper, two-time Oscar winner, had rested her pale, lovely head on his shoulder and cried. His arms had gone around her, startled by how fragile she seemed although almost his height. Winnie felt solid in his arms and in his bed. He worried he could crush Daisy, but when he relaxed his grip, she snuggled in closer. At the time he was lucky to get any kind of acting gig. His two film roles hadn't gotten much notice. His agent wanted him to audition for a brand new game show, *Tie the Knot.*

"Don't be a game show host," she whispered. "You're too good for that." And one slim-fingered hand slid inside his pants.

No wonder Winnie was such a goddamn basket case. Since the divorce, she said Daisy didn't call as much. They had lost touch. But that wasn't his fault.

He heard the noise again. He peeked outside. It was just a neighbor from across the street rolling out his trashcans. The guy was young, white, and looked like he'd just gotten out of bed. Another Los Angeles screenwriter or director or producer out of work and home in the middle of the day.

"I gotta go," Jonathan said to the dog. "I wish I could stay longer, but I can't."

He crouched and inhaled the salty, dirty dog smell. He closed his fists around Buddy's ears and held on tight. He pressed his forehead into the back of Buddy's neck. He needed to buy socks, but he couldn't remember where Jessica had told him to go. He and Winnie had danced in the aisles to the Muzak at the 99-cent store.

"Do you think I'm too old for a tattoo?" he asked Buddy.

Buddy wagged his tail.

As a present for their third anniversary, he was thinking of surprising Jessica with an intricate "J & J" tattooed onto his shoulder. It had to be high enough so a short sleeve would cover it next time they did *Tie the Knot* in Hawaii. He had asked the production assistant at work, a college student with ink up and down both arms, if it hurt.

"Shoulder's not too bad," the kid said. "No offense, but it hurts more when you're old—older."

"How old do you think I am?"

The p.a. had just shrugged, too smart to say what he really thought. "It's cool when older guys get tats. You know, ones that mean something to them, not just like, for beauty."

As if beauty on Jonathan was a ridiculous notion. But it was going to be a drop-dead gorgeous tattoo. Romantic, but not too flowery. Jessica had already told him the best place to go, where all her young friends were doing it. Jessica had an amazing flower thingy in the curve of her lower back, just above her butt. A tramp plant or fan stamp or something. Of course if he put his tattoo up high enough for a sleeve to cover it, no one would ever see it except Jessica. He wanted people to see it. He wanted the p.a. at work to see how beautiful it was. It was a complicated decision. He still had a month to make up his mind.

7.

Dave "Kidney" Hollister made sure the curtains were closed and the door of his motel room locked before he gently lifted his gray Samsonite suitcase onto the bed. He tunelessly whistled Michael Jackson's Thriller as he ran his hands over the hard plastic. He took the time to do an MJ type hip thrust and a spin. He attempted the moon walk. It was all a little ridiculous in a sixty-five-year-old overweight man in JC Penney jeans and a safari jacket, but he couldn't help himself. Today was his day.

"Okay, okay, I'm coming," he said to the suitcase. "Daddy's coming."

He undid the combination lock and slipped it from the handle. He rubbed his hands together before sliding back the catch. The top popped open. There were clothes inside, nothing but very dirty clothes, a lot of them smeared with a suspicious looking mustard colored substance. The perfect ploy, Kidney knew, to keep customs officials from digging too deep. He tossed the clothes on the floor and carefully, gingerly removed the suitcase's false bottom.

Five beautiful black-headed pythons, each in its own partitioned space, undulated and hissed at him. Three were the more typical tan with brownish stripes, but two had unusual cream and red markings. He was looking at a fortune in snakes. His fortune. They were exquisite, perfect living specimens. Reluctantly, he closed the suitcase so they wouldn't escape. He could have stared at them all day, but they had been on a long, strenuous journey with him from Australia and he needed to feed them quickly before they attempted to eat each other. He took a Ben & Jerry's ice cream container from his backpack. That morning he had gone out behind the motel, in the dead grass bordering the 405 freeway, and collected some common western fence lizards. He opened the ice cream bucket and looked inside. Only one lizard had died. The others were busy gnawing on it. Good. They would be well fed when they became food. The circle of life.

Kidney opened the suitcase again and with his bare hand grabbed lizard after lizard, dropping them in, one by one, a meal for each python. He replaced the false bottom and closed it up. He didn't think his babies would mind dining in the dark. There was one lizard left in the container, plus the dead one. He put the top back on and put it in the motel fridge's tiny freezer. He grinned thinking about housekeeping finding his treat.

He whistled and danced a little more, looking at himself in the mirror over the dresser. His jacket said it all: adventurer, wild man, ready for anything. He would definitely wear it when he went out to celebrate tonight. He masqueraded as a photographer. His camera bags were all outfitted with false bottoms and hidden compartments. Today they were filled with blue-tongued skinks from New Guinea and chameleons from Madagascar. In the most protected pockets, he had geometric turtles, endangered and therefore worth a pretty penny, from South Africa. He had become a top-notch reptile smuggler with a superior reputation. He'd always—since he was a kid—been good at catching reptiles. Now he was good at bringing them into the country and selling them. Of course it was illegal and the penalties if caught were massive fines and some serious jail time. Fuck it. He couldn't think about that now. And anyway, his country owed him. He had lost his job of twenty-two years when they closed the Saturn plant in Spring Hill, Tennessee. Twenty-two years working the line and nothing to show for it while management made out like royalty. They were the real crooks. He smiled at the suitcase on the bed. This was much more fun. Maybe the economic downturn had done him a service.

His penis was talking to him. He needed a woman. He wished he didn't have to pay for it, but the ones he liked never liked him. Not all on their own. If he was willing to spend the cash, he could get the hottest slut in town. Cash for the slash. But it was fucking expensive. Eighty bucks for a blow job in the back seat of his rented Ford Fiesta was criminal. A fool and his money are soon parted, his father used to say. He was not a fool, but he needed a little release. It was easier away from the States. The women of the jungles where he did his business were happy to oblige and they were usually free. He had gotten hooked on the taste of dark meat. He might even settle down with a couple of women on a plantation in New Guinea or someplace, but here he was in L- fucking-A, beauty capital of the world, and he wanted a hot little honey to ride. And he would have one, even if it cost him.

"Hey," he said to his reflection. "Hey, baby." He did the signature Michael Jackson move: pulling down on his imaginary fedora. He spun again, stumbling a little on the carpet. He caught sight in the mirror of his jowls flapping like the tails of his jacket, but he just laughed. He knew the chicks he wanted were only interested in the size of his wallet. "And after today, baby, it's gonna be gi-normous!"

He had meetings later, but first he had to call that kid and collect the money for his iguana. The kid said he wanted wild, not captivity raised, to strengthen the gene pool. Kidney told him that was wise, but he really had no idea. He wasn't a scientist, but the kid wanting a great green iguana from him instead of a legal buy from a pet store meant a special trip to Paraguay next week and that meant extra goddamn money. Jesus, he was making a killing this time around.

He popped out his cell phone from the special phone pocket on his jacket and texted, "Photos of your girlfriend are ready." Cell phones weren't safe, everything had to be in code, but he'd explained the drill to Oren when they had met six months ago at the Sacramento Reptile Expo. His website said 'wildlife photographer' and 'reptiles my specialty' and 'all types available.' The in-crowd knew what he meant. He worked hard to keep his business very private. Nobody even knew his real name. They just called him Kidney. It had been his moniker since he first began collecting reptiles, years and years ago, and he had told a group he'd give his left kidney for a Duvacel's gecko. He repeated the phrase often enough, about enough different reptiles, that everyone started calling him Kidney. Fine by him. It was simpler this way. And safer.

He sent out three more coded messages to clients, also about "photos," and decided to go out to the pool to wait for the replies. The Southern California weather he had heard so much about was looking nasty, but he grabbed a beer from a brown paper bag on the floor and figured at least he could say he'd been to LA and had cocktails by the pool.

8.

Winnie was dreaming. "I don't know what to say," she complained. "I don't know what to ask."

"Sssssssilly girl," the voice said. "Assssssssssk."

Winnie had recently visited a psychic and while it hadn't been a very satisfying experience, the plump, Armenian fortune teller had figured prominently in her dreams since then. In every dream, just as it had been in real life, Winnie knew she was doing it all wrong.

In the dream, Madame Nadalia was hissing like a snake. "Assssssssssk your quesssssstionsssssss."

"You're the psychic," Winnie said. "Can't you tell me what my question is?"

"Oh yesssssssssssss."

"I wish," Winnie said in her dream. "I wish."

Winnie drove past the psychic advisor every morning on her way to work after she dropped Lacy at school. The white clapboard house had plastic flowers in pots along the walkway and a purple awning decorated with stars and moons. A sandwich board offered help for every possible problem: love, career, money, and weight loss. Every morning she thought about stopping. That morning it had been raining. Traffic was stalled and as she sat in her car the purple neon star lit up suddenly and turned the raindrops on her windshield to lavender. It was a sign. There was an empty parking space right in front. The car next to her let her get over. It was meant to be.

Madame Nadalia and Winnie sat in purple folding chairs on either side of a card table covered in a dark blue tablecloth with gold fringe. The dining room was set up as the fortune telling domain, glittery stars pasted to the walls, fake tapestries covering the windows, but through a beaded curtain, on the kitchen counter, Winnie saw a child's GI Joe lunchbox, a can of Progresso clam chowder, and a blinking cell phone. From a back room she could faintly hear a morning television talk show.

"I'm sorry," Winnie began. "Should I make an appointment?"

"Please. I was expecting you."

Madame Nadalia spoke with Dracula's accent. She wore pink sweatpants and a red T-shirt appliquéd with an American flag. Her fuzzy slippers shuffled against the worn brown shag carpeting. She pulled a tissue from her pocket and dusted off the crystal ball.

"Ask." Madame Nadalia sounded annoyed. "Come on. Ask."

Winnie sighed. What did she really want Madame Nadalia to tell her? 'Go to the grocery store on Tuesday. Make spaghetti for dinner. Buy the expensive laundry detergent. It costs a little more, but you'll be happy you did. If you put a belt on that blue jacket it will make you look five pounds thinner!' Those were the things she needed from a fortune teller. What to wear, what to cook, what to say to her daughter. She did not really want to know the future; she was afraid she already knew the answer. No, she and Lacy would never be close. No, there would never be another man in her life. No, she would never leave her boring job. Her life would go on exactly as it always had and then she would die.

"Oh God," Winnie said.

She looked out the psychic's living room window. The rain

came down from gray cauliflower clouds. On the wall behind Madame Nadalia's head was a paint-by-number portrait of Jesus. His blue eyes looked in two different directions, one at the ceiling and one frowning toward the kitchen as if the unanswered cell phone bothered him. His crown of thorns was made of little Christmas lights. A white cord dangled down to the socket.

"You like that? My grandson made it for me." Madame Nadalia got up and plugged in the cord. The white lights blinked on and off.

"Beautiful."

"Yes. Good. Okay." She took a deep breath and closed her eyes. Her eyebrows were painted on. Her dry auburn hair sat crooked on her head. A wig. "Give me your hands."

Winnie put both hands on the table. The woman took them and turned them palms up. She blew on each one. Her breath was warm and smelled of burnt corn.

"You have a child."

That was not impressive. It didn't take a clairvoyant to know Winnie was a mom. Her oversized shirt hung over her jeans; she wore sneakers and her hair was in a messy ponytail—plus she had parked her station wagon right out front.

"A daughter," Madame Nadalia continued.

She had a 50/50 chance of being right. "Yes."

"Her father is gone. Wait. He lives far away."

Winnie frowned. Most Friday afternoons she made the trip across town to deliver Lacy to Beverly Hills. Some days it took forever to get there and even longer to get home, but it was not far in miles. In other ways however, Jonathan's side of town could be considered another universe. Wealthy people, teams of gardeners, valet parking at the grocery store. Still, it was not as if he lived in another country.

"Not that far away."

The fortune teller nodded. "No, but he thinks he does."

She was right about that. Winnie surrendered. "Tell me," she said. "Go ahead. Tell me everything."

Madame Nadalia pulled a deck of battered tarot cards from the pocket of her sweatpants and put them on the table. She blew her nose on the tissue she had used for dusting and put it back in the same pocket.

"Shuffle these three times. Then cut once to the left. You must concentrate on your question."

"What question?"

Madame shrugged. She lifted a knobby arthritic finger to scratch under her wig. "What do you want?"

"When you put it like that—" Winnie began, but then her cell phone rang. She dug in her bag for her phone and looked at the number. "Sorry," she apologized. "It's my mother."

She got up and walked to the front window. "Daisy."

"Where are you?"

"This phone is for emergencies."

"You weren't home," Daisy complained.

"Are you okay?"

"Where are you?"

"I'm at a psychic."

Her mother snorted. "A good one?"

"Near home. I drive by every day."

"I can recommend the best. Gary. My Gary. He's amazing. He's here in New York, but he can read you over the phone."

"Is something wrong?"

"I can't believe you just walked in off the street. Look around. Does it look like the house of someone who knows the future?"

Winnie looked at the ugly carpeting, the sagging floral couch, the glass shelf filled with porcelain angel figurines.

"Well—"

"Don't give her any money. Go home. I'll give you Gary's number." Her mother paused. "You don't need a psychic anyway. You need a dating service."

Winnie sighed. "Daisy."

"Listen, I'm insanely busy. Can I talk to you later?"

"You called me."

"I guess I just had a feeling I should. Go home."

Winnie hung up and walked back to the table. "I'm sorry," she apologized again. She sat down, but Madame Nadalia stood. She scratched under her wig. She looked at her watch. She started for the kitchen.

"Wait," Winnie said. "Are you coming back?"

"The things I have to tell you, you will learn anyway. Soon enough you will live them. You will meet a man. There will be much excitement, a trip to another place."

"All that is going to happen to me?"

"I am only the weather report," Madame said. "I can tell you it's going to rain, but you'll forget your umbrella anyway."

"No. I won't. I promise."

Madame Nadalia shook her head as she went through the beaded curtain.

"So?" Winnie tried to laugh. "How big an umbrella do I need?"

"Ask your mother."

She disappeared around the corner. The TV got louder and then a door closed and it was muffled again.

Jesus twinkled. His right eye seemed to be staring at Winnie. She breathed an odor of infection, like the yellow pus of a child's skinned knee. The rain fell harder as she opened the front door to leave. She almost laughed, she did need that umbrella.

As she drove away from the psychic, Winnie wondered what it was she really wanted. She should want to go to college. She always meant to get a degree in something, but she kept putting it off and then she met Jonathan. Eight months later she was pregnant with Lacy.

As a child she had wanted to be a clown. She loved making people laugh. She knew she wasn't beautiful like her mother, but she was strong and flexible. She taught herself to walk on her hands and sometimes, when Lacy was at school or sleeping, she still flipped upside down and turned the pages of the newspaper with her toes. There was always clown college—two birds with one stone.

She had never wanted to be an actor. Never. She knew too many, Daisy and her friends, and they were boring, myopic, and self-absorbed. Most of them were stupid. Of course her mother assumed she thought she wasn't good enough, that she didn't try because she knew she couldn't compete. And that was fine with Daisy.

"Don't worry, darling. We can't all be important. Maybe you'll marry someone fabulous."

And then, to her mother's smug satisfaction, she married Jonathan.

Winnie thought she wanted a new man in her life, but then again, maybe not. The thought of sex on the dining room table as wine glasses crashed to the floor or bent over a kitchen chair with her skirt lifted just made her tired. The idea of loving anyone as much as she had loved Jonathan was exhausting. She had been addicted to him. They would spend hours together, eating, playing, cooking, screwing. Finally, he would drop her off at her apartment, kiss her, and tell her he'd see her tomorrow. She would go inside and walk in circles in her living room, unable to sleep or even sit down, and then she would get in her car and drive back to his place. She had no shame. She banged on his door begging for more. More, more, more.

The only thing Winnie knew she wanted was to still be married. She had always wanted a lasting, meaningful marriage and Jonathan had ruined that. Daisy went through men like maggots through shit. Winnie had wanted to be steadfast and true, loyal as a dog and in love forever. It was the one thing her mother was not good at.

"You're the pot of jewels at the end of my rainbow—or whatever that expression is," Jonathan had said on their very first date.

"You make me feel invincible," he said that same night in bed.

"You're dragging me down," he said eleven years later. "You make me feel like a failure."

They were in the kitchen. She was making coffee and she went on making it. His game show had taken off; the ratings were astronomical. He had met Jessica, but she didn't know it yet, only smelled something floral in the creases of his neck and saw a new satisfaction in his chest and shoulders. She thought it was the show, the makeup, his success.

"I think you can do better," she said, meaning better than the game show, not better than her and Lacy. "When is your contract up?"

"You're so negative," he said, "You're putting that harmful energy out into the universe."

"I can't believe you just said that."

"I'm leaving."

"What about Lacy?"

"I'm not running from the past, I'm going forward to my destiny."

"Where did you get this crap?" The answer streaked across her mind like a shooting star. "What's her name?"

And, a year later, long after Jessica had moved in with him,

Winnie was still driving by his house. She would get a babysitter so she could watch through the windows as they cooked dinner, practiced yoga together, and went up the stairs to bed. A year later she was still calling in the middle of the night just to hear his voice. She bought every magazine with an article about Jonathan Parker, host of television's most popular game show. She drew mustaches and warts on the photos of Jessica.

But finally, eventually, more than two years after he had left her, she stopped. She did not drive by his house. She did not wait for the phone to ring. And she discovered she no longer wanted anything. She stopped masturbating, after twenty minutes of effort and even accoutrements she was still making To-Do lists in her head. She did not care what she ate, if she saw her friends, or what would happen next. She did not cry at movies. She was never frightened. She was numb. Perhaps that was what she should have asked Madame Nadalia. "Will I ever feel anything again?"

9.

"Fuck!" Oren shouted. The text had come too soon. Kidney wasn't supposed to arrive until next week. Next week. When all of this would be over. "Fuck!" he said again. Now what?

He opened the door to the bedroom. She was still out, snuffling a little as she breathed. She was tied down. Could he leave her? He couldn't. It would take an hour to get all the way down by the airport and an hour to get back and he had his plans. His plans.

"Can't wait to see the pix," he texted Kidney. "Working today. Tomorrow?"

The answer came back almost immediately. "Today only."

"Fuck!"

He knew Kidney was the best. He knew Kidney would get him the best iguana possible, but Oren didn't even have all the money. That was part of the plan too; get this rich mom to fork over the thousand dollars he was missing. He was sure she would give it to him later, after they had talked, when she understood what he needed from her. The money was the least of it. She would be grateful to him. She would thank him for opening her eyes. She would think a thousand dollars well worth it, cheap even. Shit, shit, shit. When would she wake up? He leaned over her and hissed her ear. The way his mother used to wake him, "Sssssssssss."

He looked down at her dark head. Her scalp was visible

through the damp hairs. She smelled bad. Later he would let her take a shower. Good, he thought. She would appreciate him. She would know he was not a bad guy. He had thought carefully and prepared a list of questions. Eventually she would begin to understand the meaning of this—the good cause it was for. Years from now it would be a story they would tell. He had not imagined that before, but all at once he could see it. Sitting around the table, maybe it was a holiday, Thanksgiving or Christmas. A long table filled with food and everybody drinking expensive champagne. There would be children and old people too.

Tell it again, someone would say, Oren, tell how you met Winnie.

He took a deep breath. It would all work out. It was still early. She could wake up now and he could take her with him and they would have time for everything. He put his mouth close to her ear and hissed again. He tried not to breathe in the cooked vegetable smell of her dirty hair.

"Ssssss," he said. Like a cat when it was angry. "Sssss."

But she did not move. What was the difference between being asleep and being unconscious?

He went through everything step by step. He would have to force her into the car. He would have to keep her tied up; otherwise how could he drive?

He needed the gun from the box in the closet. It was not a real gun, just a cheap bit of plastic. It was as light as air, but it was flat gray and a very realistic copy of a Glock. He had bought it for a Halloween costume and even the people at the party had thought it was real. They had stepped away from him, smiling as if to keep him happy. Two girls had left the party as soon as he arrived in his trench coat with the plastic gun. As if he were the type to have a gun. He did not do drugs or even drink beer. He did not speed. He never broke the law.

"Sssssss," he hissed again.

Maybe she would cooperate just because. Because he brought her the water and the aspirin. Because he was nice, a nice guy. He had no idea if he would hurt her if he woke her up. He had moved her when he wasn't supposed to, and she was still alive. The bump on her head wasn't that bad. Waking her was probably fine. And he had to. He did. Today only, Kidney had said. Today was the day.

"Get up," he spoke through clenched teeth. "Wake up!"

Winnie's eyes fluttered open. When her eyes focused and she saw it was him, she tried to turn her head. She tried to get away. It hurt her to move. He could see that.

"Wait," he said.

But she closed her eyes and slipped away from him.

"I wish," he thought he heard her say. "I wish."

"Wake the fuck up!" Oren said to her. He jostled her shoulder again. Her head flopped and she frowned in her sleep. "Wake up!" Was she pretending? Her eyes had opened for a moment. He touched her again and she flinched and moaned.

Why me? He thought. What am I going to do? He pounded his fist into his leg. And again. Stop it. Stop it!

He couldn't wait anymore. She had to get up. He tipped the glass of water over on her face. Not all of it, but most. She coughed and sputtered, her eyes opened.

"Come on," he said.

She looked up at him and he saw how frightened she was. This was not working out. Not at all. She had to understand him, to learn from him, to realize that what he wanted was best for everybody. It would not happen if she was too scared to listen.

"I'm sorry I had to wake you up."

She threw the blanket onto the floor. That wasn't nice of her. It was a clean blanket. He had put it over her to make her more comfortable. Now he could see her, all of her. Her bloody shirt was clinging to her chest and stomach; her ponytail was wrapped around her neck in a wet black clump. She struggled against the ropes tying her to the bed and the flesh on her thighs wobbled. Her eyes went up to the fairy hanging from the light fixture, then back to him. If anything, she looked more terrified than before.

"I brought you water," he said. "There's still some left. And aspirin."

He put the glass down again on the bedside table. He picked up the bottle of aspirin and shook two of them onto the bed.

She was so slow. Usually he had a lot of patience, it was one of his strengths, but today it was all he could do not to grab her and yank her to her feet. She was looking around, examining the bare room. Was she stupid? Handicapped somehow?

"Take them," he said. "We have to go."

10.

Winnie looked up past her kidnapper. A dried and shriveled monkey skeleton with wings hung from the overhead light fixture. Monkeys don't have wings, she thought, do they? Her head hurt so badly she could not remember. No, monkeys do not have wings, but there was definitely one hanging from the ceiling. It was something he wanted to do to her. Some kind of hybrid experiment. In a basement operating room, he would amputate her legs and hands; attach bicycle wheels to her knees and feathers to her wrists. He would hang her from the ceiling when she died. She clenched her teeth to keep from screaming.

She sat up slowly and took a deep breath to keep from vomiting. She tugged at the ropes around her ankles. The knots were under the bed. Without thinking, she lifted her shirt to inspect the cuts on her stomach and pulled the barely formed scabs away with the fabric. They began bleeding again. There would be scars on her stomach, if she lived long enough to heal. Or would she mend after death, the cells rejuvenating like hair and fingernails that continue to grow in the coffin? Her hand went to the enormous bump on the back of her head. A real goose egg. Stuffed goose. Only six weeks from now she might be his Christmas dinner.

"What do you want?" she mumbled thickly.

"Take the aspirin."

She forced herself to think. He wanted her to take these

pills. The light escaping from the curtained window was bright. Was anyone missing her? Probably not yet. She had told Jonathan she was too busy to have lunch. Lacy was at school and then orchestra. The tennis teacher would be pissed but not concerned. She could not think of anyone who would worry, not for a long time.

Her stomach growled. She had to pee. Bizarre that no matter what, threat of murder and dismemberment, after kidnapping and violent confrontation, her body continued as it always did. Hunger. Elimination. Only death would stop its functions. She would wet the bed and then he would kill her and she would die on a mattress soaked in her own urine and stinking of sweat.

She had been a fool to get into his car. She should have waited for the van. She caught her breath. The van. The van would have come to get her and when she wasn't standing outside, the driver would have gone into the shop. The manager would say he thought she was waiting. She had said she would wait. They would be the first to be concerned. They would call the rental place to see if she had walked there. The van driver would look for her as he drove back. When she never showed up, they would call the police. People were already searching for her. She knew it. She had to know it. And she was still alive. There had been plenty of opportunity to kill her, but it seemed he wanted her around.

"C'mon," her kidnapper whined. "We have to go."

She wanted the water and aspirin so badly. Her tongue was dry and swollen. She held the glass up to the dim light, looking for powders or pills.

"You idiot," he said. He took the glass out of her hand and had a drink. "I'd swallow your aspirin too, but then it wouldn't do you any good. Look. It says fucking 'Bayer' right on it."

He gave her back the glass. She took it. She picked up the

aspirin and put them in her mouth and had a sip of water. It was cool all the way down her throat and through her chest. She had never tasted anything so delicious. She took another drink and closed her eyes for just a moment, holding the water in her mouth, letting her tongue soak in it.

"Thank you."

The asshole almost smiled. His shoulders were knobby, his collarbone pronounced. He looked fragile, his body still that of a skinny ten-year-old. His back curved in a letter "C." Not so long ago he had been watching Sesame Street. He shook his hair off his forehead. He was barely more than a child. And all the more terrifying because of it. Children don't know right from wrong. Children don't understand that a person stabbed by a knife was dead forever.

"Now I really do need to go to the bathroom," she said.

"What?"

"I didn't before. I admit that. But now I really do."

"I'll bring you a pot."

He moved to the side of the bed. He stood close. His eyes slid from her thighs to her breasts, then back to her belly trembling under her thin bloody shirt. Winnie squeezed the empty glass willing it to break. He pulled it out of her hand. He had gotten too smart for her heroics.

"We need to talk," he said. "Maybe in the car."

"We're going somewhere?"

"I have... I have to—"

"How old are you?"

"I have a plan."

"This is going to ruin your life."

"Shut up."

"Where do your parents live? Are they nearby?"

"This has nothing to do with them."

"You'll go to jail for a hundred years and you'll never see them again. You'll never see your mother again."

"Shut up!" He slapped her.

Her neck cracked and she saw flashes of white. She fell over on the bed, hiding her head with her arms.

"Get up. We have to go. I mean it. I have to take you with me."

Winnie nodded. It was better to go. If they were out someone would see her and realize she was in trouble.

"You have to untie me."

His face had gotten darker and darker until it was a black mark looming over her. The room had grown darker too. The sun could not have set so fast. The water in her empty belly mixed with her strong need to pee.

"Please," she whispered.

"Please what?"

He stepped closer. One freckled hand grabbed her upper arm. Her flesh collapsed like Play-Doh. Her gaze was just at the crotch of his jeans. She looked down to his feet in brand new sneakers; the laces were so white they glowed. When had he bought them? Did the salesman know he was selling shoes to a psychopath? She moved up his body to his face, his mouth open and his breath coming fast. He had missed shaving a small cluster of reddish hairs under his chin.

"Please may I go to the bathroom?" He wouldn't take her in his car if she wet her pants. "I'll leave the door open. Please."

He sat down beside her without letting go. "You play tennis with these arms?"

"I told you I'm not very good."

He bowed his head. He changed then, as if he had taken a step back, forced himself to breathe. His voice was calmer. "I have an errand I have to run."

"You can leave me here."

"I don't think so." He stroked her arm. "Your skin is soft."

"You're softer than I am." Winnie ran a finger across his bicep. "You're so young. You still have perfect skin."

They paused like that, his hands on her upper arm, her hand on his. They were close enough to kiss. He studied her as if searching for something in her cheekbones, her eyebrows, or the curve of her jaw. Winnie learned the constellation of four freckles on his cheek. She saw the tiny pimple beginning beside his nose. A boy, she told herself, just a boy. If she fucked him, would he let her go?

Oren touched the tiny scar above her ear behind her hairline. "That your plastic surgery scar?"

She pushed his hand away. "I have not had plastic surgery. No way. I am not that vain."

"All women are vain."

"Not enough to want plastic surgery."

"You're only thirty-eight. Wait 'til you're fifty."

"Am I going to be fifty? Huh, Shithead? Am I going to make it to fifty?"

He squeezed her arm hard and she hit his cheek as hard as she could.

He leapt away from her, one hand to his stinging cheek. "You hit me. You keep hitting me."

"Of course I do." Winnie tried not to, but she began to cry.

"Don't do that."

Fuck him, she thought, covered her face with her hands and sobbed.

"No crying. No, no, no. It's fine. Listen, okay? You can use the bathroom on our way out. Shh. Shh. I'll untie you."

He got down on his stomach and reached way under the bed to undo the knots. She wished she had any kind of a weapon, an object like a lamp or even a heavy book, but her hands by themselves weren't strong enough to hurt him.

"Fuck it." He got to his feet and took his knife out of his pocket.

Winnie flinched and her stomach roiled. His grim smile was no help. He leaned toward her slowly with the blade out. She closed her eyes. He would cut off her legs, he would kill her because he had to leave and he couldn't undo the rope.

But he bent and cut the rope around her ankles carefully and did not even graze her skin with the knife. "There. Get up."

She tried, but her legs had fallen asleep. Past the pins and needles stage, they were like logs attached to her hips.

"Get up," he said again.

"My legs are asleep." She rubbed them, wiggled her ankles and pulled one knee up and then the other. "What is that thing on the ceiling?"

"A fairy." He said it without looking. "It's my uncle's."

"It's a monkey."

"Monkeys don't have wings. It's the skeleton of a fairy."

"A fairy? Like in the woods?"

"Girls like it."

"Bullshit."

"Why do you talk like that?"

"You think you're going to attract a girl with that? It looks like a monster."

"I told you, it's my uncle's."

Oren walked over and opened the closet. She couldn't see inside as he rummaged around. The door was in the way. She tried to get up and run, but her legs were almost useless. She slid off the bed onto the floor as he turned around. He was holding a gun.

"Where do you think you're going?"

Winnie knew she was done for. The gun ruined any chance she had. She was only surprised he had not used it earlier when she was half way out the bathroom window. She had to assume he had been saving it. Later, he would spread a dirty shower curtain on the floor to keep things clean. He would make her stand in the middle of the plastic. She would beg him not to. She would offer deals to him and to God, but neither would be interested. Then he would take a pillow, some old pillow with a blue flowered pillowcase, and hold it over the muzzle and shoot her. She imagined it would hurt. She imagined it would not be graceful. She knew dying for real wasn't like it was in the movies. She had watched her mother die in one of her early films, but in that movie the rapist had strangled her. Daisy had died naked, slowly and beautifully. Her bowels had not let go. There was no blood or vomit. Perhaps his plan was to make a snuff film. She almost smiled. She would finally have a starring role. What was the old joke? Hey Mom, good news: I got a big part in a movie. Bad news: no chance for a sequel.

The first time she saw Jonathan act he had carried a gun. It was bigger than this one, but it was not real. It was a lousy play, he wasn't particularly good in it, but when he saved his co-star, a buxom blond hooker with a heart of gold, it was real to Winnie. He was a savior; he had saved the blond and he would save her. Never again would she be nothing but Daisy Juniper's daughter. Never again the afterthought; the 'I didn't know she had a child;' the dark-haired oddity in the corner. She would be Jonathan Parker's girl. He was handsome and on his way. He didn't care who her mother was. Her past was wiped clean. He was her knight in shining armor who pulled her up on his white horse and galloped away with her. Jonathan Parker's girl.

But he could not save her this time. Even if he wanted to. No one could save her now. Two defeated tears slid from the corners of her eyes.

"No more crying."

A gun would not hurt as much as a knife. One blast and it could be over.

"Get up," he said.

She held onto the side of the bed and stood, awkwardly, trying to keep her skirt down and her ass hidden. She took one step, stumbled, and grabbed him for support.

"Hey, hey. Watch it."

"I'm sorry." She let go, but her legs were not steady.

"Okay," he said, "You can hold onto me."

"Thank you."

They hobbled out the door, a grandmother leaning on the attendant at the nursing home. If she lived through this, she would never complain about getting old again. Please, God, she thought, let me be old.

He sighed as they crept up the hallway. "Why did you get divorced?"

Winnie's head came up in surprise. "What?"

"Did you get divorced because of your daughter?"

She didn't want to talk about Lacy. She didn't want him to know anything about her. She refused to answer.

"She got in the way, didn't she? You had to stop being an actress."

"I never wanted to be an actress." Why did he think that? She never told him anything like that. In the car? No, they had chattered about nothing. Nothing. She should have asked him a question, his name at least. She could have asked to see his license. If her head would stop pounding she could think. What had she told him in the car?

"Don't lie to me," he said. "If there's one thing I hate, it's lying."

"Really," she said, "I'm not an actress. My husband, my ex,

I told you, he's the actor. He was going to be a movie star, like Anthony Hopkins or Paul Newman. He loved them. He wanted that. I loved being a mom, being married, having a home."

"I don't believe you." His hand tightened around her arm. He pulled her faster down the hall.

"I swear, please. I swear. It was Jonathan, my ex. He left me for a girl he met on his show."

Jessica had been a contestant on *Tie the Knot*. She was young, pretty, and corn fed, fresh from Iowa or Idaho, one of those Midwestern states famous for growing carbohydrates. She was a yoga instructor hoping to teach Downward Dog to the stars. Her energy, Jonathan said, that's what attracted him. What a cliché.

"She's ten years younger than I am. Not much older than my daughter."

"That's harsh."

"She has red hair, darker than yours, but irresistible, I guess." Winnie paused. "I bet the girls just love your red hair."

He smiled and blushed. Good. She wanted him to feel good, stay happy with her. They reached the bathroom door. He had re-hung the shower curtain—it was just one of those rods with suction cups at each end. He had gone outside and replaced the screen.

"You fixed everything," Winnie said. She hoped he could not hear her disappointment.

"I did."

No evidence of their fight or her attempt to escape. Nothing for a neighbor to notice. Winnie put a hand on the wall to steady herself.

"Leave the door open a little." He gestured with the gun. "I'm staying right here."

As she stepped into the bathroom she suddenly had to go so

badly, she wasn't sure she would get her pants down in time. The tennis panties were tight and sticky against her hot skin. She had to wiggle and dance. But she made it. She sat and released the warm stream of urine. It had to be the best moment of her life. It was a joy to have a clean toilet and a semi-private room and this feeling, this feeling of relief.

Thank you, she said silently, to him, to the universe, to herself. Thank you for not letting me die in my own urine.

"Jesus," he said from outside. "You really had to go."

Winnie almost laughed. She finished, flushed, and washed her hands, then her face. The cold water coming from the tap was another gift. Please, she prayed, if I live through this I will never take water for granted again. The gold streaks in the fake marble were like veins in raw meat.

"I'm just washing my face," she called.

Quietly, with the water still running, she pulled open the medicine chest, but inside there was only a box of Band-Aids, a tube of antibiotic cream, and two things of dental floss. In her own medicine chest, crammed full of crap, she could have found a weapon. Perfume to spray in his eyes, an ancient rusty razor blade, a nail file. The cabinet under his sink held only a package of toilet paper and his carefully coiled electric razor. Her life was so full, every corner chock o' block with stuff. His seemed absolutely empty, except for Cookie, that monkey fairy skeleton, and now her.

She used his towel and carefully folded it over the rack just the way he had it. She felt better. The aspirin was beginning to work. She knew if they got in the car she would get away. Her purse was in the car. She could poke him in the eye with her house key. She stepped out and he grabbed her arm.

"In here."

He tugged her to another closed door in the hallway, the last door before the living room. Her resolve evaporated. She did not want to go to some new room, a chamber devised for her torture or demise. Fairy skeletons for his girlfriend, monkey legs, lizard skin. Winnie's teeth began to chatter, goose bumps erupted despite the heat. She forced herself to stay upright.

"Wait—" she began. She could not say more.

Oren opened the door. "Go on," he waved her inside. "Go in."

Winnie lurched into the room, but it was just a bedroom, his bedroom, as clean and sterile as the rest of the house. There was no steel operating table, no open case of torture tools. Thank God, she thought. His laptop was open on the bed. He stepped past her and closed it quickly. The double bed had no bedspread. It was made military style, corners just so, the white sheets and blue blanket perfectly straight. Only one pillow. Maybe he wanted sex. Involuntarily, her legs squeezed together. Then again, maybe it would distract him. She searched for something she could use to hit him as he lay on top of her, a lamp or an ashtray, but the dresser top was empty and dusted. A TV and a DVD player were on a stand at the foot of the bed. No reading lamp, not a single book anywhere, only a framed photo on the nightstand. She looked closer; it was a picture of a tiny lizard perched in a man's hand.

"Don't touch anything," he said.

But she picked up the photo. She could hit him with it if she had to, even though the frame was just cheap plastic. "Is this Cookie?"

Surprisingly, his shoulders relaxed and he grinned. She exhaled.

"Can you believe it? Hard to imagine now that he's so enormous."

"Is this your hand?"

"My father's."

"Where was this?"

"The Amazing Amazon. Not in Africa, but a show, like a reptile show. My dad owned it when I was a kid."

"You've had Cookie for so long."

"He's my best friend. I know that sounds silly."

"Not at all. I love my dog."

"Oh yeah, right."

"My daughter named him something long and complicated when we got him. I just call him Buddy. Honestly, he's good company." Bullshit, she thought, I hate that damn dog, but at that moment even cleaning up the poop in her front yard sounded good.

"Buddy," his voice got quiet. "Buddy is not a nice dog. Buddy is a pit bull. Trained to attack, to bite, even your daughter."

"What are you talking about? He's a mutt. A sweetie. I know exactly how you feel about Cookie," she blathered on. "Buddy and I spend a lot of time together. He has the softest ears."

"I told you I hate lying."

"I'm not. I'm not."

He was jittery and frowning and Winnie saw she had upset him again. He put the gun down on the dresser. He opened a drawer. He was searching for something. He used both hands to rummage through a stack of seemingly identical white T-shirts.

Winnie jumped from the bed and pushed him away. She grabbed for the gun, but he whirled and kicked her hard in the stomach. She flew back and collapsed on the rug. The wind was knocked out of her, she gasped for air.

"Oh God. I'm sorry," he said to her.

She rolled away from him and turned her back. She tucked her head and knees into her chest, protecting herself as much as possible from the next blow. She fought back the bile.

"Don't kick me again."

"I had to. Don't you see? I had to."

No, she didn't 'see.' There was nothing clear about any of this. There was a dusty sock under his bed. He was not as fastidious as he believed. He had lost a sock and it probably drove him crazy looking for it. It made her feel a tiny bit better. She would never tell him the sock was there.

"Put this on," he said. "You can't go out like that. C'mon." He nudged her with his toe.

She unwound slowly and looked up at him. He held a white T-shirt out to her.

"Get up now. C'mon. Get up." He was whining at her. "We're going to be late."

Winnie unfolded and rolled over slowly. She did not wipe her tears away as she got to her feet.

He shook the shirt at her. "Put this on. I can't look at that one anymore."

The blood was evidence, she saw, proof that he had hurt her, that what he was doing was wrong.

"Hurry," he said.

Winnie took the T-shirt and turned her back to him. The fact that he wanted her to change made her feel better. He wouldn't give her a clean shirt and then kill her. He was saving her for something. She lifted her nylon tennis top gingerly, carefully over her head. Then she decided to turn back to him, to show him the long deep scrapes on her stomach, the stripes of crusty blood. She saw him wince. He avoided looking at her breasts in her jogging bra and she realized sex was not what this was about.

"You hurt me," she said quietly. " You keep hurting me."

"You hurt me too. My shoulder hurts. And my leg where you kicked me. You do this to yourself."

"What the hell do you want?"

"Put the goddamn shirt on!"

She put it on slowly, watching him every minute.

"Why are you doing this?" she asked. "I haven't done anything to you."

"If I was your daughter," he said, "I would hate you. I would."

"What?"

"Your daughter hates you. Right now. She is hating you."

"No, she is not." Winnie thought of Lacy slamming the
car door just that morning, those hours, that lifetime ago. "My
daughter loves me."

He gestured with the gun for her to leave. "We have to go."

She watched him cringe as she dropped her bloody shirt
right on his pillow. Then he stepped back to let her go first and
she kicked him as hard as she could between the legs. He gave a
little cry and fell back.

She ran through the living room, the empty dining room
and into the kitchen. She had seen the backdoor; it had to open.
Cookie was up on his log against the opposite wall. She rushed
to the door. It was locked, but the key was right in the lock. Had
no one ever told him that was the stupidest place to keep a key?
In her hurry she pulled it from the keyhole and dropped it. She
crouched and felt for it desperately among the damp newspapers
and badly soiled sand. This area was Cookie's bathroom. She had
to find that key. She had it in her hand as Oren lurched in.

"Stay away from that!"

She got the key in the lock. She turned it, heard the bolt
slide back and had her hand on the doorknob when he seized
her from behind. She held onto the knob as he tried to pull
her away. Through the window, she saw the grassy backyard of
the house behind them. A swing set. A yellow light on in the
kitchen. Maybe a mother was home making lunch. Maybe a

toddler was sitting at that kitchen table hungry and refusing to stop banging her spoon. The mother was sighing and wishing she were in Paris or Hawaii or even at the pizza place down the street. He began to pull her away. She balled up her fist. "Help me!" she shouted to the mother, to anyone, "Help!" She hit the window with her fist. She hit it again. Pain shot up her arm. Again and again. How could the glass not break?

"Safety glass." He read her mind.

He turned her to him and threw her through the swinging door into the dining room. She leapt toward the door to the garage. As her hand touched the knob, he grabbed her and tossed her down.

"Bitch!"

Her hand hurt. And her neck. And her arms and shoulders and her stomach and her head. She had banged her knee. She saw his angry red face, then rolled to all fours and tried crawling away from him to anywhere. He grabbed her ponytail.

"We are leaving and you will behave."

She saw the gun in his hand. She surrendered. But not for long.

11.

Lacy was learning to blow smoke rings. Buster showed her how as he drove. He flattened his lower lip and popped them out. Perfect rings. She could not get it right.

"Maybe marijuana smoke is different," he said. "Heavier or lighter or something."

"More circular," she joked and he laughed and so did she.

They arrived finally at his special place. It had taken a while through winding back streets, neighborhoods she did not know, each street getting bumpier and more neglected, the houses smaller and shabbier.

"We're here," he said.

He parked the car in front of a chain link fence. Junk was piled against the fence as high as possible. Chairs and boxes and car rims and an old birdcage stuffed with clothes. She couldn't see past the trash.

"Where?"

"Look up."

She could just glimpse something glittering.

"Shiny," Lacy said. "Whoopee."

Buster hung his head. Lacy felt terrible. She had crushed him. She had tried to be cool and it was just stupid.

"I'm sorry," she said. "I just can't see anything from here."

"I thought you were different."

"You did?"

He looked at her from under his shaggy hair. His eyes were red-rimmed, but a soft, rich brown. His skin was tan and blemish free; as smooth as if he had never shaved even though she knew he was a year older.

"Well, come on." She smiled at him. "Show me."

"Better take your backpack," he said. "I can't lock my car and in this neighborhood…" he shrugged.

She was glad she had left her flute at school. "I have orchestra this afternoon."

"I'll get you back in time, Miss Flautist."

"You remember I play the flute?"

"I remember your crazy curly hair too—and I grieve at its demise."

"If you knew how hard I work to make it straight."

"And why?"

If he didn't understand, she couldn't tell him. He was just a clueless stoner anyway. Still, it was funny he remembered her hair and that she played the flute. He led her around the corner. The chain link continued, the junk wall as well. Across the street an older Mexican woman, thick set with a broad, Indian face, was sweeping her porch. Buster waved at her.

"Do you know her? Do you live around here?"

"She is the Sweeper. Every time I come, there she is. Sweeping."

"You come here a lot?"

"Not often enough. Now, shhhhhh."

There was a tear in the fence right at the corner and a little tunnel under a wooden ladder with flowerpots of dead plants on every step. Buster held open the fence and nodded for her to go through. Lacy pulled her backpack around in front of her. She made herself small and waddled through the fence and under the ladder. She looked back at Buster and he was grinning.

"Is this legal?" she asked. "Are we going to get shot?"

"Depends."

There were butterflies in her stomach, but not in a good way; she shivered and she frowned. Inside the fence there was just more crap and a very narrow path past an old sewing machine, stacks of moldy magazines, and some odd equipment she didn't recognize. She could not see a house. She hesitated.

"We'll be fine," Buster said. "I know this place like the proverbial back of my hand. Like I know my own name." He paused and leaned close to her. "Like I would like to know your face."

Lacy blushed.

"Close your eyes," he whispered.

She did as told. He took her hand and led her down the path. His hand was warm, soft, and dry, not gross at all. A dog barked angrily and she jumped, but now she was not afraid.

"Almost," he said. "Almost."

He stopped and she stopped beside him.

"Open!"

She opened her eyes and gasped. They were in a beautiful garden made entirely of glass. All colors of glass. Most were old bottles—blue, green, brown, red, and clear ones filled with yellow liquid. Some were woven into a wire frame to make a mosaic of a mermaid. Some were cut and glued together to make flowers. Lacy spotted a four-legged animal taller than Buster with bottle caps for eyes.

"Do you like it?" Buster asked.

"I can't speak."

"And for you, that's something."

She pushed him and he danced away from her. He spun around and around with his hands outstretched. She twirled too and the colors blurred and sparkled. Then she was dizzy.

"This way," he said and skipped off.

There were paths and benches and a little fountain, all with glass imbedded in the concrete. He ducked inside an archway and she followed.

"Your face is blue," he said to her.

"Yours too."

They stared at each other and then her stomach growled. She was mortified, but he just laughed. "Lunch time. How about a glass salad? Or some glass fries?"

"I actually have a sandwich. Want half?"

They sat and she pulled her lunch bag from her backpack. She unwrapped her peanut butter sandwich and gave him half. He took an enormous bite. He was so skinny. Did no one ever feed him?

"Delicious." He smacked his lips. "You make this?"

"My mom."

"Your mom. I remember her. She's pretty hip for an old lady. An artist, right?"

"Mom just works in an office. She's nothing."

"She has an artist's soul. Even if it's buried down inside. She's cool. I remember. She always had us laughing on those field trips."

In elementary school, when her parents were still married, before her mom had to work, she went on every field trip as a chaperone. She drove or she rode on the bus and she sang songs and on the way home she would mimic the museum docent or the tour guide or even one of the teachers. Lacy's friends loved her and Lacy had been so proud of her.

A lizard darted out onto the path in front of them. Lacy started to tell Buster, but he put his hand on her thigh to keep her quiet. He saw it too. They watched. The lizard froze except for his little eyes rotating in his head looking this way and that. He pumped on his tiny legs, listening.

"So flipping alien," Buster whispered.

The lizard twitched and looked up at them. Lacy thought of her online boyfriend, Oren, and the photos he had sent her of his pet, Cookie. Cookie was scary. This little thing was creepy too. A snake with legs. In her English class they had read the part in the Bible about how the snake had been a lizard until God took away his legs as punishment for giving Eve the apple. Lizards looked evil. Wiggly. Slimy. Green. What had Oren told her? They're not slimy. They're smart and friendly. They have personalities. She could see the tiny lizard's muscles working. She could see it breathing. Why did Oren love them? What did it say about him that he loved an iguana more than anything else in the world? It was nice that he was so attentive to her, always calling and texting and emailing, but really, when she thought about it sitting there with Buster, Oren was kind of creepy too.

Buster whispered, "Legend has it when you see a lizard it means someone from your past is thinking about you."

"I don't know who that would be."

"Remember that girl in fourth grade who followed you around? She started combing her hair like you and wearing the same socks? I bet she thinks about you all the time."

"Yeah, right." Lacy giggled, but she thought again of Oren. He was probably thinking of her. He said he thought about her constantly. She had lied to him about everything and he had believed every ridiculous story she had told him. What a jerk. The lizard darted away.

"Hey," she said to Buster. "Hey."

"What?"

"Thank you. Thank you for remembering everything and for saying nice things and for bringing me here."

"I like you, little Miss Lacy. I always have."

He turned to face her with his hand still warm on her thigh.

His eyes were the best brown. She could smell peanut butter on his breath. She had never even met Oren, but Buster she had known forever. She leaned toward him and they kissed. His lips were soft and he opened his mouth just a little. He tasted like the sandwich and marijuana. She pushed Oren out of her mind. He was in her past. He was probably thinking of her, but she was done with him. She tentatively touched Buster's tongue with hers. A first. A first kiss and a first French kiss. Not bad. He sighed happily as the kiss ended. She dove back into him for more. Kissing was good. Kissing was great. This was her first time and she was loving it. She didn't want to talk. She didn't care where they were. She just wanted to keep on kissing him. She felt it in her breasts and between her legs and in her knees. Her toes curled inside her shoes. He stopped first and she almost fell into him.

"Did I do something wrong?"

"Look," he said.

He turned his face away and she felt sick. He had a girl-friend or she was not a good kisser or she was too ordinary for him. She had not liked the glass garden enough. But she did, she did. How could she tell him?

"This place—" she began.

"We have company."

She followed his gaze. Three young Latinos were coming down the path. Shaved heads, tattoos, serious expressions. The overweight one lagged behind. The most muscular took the lead. They weren't carrying guns or tire irons or anything Lacy could see, but who knew what was hidden in their baggy pants or under their long flannel shirts. She had nothing they might want except her cell phone and her virginity.

"Hey," Buster greeted them.

The leader nodded. "You know this place?"

"Mr. Rodriguez is a friend of my grandfather's. I've been coming here since I was little."

"Who's your grandfather?"

"Milton Goldstein. He had the liquor store on the corner."

"It's not the same around here anymore."

"Man, this is my favorite place in the world. I just wanted to show it to my girl."

Lacy wished he hadn't mentioned her. The dark eyes slid to her, surveyed her like an ad in a magazine. She was wearing incredibly expensive blue jeans and a T-shirt. Her heeled boots were just what everybody was wearing—everybody who could afford it. Her dad paid for all her clothes. She tucked her hair behind her ear hoping her multiple piercings would count for something.

"Hi," she said. "This is amazing."

"See," the leader began, "The thing is, this is our place now. And you show your girlfriend and she tells someone else and so on and so forth and pretty soon we got a problem."

"I won't tell anyone!" Lacy spoke without thinking and then clapped her hand over her mouth.

The fat one laughed. "I can tell. She's the kind that don't shut up."

"No, I'm quiet. I never say anything to anybody. Isn't that right, Buster? I mean people have to beg me to talk. I'm so quiet."

Now they were all laughing, but not in a good way.

"You put up with this?" The fat one asked Buster.

"I find her endlessly entertaining," Buster replied.

He looked at Lacy and smiled and despite her fear she could not wait to kiss him again. If they lived. If they survived long enough to get the chance.

The leader was not laughing anymore. He nodded. The quiet boy, the one who had not yet spoken, stepped up beside him. His head was flat on top, as if hit by a cartoon anvil. He worried a pimple on his cheek as he leaned close and said something in Spanish.

Lacy scooted closer to Buster. He raised his eyebrows. They were both taking French—fat lot of good it did them.

"What're we gonna do?" The leader looked around as if the glass would answer him.

"Hey, man, I know. Let's get high." Buster pulled his bag of pot and a little pipe from his jacket pocket.

Lacy stared at her feet. That seemed ridiculous, absurd, the last thing these guys wanted was to smoke with Buster.

"You just carry that in your pocket? Shit." The quiet one spoke perfect English. "You are a white boy."

"No, no. Cops hassle us hippies like it's still 1968. But this time—" Buster sort of nodded at Lacy as if he had intended to take her to the garden and get her high. "She doesn't partake, but I was hoping—you know—the magical place, the handsome guy—"

They laughed at that one.

"Let's see if it's any good," the fat one said.

"Let's see if the hippie is any good." The sullen one talked to his leader, but kept his eyes on Lacy. "Doesn't look like he's much good for anything."

12.

Kidney waited in the Tip-Top Coffee Shop on Lincoln Avenue. It wasn't a very upscale kind of place, but he chose it for its easy access to the freeway. He liked to keep his options open. He had a rule against meeting his clients at the motel where he was staying. Too dangerous. You never knew who Fish and Wildlife had their eye on.

The wood grain Formica tabletop was pitted and peeling at the corners. The coffee was okay. There were people in his business who lived the high life, who treated their clients to shark fin soup and gave their girlfriends combs made of endangered turtle shell or lizard skin boots. They were asking for trouble, begging to get busted. Still, he wouldn't mind moving up a notch next time. Nothing too fancy, but maybe a Holiday Inn instead of the No-Tell Motel where he was; maybe a real restaurant instead of this crappy place. He looked out at the gray haze blurring the horizon, making even the gas station across the street fuzzy. What was in the air? Not moisture. He figured it had to be the famous Southern California smog. The sun was barely peeking through the gloom and it was 60 degrees, tops. The birds of paradise and all the bushes outside the window were dying. He had not expected LA to be so ugly. It was all strip malls and freeways and garbage in the gutters. There were fucking homeless people standing at every intersection begging for a handout. He realized the area around the airport was not Beverly Hills, but shit, this was the home of movie stars and Disneyland. He had imagined bright colors and warm sun. Happy tourists even in November. Maybe the people in Kantoba, New Guinea didn't have HBO or hamburgers, but it was lots prettier and the poverty didn't bother them or him. He'd only been in LA overnight and already his legs were twitching, he was so anxious to get back to the jungle. He was happiest out there collecting specimens. The jungle had a tangy, moist, exotic smell and the air was rich with a taste like almonds. The earth was black and damp and the leaves on the plants were shiny green and thick as flesh. They cried when you cut them, the water leaked from their stems like tears. And the creatures. Everywhere you looked. Bugs the size of mice. Birds as multi-colored as circus clowns. And luscious, lovely reptiles everywhere.

In each of the two jungles he frequented he had a woman waiting for him. A cinderblock house, a bed that slumped in the middle, neither of his dark skinned girls wanted expensive gifts or more than they had. It was their pleasure to serve him and it was his pleasure to be served.

He had to remind himself he was in LA for a purpose. He'd be on the plane home to Tennessee tomorrow, a few pockets lighter and a whole lot richer. Do some laundry, bang the wife, and back to the wild.

His first delivery had gone well; the client, a weird old Chinese lady with a "personal menagerie," had been thrilled with the blue-tongued skinks. One of them was looking a little worse for wear by the time he handed it over, but luckily that was her problem now. He had her two thousand dollars in his pocket and one of the good things about illegal transactions was the no returns policy.

"Can you get me something two-headed?" she had asked.

"Are you serious?"

"Do you think me terribly macabre?" She giggled like a teenager.

He wasn't sure what macabre meant, but if it was crazy he was with her.

"I have everything," she went on. "The entire reptile genus is represented in my home zoo. Now I need something unusual."

The unusual didn't live long in the wild. In fact, the only freaks he ever saw were dead. "I'll see what I can do," he said. "It'll be expensive."

"You know me," she giggled again. "Made of money."

She had actually been flirting with him. She was seventy-five, if she was a day. He shook his head. He absolutely could not tap that, no matter how much he wanted to see that zoo of hers. Little withered Chinese tits, thighs sagging like the bedroom curtains. Plus, then she'd want special favors, special prices. Nope. This was business and later tonight he'd find someone young and hot to help him celebrate.

He ordered another cup of coffee. Two of his chameleons had died on the trip, but the rest had gone to Dr. Herp's Emporium just off the Venice Beach main drag. Kidney didn't know what to expect, but it turned out to be a sweet little place and he was glad to make a new client. The Doc looked like a brainless surfer, right down to the flip-flops and puka shells, but he was very happy with the chammies and impressed by their quality. Then he showed Kidney his secret room where he kept an incredibly rare *Anomochilus weberi*, known to the common folk as a Weber's dwarf pipe snake. Kidney's mouth had literally watered looking at the little thing. It was only about a foot long and black with pinkish spots.

"One of nine that's ever been found alive," Doc said.

"Where'd you get it? You go to Sumatra?"

"Traded for it. Let go an entire clutch of *Nephrurus Wheeleri Cinctus* and a cage full of my favorites."

Kidney was impressed. "Would you sell it?"

"You can't afford it. No one can. Maybe Bill Gates." The Doc had laughed. "No, dude, I wouldn't part with him for love nor money. Just look at him."

Together they had watched the snake do basically nothing for about fifteen minutes. That was the thing about snakes, they didn't do much. It was one big reason Kidney liked them. He had a puppy when he was a kid. It never sat still, then it ran out in the street and got hit by a woman in a car who had a fit and yelled at him about it. Like it was his fault.

Kidney patted the Doc on the back. "That's something." He vowed to put Sumatra on the list for his next trip. "I'm gonna try to find one."

"Good luck, dude. Great surfing in Sumatra!"

The black-headed pythons were still at the motel digesting their lizard lunches. They were rare, but their beauty was nothing compared to the Doc's secret snake. That morning he had thought he would be sad to sell his bevy of pythons, but now he was anxious to be rid of them. The delivery was for late this afternoon. It was a special deal. The guy had serious cash. Kidney had agreed to drive them to the guy's house up above Sunset Boulevard, in the nice part of town. He wanted to shower and put on a fresh shirt before that. Now he was waiting for Oren and his money. Oren had texted he was on his way. With the forty-five hundred dollars Oren was paying him, he could finance a trip to Sumatra. He could buy Oren a good-looking female iguana for two hundred bucks in Florida on the way back. Oren would never know the difference and capturing an *Anomochilus weberi* would make him the fucking Michael Jackson of reptile collectors.

An official looking SUV drove past before he could read the insignia on the door. Kidney craned his neck to watch it go. He had to be vigilant. He was careful, but anything could happen. Dr. Herp's place was pretty public and Kidney had walked in with a big camera bag. He was smart; he also carried a manila envelope of photos that he left behind. They were downloaded, printed, and color copied, but he never told anyone he was a good photographer. He left the pics behind every time he did a delivery. He was very, very careful, but sitting in the coffee shop, the thought of jail made his bowels constrict and his throat go dry. He was older and not pretty by any standards, but he knew jailhouse rape was about power and control. He would pay whatever fine the Feds asked, have his passport revoked, leave his wife, run away and live in Mexico forever, as long as he didn't have to go to jail. Fish and Wildlife was cracking down. Reptile trafficking ranked second behind drugs for the amount of money that changed hands. It was a six billion dollar a year business and that meant the Feds hated it. And why? Kidney tapped the tabletop in frustration. 'Cause he was making money and they weren't. They pretended they were worried about the animals. If they only looked at the facts, they'd see he was helping the reptile population by protecting some of them from their natural predators and making them available for breeders. To say nothing of the people who could never travel to Borneo or Peru on their own. Oh God! Jail! They were gonna legalize marijuana. Why not reptiles? When Kidney was a little bean, his pop had gone to Australia for work and come home with a pygmy python. Pop had spent the equivalent of ten bucks and carried it home on the plane in a glass jar as a gift for his son. Now transporting any reptile from Australia was verboten.

The SUV continued out of sight. Kidney checked his watch again. Oren had said an hour. Ten minutes to go.

A couple walked into the coffee shop. She was blond and skinny. He wore a fedora. They were both in sunglasses. They were somebody, weren't they? Other people turned to look. He took out his phone to take a picture, then turned away and stared out the window again. What would movie stars be doing in a dump like this?

13.

First he tied her hands behind her back, but then she couldn't sit in the car comfortably, so he untied them and retied her wrists together in front. He started to put her in the passenger seat, then changed his mind and made her sit in back, then changed his mind again, made her get out and get in front. All the while he muttered and cursed under his breath, "Shit" and "Why the fuck is this happening to me?"

"Why the fuck do you think this is happening?" Winnie finally said. "Are you an idiot?"

He slapped her, not as hard as any other time, but she decided to stay quiet. She sat still in the front seat while he tied her ankles together. He wore a ridiculous orange baseball cap with a pet store logo; she couldn't see his face but his hands were shaking and he seemed nervous. Something was not going right for him and she was glad.

It was a relief to be out in the cool air. He had let her put her jacket back on. He had given her a brush to straighten her hair. She felt better. She was out of his horrible house. She could get away from him now that she had fresh air to breathe and room to think.

She couldn't help asking, "Where are we going?"

"That's for me to know and you to find out."

Without thinking, she sneered, "What are you, ten?"

She cringed away from the smack she was sure was coming,

but he just slammed her door shut and went around to his side of the car. She watched through the window as he took an envelope out of the pocket of his leather jacket. He opened it and she could see money inside. A lot of money. If he had money, what was he doing with her?

"What's your bank?" he said as he slid behind the driver's seat.

"What?"

"Which bank do you go to?"

"Citibank."

"I want you to get me some money."

"More money? Looks to me like you have plenty."

"Yes. Mom. I need more money."

"Okay. Okay."

At the bank she would be able to communicate with someone. She would show someone the cuts on her stomach, the marks the ropes were making on her wrists. A teller would know what was going on. They were trained to know.

He closed his door. He put the key in the ignition, but then he just sat there, without moving. It was as if he had stalled. He stared at the garage door without blinking. Finally, he laid his head back and closed his eyes.

Winnie landed on the horn with both hands.

He punched her hard. She flew across the seat and her head hit the window. She crumpled against the door. She couldn't hear, she was underwater and the sounds undulated and throbbed. She began to cry.

"Fuck!" He banged the steering wheel. He reached above the visor and hit the remote.

Winnie pressed her tied hands against one ear as the door lifted and the neighborhood appeared. Empty. No one on the street. No one had heard the horn. Not a dog or a bird. Life had evaporated.

"Stop crying. Stop it. Or I'll give you something to cry about."

How many times had his mother said that to him?

Winnie had been hit by another guy, a boyfriend, long, long ago in Manhattan. She'd thrown a full beer can at him and only just missed hitting him in the head. He had grabbed her throwing arm and slapped her face. What she mostly remembered was how anticlimactic it had been to slam the door of his apartment behind her and then have to wait for the elevator. She stood in the hallway with his handprint on her cheek and her smeared lipstick and red, snot filled nose. She prayed he would not open the door and see her tapping her foot. The elevator finally came; the doors opened agonizingly slowly and revealed a small man inside with his very small dog. He politely said nothing as the tears dripped off her chin. The white, fluffy dog licked her shoe and then her bare ankle. She remembered the rough dryness of its tongue. She had been seventeen. One year older than Lacy. At seventeen she had already slept with three guys, one of them old enough to be her father. Maybe he was her father. He was a lawyer. Her father was a lawyer and Winnie couldn't remember what he looked like.

"Mom," Winnie said when she got home.

"I hope you hit him back." Daisy was reading a script at the kitchen table.

"I threw a can of beer at him."

"Get him?"

"It hit the wall and exploded." The stain had looked like fireworks.

"They're all the same," Daisy replied. "Shits, all of them. Except this new one of mine. He is—amazing."

"I think I'm bleeding."

"Where?"

"Inside my mouth."

"No scar, no worries. And if it's hard to eat, you'll lose weight."

She must have been joking, but Winnie could not remember. Daisy came over to give her a rare hug, but Winnie waved her away. "I just need a shower."

She hated her mother's touch. Daisy's hands were always cold, her fingers like frosty twigs. She was so brittle, one squeeze and she might shatter. She cultivated her Ice Queen image, never getting a tan, always wearing her white blond hair in a straight, chilly flow down her back. People used to ask if Winnie was adopted. Now they asked Winnie if Lacy was. Both of them, Daisy and Lacy, had such pale skin, platinum hair and big eyes the color of sky reflected in snow. Standing between them Winnie felt like a clump of dirt bookended by glaciers.

What would Daisy do? That was the question teenaged Winnie always asked herself. How would Daisy handle this? Even now, curled against the door of a crazy man's car, she could not stop her brain from asking what her mother would do. Daisy would never let a kidnapper kill her. Daisy would charm her way out of it. Winnie had never been very charming. She would end up dead. The thought of her mother's final and eternal disappointment made her cry harder.

"I said, stop it," he growled. "I mean it."

He was turning out of the neighborhood onto a street with shops. She saw the post office and a grocery store. She sucked in her snot, wiped her eyes with her tied hands and sat up straight. She saw people walking in and out of these buildings, going about their day as if everything was just the same as always. She stared at a woman, about her age, in jeans and a striped sweater, talking on a cell phone in front of Starbucks. That woman could help her.

"Don't," he said.

"I wasn't—"

He took the gun from his pocket. She had forgotten about the gun. How could she have forgotten about it?

"If I'm going down," he said, "you're going with me."

"Did you hear that on a television show?"

He jabbed one finger deep into her thigh. She grunted, opened her mouth to scream.

"Don't. Just don't," he said.

She saw a branch of her bank up ahead. It was small, with a single walk up ATM out front, but there it was. The rotating sign was like a hand waving her in. Security guards, tellers with buttons under the counter. She almost giggled, giddy suddenly with the promise of rescue. But he was driving past.

"That's my bank," she said.

"Shhhhh." He shook his head. "Just shush."

"I thought you wanted money."

"Not there."

He drove on. A different bank appeared. He turned in to the drive through entrance.

"This isn't my bank," she said.

"You think I'm going to let you get out of this car and talk to a teller? You really are stupid."

Winnie's despair blocked her throat. The tears came again. Of course he would pass her bank to go to one where they could stay in the car. Of course.

He reached in the back and got her purse from where he had thrown it earlier. He fiddled inside until he found her wallet. "Get your card. C'mon."

Her only hope was to take a long time and let someone pull up behind them and get annoyed, but it was the middle of a weekday, not many people banking.

"C'mon, c'mon." He looked at his watch. Tapped the gun against his thigh.

"They have cameras," she said. "These machines have cameras."

"Why do you think I'm wearing a hat?"

It was true. The cap's brim would hide his face from the small camera positioned at the top of the ATM. He grabbed her wallet out of her hands and dumped it in her lap. He picked out her Citibank card and stuck it in the slot.

"What's your number?"

She thought briefly about giving him the wrong number. Three or four times and then the bank kept the card, but what good would that do? "1422." She slumped back against the seat. One daughter, born April 22. Her throat was closing, she had to concentrate to swallow.

"What's your limit?"

"I don't know."

"Five hundred? A thousand?"

"I have no idea. Really. Why should I care?"

"You rich bitches are all alike."

He punched in a thousand. The machine grumbled and a message appeared. He read aloud, " 'The amount requested exceeds available funds.' Fuck!" He gritted his teeth as he read on, " 'Would you like to use overdraft protection?'"

"The fee is so high," Winnie complained without thinking. "I get paid tomorrow." Stupid! she berated herself. As if he could wait, as if she wanted to still be here tomorrow.

"How much money do you have?" He seemed confused.

"I think about six hundred dollars."

She could tell he didn't believe her. Behind him the machine waited for his response. Was anyone watching this transaction?

Wouldn't it seem odd it was taking so long?

"I'm not lying," she defended herself. "I don't know why you think I'm rich. I'm not. My ex is rich. I am not."

"No savings account? Other banks?"

"I have a savings account," she said. "But it's not connected. I'd have to go in to my bank. It's for Lacy. My daughter."

She was sorry she had said her name. She didn't want to give him any bit of her. He shook his head as if to clear it. He chewed on a fingernail. Then he sighed and pressed "yes." The machine churned and another message came up.

"Fuck!" he hit the steering wheel.

"What?"

"Transaction is too big for overdraft protection."

"Check the balance and take what I have. Go on. Just take it. All of it. Who cares."

"I'll be short," he sounded like a child. "I won't have enough."

There was nothing she could say.

He pressed the appropriate buttons. "I left you seven dollars."

"Such a gentleman."

The machine whirred and spit out the money. He put the cash and her card in his left pocket along with the gun. He pulled forward, but had to stop. "Oh, c'mon."

An old man crossed slowly in front of them. He wore brown pants and a brown sweater and he walked a short-legged fat brown dog. The wind blew and the man pulled his sweater closed. The little dog bent his head against the gust. Winnie shivered. No place was colder than right there, right that minute. Not Alaska or Siberia or the Arctic Circle. His hot house had sucked the warmth from the world. The old man turned his face out of the wind and glanced at them. Should she try the horn again? Should she scream? Roll down the window and scream?

She looked at the button, took a deep breath.

"Listen," her kidnapper said.

He knew what she had planned. She'd been too obvious.

"Listen," he said again. "If you try anything, I will go get your daughter. I know where she is. I will drive from here right to her school and I will get Lacy."

How did he know? "She's not in school," Winnie was frantic. "She lives far away with her father. She's grown up."

"I hate lying. I told you I hate lying."

"Leave her out of this."

"She hates you."

"You keep saying that."

"You're a bad mom."

"No, I'm not." She wasn't.

In the middle of the night, Winnie had woken to Lacy crying in the bathroom.

"Lacy? What is it? Sweetpea?"

Lacy had opened the door in her underpants with her tank top pulled up. She had her hands cupped over her bare stomach.

"It hurts, Mommy. It hurts so badly."

"What?" Appendicitis, drugs, the morning after pill all whistled through Winnie's mind.

Lacy moved her hands. A gold ring pierced her belly button. The incision was oozing watery pus, the skin around it swollen and red.

"Oh, Sweetie." Winnie could not be angry. Lacy was too miserable. "It's infected. It looks so painful."

"It's just… just… I sleep on my stomach and…" Lacy sobbed. "I thought it would be so beautiful."

Winnie kept her opinion to herself. She found the rubbing alcohol and the antibiotic cream. She cleaned the two red, ugly holes and the hideous tiny ring and kissed her daughter's perfect flat stomach and together they fashioned a very strange bandage using the cap from a water bottle to keep everything and anything from touching her navel. They were laughing by the time they finished. Lacy hugged her goodnight and said, "Thank you," and "I love you, Mom."

But in the morning they fought. Winnie shouted, "Why don't you just put a bone through your nose?"

"Maybe I will."

"Do you want to look like a tramp?

"Yes!"

Winnie knew it; she knew that Lacy thought dressing like a slut would make her popular. It broke her heart that her daughter wanted so desperately to be cool. Lacy had been friends with the kids in orchestra, but now she avoided them. She continued to practice her flute and play in the orchestra twice a week, but she would not go out for pizza after rehearsals or to the first violinist's birthday party. As if being a nerd was contagious. So she had no one. The phone never rang. She did not go anywhere on the weekends except to her dad's house. She talked a lot about some girl named Marissa, what she was wearing, what she said, but Marissa had never called or come over. Winnie was positive Lacy was still a virgin, but doing her best not to look like one.

Her beautiful girl. She had fine blond hairs like down on the back of her neck and on her arms. Her daughter was a peach, firm and white and not yet ripe. Lacy needed her.

Winnie straightened her shoulders, ignored the thump in her head as she turned to Oren. "So what is this all about? It's not money. Do you have some stupid idea that this is going to make you famous?"

"No!" He spoke through gritted teeth. "I'm not stupid. I'm

sick of people saying that. All the time telling me I'm a dumb shit. I am not. I'm not! I have a job. A good one. I have a real house to live in. What have they done? Huh? With their dumb little lives? Huh?"

"Who thinks you're stupid?" she asked.

"None of your beeswax."

"At work? Where is that?"

"They like me at work. The Carpet Barn."

"I know that place." A big, red barn-like building with rolls of carpets stacked out front. She had passed it many times. What other places had she driven by with kidnappers and murderers inside?

"I'm an account rep," he said defensively. "Not just an installer."

All the people we meet, Winnie marveled. Any cheerful face ringing up her purchases or bagging her groceries or telling her to have a nice day could be a psychopath. Anyone, everyone was suspect.

"Listen," he began. It seemed to be his favorite word. "Listen."

But then he said nothing. He drove the speed limit down the street, heading for the freeway entrance. Winnie stared out the window at the signs for restaurants, nail salons, and a hardware store. It was beautiful, all of it. She held her breath at the colors in the graffiti on the white wall of the 7-11. The pigeons in flight brought tears. It was all so perfect, so defined. She had never noticed before, but now the world outside the car was crystal clear. She saw a father and young son and instantly knew everything about them. She could taste the pancakes they ate for breakfast, the maple syrup thick and sweet from the plastic pitcher. She felt the little boy's teeth growing in his mouth and the sugar buds drilling into baby enamel. She saw the metal grill of the braces he would wear in a few years, felt the cut on the inside of his lip. She knew his pain when his wisdom teeth were removed one vacation when he was home from college. She saw the stained yellow of his adult incisors, and then the way his tongue rubbed the worn, flat edges of his front teeth as he waited in the nursing home for his own children to visit. She was the one who was going to die, but everyone else's life was passing in front of her. Out there it was all so clear. Inside this car it was a mystery.

She moisturized daily, but that wouldn't help her here. She said no to that piece of chocolate cake, even though she wanted it so much and her friend said it was the best she'd ever eaten. She said no, but that wouldn't help her here. She bought the expensive biodegradable dishwashing soap. She let the old lady go first. She gave up the parking spot. She never ever littered. She wished on first stars, eyelashes, white horses, pennies, the turned up hems of her shirts and skirts. None of it would help her here.

"Little Lady," her southern grandmother used to call her. "Looky there."

She looked down and the hem of her party dress was folded up. She started to straighten it, but her grandmother stopped her.

"Turn around three times and make a wish." Her voice as broad as her hips. "It'll come true. Always does."

Her grandmother in heaven. Her mother in New York. Sitting on a cloud or sitting on a couch, painting the sky or reading a script. Each of them, today, right now, were easier to see than she could see herself. She had left that penny lying on the street outside the mechanic's as she got into this car. What would she have wished for? Just four hours ago, what would her wish have been? A better job? A boyfriend?

He was pulling onto the freeway. They were leaving the shops and people behind. Her chance for rescue was diminishing with every mile. She had to make him understand. She would give him whatever he wanted if he would let her go.

"Listen. You listen," Winnie said to him. "My mother is rich. She really is famous. You've heard of her: Daisy Juniper." She named her mother's most popular film, "*Dawn of Delilah*."

He shrugged. "I didn't think it was so good. I rented it."

That stopped her. "When?"

"Couple days ago, three or four."

"By coincidence?"

He shrugged again.

And then, as if suddenly the truth was sitting on her chest, pressing her back into the seat, she realized: she had not been kidnapped randomly.

"You know who I am!" She could not get her breath. She coughed. "This wasn't by accident, was it? You were after me."

He turned his head and looked at her and his eyes were small and dull. They were a sour moldy green and his eyelids were heavy.

"I was after you, Winnie Parker," he said. "I need to teach you a lesson."

14.

Jonathan stood at the sock counter of Mario's Menswear in Santa Monica. He had called Jessica and she had reminded him that this was the place. He was surprised. Who would have guessed this hole in the fence, squeezed between a bar and a locksmith, had the best men's socks in Southern California? How did she know these things? Only six years in LA and already she knew everything. He had grown up just over the hills in the valley and Los Angeles was still a mystery to him.

He held two pairs of socks, a black pair and a different black pair. "Onyx," the sales guy had called one, and the other, "Ebony."

"I guess I'll take them both," Jonathan said. He didn't know which was better. He wore black socks very occasionally, but the pair he had had a hole in the toe. He hated socks. It was a joke at work that he was the only on-camera host in TV who wore a suit and flip-flops. Of course he didn't wear flip-flops, but he did wear his expensive Italian loafers without socks. On the other hand, or foot, if he wore socks, these were the socks to have. That's what Jessica said.

"That will be $151.20."

Jonathan took his credit card from his wallet. He would not call Jessica and clear it with her. He could buy socks. He didn't remember the world before credit cards, but he did remember not having enough credit to get one. He remembered his bank account slipping down to negative numbers almost every month, mooching off his friends for beer and parking meters at the beach. Now he had no idea how much money he had. His accountant paid the bills. The valet usually took his car wherever he went. It seemed he could do whatever he wanted and he always had enough money.

"Excuse me?" There was a high lilt to the voice behind him. He turned. A pretty young face, blushing, with blue eyes under brown bangs.

"Hi," he said.

"Aren't you, I mean, I hate to bother you, but are you Jonathan Parker?"

He smiled. He did not need to say yes. Her face was as fresh as a morning muffin. She made him think of a bowl of just picked blueberries and thick white cream, served in a bright farm kitchen under sunny skies and healthy appetites. He saw her lying on her stomach in front of her family television set watching him as he joked with his contestants and dreaming of the day she would come to Hollywood. Dreaming of him.

"Mr. Parker," she began.

"You can call me Jonathan."

"I just wanted to say, well, my mother loves you. She watches your show—what's it called?—every night. When she finds out I saw you—"

Behind her now he saw her boyfriend, dark hair falling across his high Asian cheekbones, snickering as he looked at five hundred dollar sweaters.

"If you could just sign something for her," the girl was continuing. She dug in her purse. "This would be fine."

She handed him a folded over grocery list. Tampax. Toothpaste. Onions. And now, Jonathan Parker.

"Thank you. Thank you so much. My mom is such a fan."

Her boyfriend couldn't help it, he laughed out loud. "Sorry, man," he said. "If you only knew her mother."

Jonathan went out and sat in his Porsche behind the tinted windows. He practiced his yoga breathing. The backs of his hands were freckled. The skin was loose and puckered over each knuckle. He had the car running and the heater on. He had come out of the store chilled and shivering in the California sunshine. A hundred and fifty dollars for socks. Long ago he had seen Marlon Brando in a restaurant in Beverly Hills. Jonathan thought him the greatest actor who ever lived. But when the 70-year-old Brando stood up and turned toward him to leave the restaurant, Jonathan had been shocked. It wasn't the weight, or the plastic surgery; it was the dark in his face. The man he had idolized was gone. The eyes were flat; the lips pressed together like anybody's grandmother. Where was the light? Where had he gone? Where was his hero?

Jonathan vowed then to stay alive. To be himself always. It wasn't hard those first few years, when he was young. Younger. Acting and surfing were all he cared about. If he had a bad audition, the ocean made him feel better. Out in the water he never fumbled his lines or missed his mark. There was no such thing as a bad day surfing.

Then Winnie came along and so quickly there was Lacy. Watching Lacy toddle, grow, learn to speak, had been amazing. He wanted Lacy to love what he loved. He took her surfing before she could walk, put her on his shoulders and rode the smallest waves. It was cool, she wasn't the least bit frightened, and he bought her a little board of her own, but once the game show started he was too busy to teach her. He was too busy to go himself. Winnie was not a surfer, but she had loved the beach and hung out on the shore in that funny one-piece red bathing suit she'd had for a hundred years.

Same old bathing suit. Same old Winnie. He had changed,

but she had not. He had moved forward, breathing, working, filled with the California sunshine. She couldn't understand that the game show was just a stepping stone; no more worries about money, no more struggling. Then he would really act. But she told him not to do it. She said she didn't care about the money. Easy for her to say. And when he came home exhausted in those first months, tired out from being a game show host all day long, Winnie had that look on her face, disappointment. She said she was happy if he was, but the light had gone out of her and she was snuffing it out in him.

Jessica came along just at the right time. She sent him surf-ing again, literally and metaphysically—phorically—whatever, to soak up the ocean's energy qi. Winnie had stopped seeing him, who he was. Jessica saw him. She really saw him.

"Shit," he said out loud. Jessica had seen him the way he thought that blueberry girl saw him before she opened her mouth. Here he was, thirty years younger than Brando was that day in the restaurant and already people were laughing.

"Call Andrew," Jonathan told his phone.

There was a movie possibility out there. He looked at his blue eyes in the rear view mirror. Still blue. Still there. Still him. I will stay alive, he vowed. I will stay alive.

"Andrew," he said. "Jonathan Parker."

"You were my next call."

Jonathan knew that was just agentspeak for sorry I've been out of touch.

"What's happening with the movie?"

There was a pause while Andrew regrouped and tried to fig-ure out which movie Jonathan was talking about.

"The sci fi thing. That young director."

"I have it right here," Andrew said, "Good news. They defi-nitely want you. Definitely."

Jonathan smiled at his reflection. His shoulders relaxed and his stomach settled. "That's terrific. Which part? The Captain?"

"They want you to play yourself. You know, Jonathan Parker. You were frozen for five hundred years or whatever and then you're thawed. See? It's hilarious."

"Very funny." Jonathan pretended to laugh. "I read the scene you sent over. Is it the scientist part?"

"This isn't that kind of film. You'll have a moment. A good moment, but they want Jonathan Parker. The real Jonathan Parker."

"A walk-on? Who do they think they are?" He was angry. He didn't want to be angry, anger was not healthy, it was not productive, but his breath was coming faster, his heart beginning to thump. He was sweating before he remembered he had the heater going on high. He punched it off.

"You'll be great. A riot." Andrew gave a hollow chuckle. "Probably the best moment in the entire movie."

"Fuck! Can't you do something for me? Something better? I'm the goddamn host of the most successful relationship show since *The Dating Game*."

"Hey, I know. I read the press releases too." Then Andrew sighed. "I'm sorry. Sorry. You're just so damn recognizable – as yourself."

Jonathan willed himself to calm down. He used his yoga breathing. Pranadama, pranayama, whatever the fuck it was called. Count to ten his dad would tell him. Then hit the other guy.

"I'm sorry, Andrew. I'm not mad at you. I'm glad I have the show, of course. But other people have done it. Gone back to real acting."

"You will. We just have to find the right thing. So do this and we'll keep looking. Who knows? This director is young, hip, a definite up and comer. Maybe he'll like you."

"I'm an actor. This host thing is just temporary."

"You just need to prove that you can be someone else."

They chatted some more, but Jonathan wasn't really listening. Andrew would send contracts over later that week. Jonathan's one day of shooting wouldn't be for a month or so. He didn't want to go to the office anymore. He didn't want to go home. He was afraid Jessica would be at the house, she would know he was upset and when she heard about his tiny cameo role in the movie she would go through the sky – or whatever that expression was. Maybe she was out. She taught super advanced yoga three times a week, but he could never remember when. She didn't have to work, but she did it because she loved it. He admired her for that. And in her classes she met lots of stars and directors and people with money. Jessica wanted to produce feature films. He had no doubt she would do it too. She knew how to work it, how to get people to like her, to give her things just because she was so pretty and so nice, honest and open and fun. He snorted. Maybe she would have a good part for him.

Jonathan turned right toward the beach. Winnie was so lucky. She had no ambition. A little job, a little house was enough for her. One day she would meet a nice man. Or not. He could admit it: he hoped not. Anyway, she seemed totally happy alone.

15.

Oren crested the hill. He could see way ahead. Traffic was getting worse. The 110 Freeway through downtown was always clogged, but this looked bad. Dodger Stadium was just over that hill. He had never been to a baseball game. He always meant to go, but he never had. The guys at work went. They invited him at first, but he always said no and eventually they stopped. He would take Lacy, he decided. And maybe even her mom. He saw the three of them in the stands, eating hot dogs, cheering for the team. All the guys would be jealous that Lacy was with him. No. He would leave Winnie home. She would never be quiet for an entire baseball game.

"You don't need to teach me anything. I mean, you already have. You've taught me so much. I've learned my lesson," she was saying, filling his car, his head with her endless yakking. "Oh yes. Yes, yes. Definitely. I'll be a better person. Starting right now. I'll stop complaining. I'll never complain again about my house or my weight or being short."

She would not shut up. He had started to tell her all the things she needed to hear. The lessons she had to learn were so simple. Stop treating your daughter like shit. Stop beating her and making her wear ugly clothes and threatening to cut off her hair in her sleep. He had so much to tell her, but she kept talking.

"Thanks to you, I really appreciate my life now. I do. I really, truly do. Thank you. Oh. Look where we are. If you pull over and let me out, I can walk home from here. I can. It's nothing. No problem. It's just over that hill."

"I thought you lived in the Hollywood hills."

"Echo Park. Close to the stadium. The 'hood as we call it."

He must have misunderstood Lacy when she told him about her mother's mansion, the automatic gates, the snobby neighbors. There had to be nice parts of Echo Park too. He imagined the house, set back, enormous, lording it over the smaller shitboxes where the regular people lived. She would not shut up.

"I live right near here, so really you could let me out anywhere."

His hands gripped the wheel so he would not poke or hit her. Traffic was almost stopped. Someone would see him and call a cop.

"So this is about money, isn't it?" she continued. "You said I was rich."

"You are rich."

"Compared to some," she went on, "I guess I am. Compared to people in third world countries, well, even people in this country. It's terrible. You said you need more money. Let's call my ex-husband. He's really rich. Jonathan can give you whatever you need. We could stop by, or meet him someplace. Jonathan will pay. Even though we're divorced, he'll give you lots of money. Thousands and thousands. No problem. And maybe my mother will chip in. I'll give you Jonathan's cell phone number. You can start with him. Let's call right now."

He just shook his head. She wasn't getting it. And, as she chattered, he saw her hands slowly going toward the door. They were moving at a crawl. She thought she could get the door open and get out without being killed. He sighed, reached over and put her hands back in her lap. She exploded.

"What do you want?" she shouted.

Just like that, she was having a little fit. Oren watched her, stunned, as she screamed and rocked in the seat. She banged on the window and held her tied hands up to the car next to her. Before he could grab her, a businesswoman in tons of make-up looked over. She was talking, obviously on the phone in her empty car. Oren saw her black skinny eyebrows rise and the look of concern.

"Call the cops," Winnie shouted to the woman. "Help me."

She was wiggling all over the seat. She looked insane. Gently, he took her hands and pulled them down to her lap. He smoothed her hair off her forehead, then shook his head sadly at the businesswoman. He mouthed, "Sorry," to her as if Winnie was a nut case, his psycho mom who needed restraint. The woman frowned, still talking. Then her lane eased forward, the car behind her honked, and she moved out of sight.

"Just stop it," he said. "Stop talking, stop moving, stop everything. Remember your daughter. Remember Lacy."

"Leave her alone. Leave her out of this you asshole, you jerk, you bastard!"

She was losing it, jumping all over the car. Bouncing up and down in her seat. He looked in his rearview mirror, at the cars on either side. He turned on the radio and cranked it up as high as it would go.

"Help me! Help me! Help me!"

He pretended to sing along, "Help me. Help me," as if it was a song. She would not stop. He didn't want to, but he poked her thigh again. And again. She gasped and folded over her legs, but she was quiet. Finally. He turned the radio off.

"I have things I need to say. Sit up."

She didn't move. He put his blinker on.

"I am not kidding," he continued. "I will go get Lacy right now."

She sat up slowly. "Don't. I'll be quiet. I promise."

She dropped her head. Her cheeks were wet, with tears or sweat he wasn't sure. There were two more fingertip-sized bruises blooming on her leg. He flipped off the blinker.

"Thank you," she whispered. "Teach me whatever you want."

She said no more. It was a relief to have her quiet for a moment. He could almost think again. If only the traffic would lighten up. If only he could move. If only the people on all sides stopped staring at them.

"I know I'm right about this," he said. "I know I'm right because of Cookie. I have taken care of him since he was a baby. He is happy and he loves me. I know what I am talking about." He had this all written down on his laptop. He had thought it out carefully, practiced even, but thanks to the traffic, and Kidney, and the money, thanks to her, yes, thanks to her, the bitch, the words were twirling around and around in his mind, like cotton candy in the spinner, nothing to grab on to.

"Listen."

"I'm listening. I am."

"No, you are not; you are talking again."

She had to shut up or he would strangle her, she would make him angry and he would not be responsible. It was not his fault. He would do everything he could, but if she did not shut up he might kill her and it would not be his fault. 'Permission' was one of the circling words. 'Trust.' 'Mutual respect.' He knew these words, but his mouth could not capture them.

"She's an adult now." He said it out loud, relieved to have caught one of the swirling phrases.

"I thought Cookie was a boy."

She was so stupid. Killing her seemed the best idea. Be done with her. No one would know. Lacy would never know he had killed her mother. Then he could comfort her. Comfort the poor girl with the murdered mother. She would call him and he would come to her and hold her while she cried. It was a beautiful image. She would turn to him of course. His mother was dead too. They would have so much to share. He looked over at Winnie. Killing her suddenly seemed like the best idea. A brilliant solution to everything.

But how would he do it? He couldn't push her out in traffic, they were moving too slowly and everyone would see. His gun wasn't real. He didn't have time to take her up in the mountains and throw her off a cliff. He had a knife, but the thought of sticking it into her, slicing her open, the smell of her blood, her intestines, the look in her eyes as he did it made him shudder. There would be so much blood, and he knew how hard it was to clean.

No, he would continue with the plan, for now. His hands relaxed on the steering wheel. He took a deep breath and almost smiled; the option of killing her made him feel better. It gave him another way to succeed if this plan did not work. He could figure out a mess-free method for her death. Meanwhile, he would be patient and keep teaching her what she needed to learn. He looked at her. Her head was down, her eyes closed. He realized this was hard for her, to understand the errors she had made raising Lacy. People always thought they were good parents. Same with reptile owners, they usually screwed up by accident. He watched her rub the bruises on her thigh. She gave a little groan. His stomach clenched, but then he gritted his teeth. She did not deserve sympathy. If he hurt her, it was only to give her a taste of her own medicine. It was not by accident that she slapped her daughter around or locked her in her room or set Buddy the pit bull on her. Lacy said there were bite marks on her ankle, an ugly scar from the six stitches she needed in the top of her foot. And the chauffeur, who doubled as her jailer, almost raped her and her mother did nothing. Every muscle in his body contracted as he thought of everything his darling Lacy had told him. He felt sick. Winnie was an ogre. He looked at the little, dirty woman sitting next to him. Funny how tyrants came in all sizes.

"Listen," Oren began again. "I know this because of Cookie; I know how you have to treat someone. Someone you care for and who depends on you to feed them and clothe them and educate them." He took a deep breath and nodded as he continued, "You want to trust them, but they have to be able to trust you. And pain does not lead to trust. Fear does not lead to trust."

Winnie looked at him, frowning, obviously confused.

"You know I'm right. Kindness is contagious." It was a phrase he had heard on television. "It's a two way street."

She shook her head like he was nuts. She opened her mouth. Oh God. If she spoke it would ruin everything, there would be a thunderstorm and he would not be responsible for what happened to her.

"Shhhh!" He put his hand up. "Shhh! Listen. Remember when Lacy was learning to walk?"

She nodded yes.

"Didn't you have to let her fall down?" His brain was working again. He was remembering the things on his list. This was one of his favorite examples. He had figured it out on his own. But her expression did not change. "You have to think of this just the same. Think of her now as if she is learning to walk. Do you understand me?"

Winnie nodded. She smiled, but he could tell her stupid smile was a lie. Mothers were liars. His shoulder hurt. He stretched his arm over his head, tried to stretch out the kink. He could not remember what he had done to it. His whole body ached, but why? He could not come down with the flu, not now.

"I know you will lie to me," he said. "I know you will tell me you love your daughter."

"Yes. I do. More than anything."

"All mothers lie."

The traffic was stopped. He had to get off the freeway. He had to. There were too many people around. They were too close. He put on his blinker and nosed over, cutting off another car. He ignored the honking and continued trying to cut across three lanes to the exit.

"What are you doing?" Her voice was small and scared.

He gave a little snort. She thought he was going to get Lacy. That was good. Keep her guessing. He pushed over another lane and waved to thank the driver of the other car. The driver was staring at him—and at Winnie—with a funny look on his face. Winnie used her tied hands to wipe her nose and Oren wanted to scream. He kept going and the next car had to stop short to let him in. The woman rolled down her window to yell at him, but he ignored her. He just wanted to pull over someplace and finish what he had to say to Winnie. It was hard to drive and talk and worry about what she would do. He had a plan and it was all going to hell. To hell. He didn't have enough money to give Kidney. He would never get a mate for Cookie. Cookie, Cookie, Cookie. At home probably scratching the kitchen door to shreds. She was fucking rich, why didn't she have any money in the bank? All the things Lacy had told him about her. The big house with servants. That bastard chauffeur for the rare, expensive car. The wild parties. The nights she cried herself to sleep. She had said her mother was filthy rich. "More money than God," she told him. The car beside him wouldn't let him in. He crept forward a little more, but the guy pulled up right in his way. The driver wouldn't look at him, ignored him, was just a plain old stupid dick.

"Why me," Oren exhaled. "Why me?"

"Why do you hate me?" Winnie whispered. "Why do you hate mothers?"

It was a good question. It would take a lifetime to answer, but for now, until he and Lacy were joined forever and there was more time, he could tell her the last part, the final moment. Then she might understand. He had never told anyone, but he would tell her. It was a good thing to do. "Listen. Listen to me."

"Yes."

"Shhhh." He moved over another lane. And another. And he was free. He sped down the exit. It dumped him into the industrial area that bordered downtown LA. The sky was the same color as the rundown cinderblock buildings. It was perfect. There were no people around except a drunk lying on the sidewalk near the bus stop. Either drunk or dead, no one to worry about. He could drive all the way to the airport through the scummy edges of Los Angeles. Not a scrap of vegetation except the weeds poking up through the cement. The security doors were all closed, the few windows painted over. Even the gangs didn't come here, the walls weren't worth tagging, the neighborhood not worth claiming. He exhaled and began.

"Listen. I grew up in a traveling carnival. My mother, father, sister, and me. We lived in a big RV."

"That sounds—fun."

He pinched her bare leg hard. She gave a little scream.

"Don't talk." When she nodded, he began again. "I grew up in the carnival. Most of the carnies were very nice. I liked them. We were like a family. We traveled year 'round from one side of the country to the other. My Uncle Nolan ran the carnival and my dad was a big showman. He owned the Haunted House, the Amazing Amazon, the Tilt-A-Whirl, and the Dragon Coaster. Plus a couple of food stands. There's a hierarchy in the carnival:

the bigger the ride, the more powerful the showman. Marcus, my dad, was powerful. Definitely. He wasn't very tall, but he was strong and he had a right hand that used to knock me down for nothing, whenever, almost on its own as if his brain had nothing to do with it. People respected him. I was proud to be his kid."

Oren's hand went to his cheek. Pride wasn't exactly the right word, but he did know Marcus was special. A special kind of asshole. The carnies stayed out of his way. Even the marks got quiet when he was around. Only Oren's mother would stand up to him. She'd yell or sometimes try to hit him and he'd catch her hand and bend her wrist backward. He smacked her sometimes too, but she didn't stop fighting him until that night. Oren was thirteen, still working at the hot dog stand, still fucking up. It was late. The rides had stopped and the games and stands and booths were all shuttered. The incessant tinny music was turned off and the workers had gone to bed in their pick-ups and RV's and trailers.

"My mom didn't want to work." Oren told Winnie as he drove down a rutted, pot-holed street. He saw her wince with the bumps. To his right, over the tops of the decrepit warehouses, the skyline of downtown LA glittered like the Emerald City. "My dad called her a princess. She was lazy. Never cleaned or cooked much. But she was beautiful, and people liked her. And she liked them. Boy, did she. She used to say she was born lonely. She was born missing someone and none of us made up for it. She said she had been looking all her life for that one special friend to fill her up. Marcus, my dad, made her the carnival clown. Jilly Bean he called her. Her name was Jill. Jilly Bean. My sweet Jilly Bean. She dressed up in a clown costume with a red nose and big shoes and sold balloon animals to kids. Mostly she just stood around and smoked."

"Where did you go to school?"

Winnie's voice startled him. He had forgotten she was there. He had forgotten what he was doing. For one blessed fucking moment he was somewhere else.

Up ahead a traffic light guarded an intersection that looked as if it had been empty forever. It turned red just as he drove up. He thought about running it, but he could not risk it. Good thing too: he and Winnie watched a dark-skinned girl, a kid really, in shorts and a Mickey Mouse T-shirt push a grocery cart filled with cans and bottles across the street. Where was she going? Why was she here? It made Oren sad. Some Emerald City. Crowded with poor people who would never get a chance to see the Wizard.

"Every night," Oren continued as the light changed to green, "my dad checked the locks on the trucks. Every night, last thing. It was not a surprise or it should not have been for my mother. I was with him, making the rounds. He went to the last semi, to the passenger side first, grabbed the door handle, swung himself up on the running board and tugged. Locked as it should be. He jumped down. I remember he grunted as he hit the ground and complained about the burrito he had eaten for dinner. He was not quiet. My mother should have heard him. She should have sat up then. She could have looked out the truck's door, explained that she fell asleep. But he walked around to the driver's side, hopped up on the running board, tried the door, and it opened."

Oren remembered the blue patterned curtain swaying behind the seats. He heard the boy first, his high teenage squeals ending in a question mark, 'Ooo? Ooo?' as if to ask, is this really happening to me? And then his mother's voice in response, "C'mon, baby. That's it. C'mon, baby."

"My mother was in there with a boy. A boy. Not as old as I am now. My dad reached through the curtain and grabbed whatever body part he could find. He yanked that kid right over the seat and tossed him on the ground. He was pink and naked, like a hairless baby mouse, a pinkie, the kind they feed to snakes. Then my father reached in and grabbed Jilly Bean. She was screaming, but he didn't care. He fell backwards out of the cab with her on top of him. Her ruffled collar was still on, and her wig and make-up, but she was naked from the waist down. Her pubic hair was as curly as the pom poms on her shirt. Her legs were all bubbled with cellulite. My sister, Fiona, came running. We watched Marcus beat the hell out of her. Her clown white smeared all over his big knuckles. The red smile around her lips turned to liquid and dripped onto her shirt. That pink rat boy ran away to his car in the parking lot, left his clothes behind. My father gave them to me, but I wouldn't wear them."

He looked over at Winnie. She was staring straight ahead. Had she heard what he said?

"I'm sorry," she said. "I'm sorry for you." She turned and looked at him, and he was surprised her eyes were so angry. "If you kill me, it won't make your mother a better person. It won't change any mother, anywhere. Is that what you want? To make a statement about mothers? This isn't the way to do it."

"You're not listening."

"I heard. Your mother was a horrible person. Your father had a temper."

"A temper?" Oren felt the blood fill his face. "He killed her."

"Oh my God."

"He killed her."

"I didn't know. You didn't say."

"You weren't listening. Blood. Blood everywhere."

"What happened? What happened to her?"

"He said he was driving her to the hospital, but he came back with dirt on his pants and on his hands. I saw the shovel in the back of the car. He buried her in a cornfield."

He watched Winnie start to shake, to tremble all over. It wasn't like before, it wasn't on purpose or like a fit, but as if she was freezing to death. Her teeth were chattering together in her mouth. The snow days were the best in the carnival. They'd hole up in someone's trailer, playing cards, making chili. The grown ups would drink and tell stories. His mother would rub his arms when he came in cold and wet from checking the rigs. She would sling one arm around him, pull him to her. Popsicle, she called him. My little popsicle boy. The sunlight through Winnie's window glowed golden around her. Strands of dark hair stuck to her cheek and looked like wet branches against the snow. There were goose bumps on her thighs; even on the purple bruises just the size of his finger. He reached for her hand and held it even though it was damp and kind of slimy.

His cell phone rang and they both jumped. He dug it out of his back pocket, looked at the number and tried to turn away from her to answer, "Hey."

"Help!" Winnie screamed. "He's holding me prisoner. Help me!"

She grabbed his arm, reaching for the phone. A girl's voice came through loud and clear, "Oren! Who is that? Oren? Are you there?"

"Help me!" Winnie yelled. "It's not a joke."

He pushed her violently. She slammed against the window. He heard her head crack one more time against the glass. He stopped the car in the middle of the empty street.

"It's just a joke," he said into the phone, "I have to go."

He put it back in his pocket. Winnie was looking all around, but Oren had checked, there was no one to help her. He got out the gun and pointed it at her. He wished his gun was real.

"Now," he said. "Now." But he had nothing after that.

She pulled her arms in front of her chest. She stuck out her bottom lip, like a child. "Okay. Oren."

He froze. He didn't realize she had heard that.

"Isn't that your name? Oren?"

"I was going to introduce myself. I was. Later." He had that part planned too, but it wasn't supposed to go like this. They should be home, sitting on his couch, talking it out. He looked at his watch. He was late. This trip to see Kidney, the money, this stupid woman was ruining everything.

"So," she said. "Hi. I'm Winnie. Nice to meet you, Oren."

"You're Winnie Parker," he said. "Your husband is Jonathan Parker. Your mother is Daisy Juniper."

He slammed his fist into his thigh as he started driving again. Damn his eyes for filling up with tears. He shook his head, rubbed his eyes, and forced himself to smile. He sang a tuneless little song, "Winnie, Winnie, don't you wanna? Cuddle up with my iguana?"

"I'll help you get the money, Oren. I will. It's for Cookie, isn't it?"

"Why do you think that?"

"He's sick."

"He's not sick."

"He's that funny color. I thought iguanas are green."

"It's mating season, that's all. He gets rusty like that to attract the female. The girls like that color." He laughed. "Like my red hair."

"Cookie needs a girlfriend. Of course he does. Everyone needs someone special to love. I bet you need money to buy Cookie a friend."

He was stunned. And then grudgingly impressed. She had figured it out.

"You can't be such a bad mother," he said.

"Who told you I was?"

"Do you lock your daughter in her room at night?"

"Her door doesn't lock."

"Do you tell the servants to not speak to her?"

"I don't have any servants. I live in a little house, a bungalow, in Echo Park near Dodger Stadium. Two bedrooms. One bath. Your house is bigger than mine."

"And that fancy European car you drive?"

"A fifteen-year-old Peugeot."

"One of two ever made."

"One of two still running maybe."

"I wish I could believe you."

"It's the truth."

It could not be. Because if it was the truth, then Lacy was lying to him and if Lacy was lying to him then everything he was doing meant nothing. No. Winnie was lying to him. She had to be. And he hated liars.

16.

Buster filled the pipe.

"More, man," the leader said. "There's a lot of us."

Buster obliged. Lacy watched him, afraid to look anywhere else. The pipe was a small, carved and polished piece of something, black and gray with flecks of blue. Lacy didn't think this kind of stone was really found in nature. She wondered how she could be thinking about this right now. She wrapped her hands around her knees. She felt the scarier, quiet guy looking at her. She tried to see him with her peripheral vision, without turning her head, but he was a little behind her. When she finally turned to him, he was staring at her arms.

"Girl," he whispered, "you are white."

She blushed.

"Whoa, watch that!" the fat boy exclaimed. "Now she's red."

"Such a drag," Lacy said. "I hate my skin."

"Uh huh, I can see why." Fatty laughed, but his friend just stared at her.

The leader had a lighter. He took the pipe from Buster and lit up. After a few tokes he passed it to the fat one. The other one did not partake. Lacy didn't either.

"C'mon, white girl," said the leader.

She shook her head.

"It's good for you," he said. "Make your toes twinkle."

"Let her be," the quiet one said. He held out a hand to her.

"Let me show you what's really cool."

Buster frowned. Lacy waited. Did she have to go? The guy gestured, "come on" with his hand. Everybody was staring at her.

"Babe," Buster began.

Lacy cut him off. He would not do well in a fight. "I'll be right back." She took the offered hand and stood up. She tried to smile. "I love this place. I do. Can't wait to see more." She wished she were back in school, that she had gone to see the principal, braved Marissa and her friends.

She let herself be pulled away from the others, through the garden until she couldn't see Buster anymore. They went up some steps and down another little path. Clouds had slipped in across the sky and without the sun nothing shone or sparkled.

"Look," he said. "Reject land."

Hidden in among the bushes and dirt were small glass mistake animals. They were misshapen and lumpy, freaks of nature, missing legs or eyes, with one ear twice the size of the other or a hump back covered in glass tumors. There was even a two-headed animal, one end a rat, the other end a bird or something, as if the glass blower had changed his mind in the middle. Her guide held her hand tightly. His grip was firm, but narrow and long-fingered like a girl. She could not help but notice how dark his skin was next to hers. His hips were slim too, almost feminine in the cheap jeans she recognized from Target. He stopped abruptly and she tumbled into him. He let go of her.

"Sorry!"

"Shh!"

She waited and listened. The wind was picking up and there was a clattering of palm fronds. She shivered. It had been so warm earlier sitting in the sun with Buster. She looked back over her shoulder. The clouds had changed the light. A greenish tint as if the day had spoiled.

"I should go," she said.

She turned to head back and he grabbed her arm.

"My mother," she whispered, "is picking me up."

"And what if you're not there?"

She held her breath. She stood as still as if she were made of glass. The breeze blew a hair into her face, but she did not brush it back. She was his height. Her blue eyes looked right into his, a lighter brown than she expected, golden in the odd winter light. His hand slipped down her naked arm and held her wrist.

She stood up straight. "Why did you want me to see this?"

"It's good for you."

"What is?"

His gaze went down and up her body slowly. Then he said, "It's good for perfect girls to see something ugly. I bet everything is pretty in your perfect life."

"I'm not perfect," Lacy protested. "I'm not."

"You don't know what you are. You don't know what I am. You don't know what any of this is."

She waited for him to tell her. His long fingers easily circled her wrist. Over his shoulder she could see a misshapen dog, or maybe it was a bear. One side of its face caved in, making a bubble in the other cheek.

"Don't you see?" he asked. His eyebrows went up. He leaned in close enough to kiss her. He smelled of aftershave and soap, minty fresh. Then, abruptly, he stepped back and grinned. His teeth were straight and white and clean. Obviously he'd had braces. He let go of her and she exhaled.

"Where do you go?" he asked.

"Kennedy."

"That arts magnet?"

She nodded, both feet back on safe ground. "You?"

"UCLA."

"You're in college?"

"Freshman."

Her surprise must've shown. He shook his head. "I'm not what you think, huh? You thought I was a gangster? And mean. A pig like this?" He picked up a little red animal and dropped it on the sidewalk. It shattered and Lacy jumped back.

"No," she began.

"Don't bother," he said. "Whatever you think about me, I don't care 'cause I think you're a rich white girl whose parents think it's liberal and cool to send their baby to public school."

"I'm not."

"I don't care."

He was so disappointed in her. She turned away and he took her hand again. Then she spun around and faced him angrily.

"You don't know anything about me. My life is far from perfect. I have worries and troubles and… and things, just like you. Just because you're Latino, doesn't mean you're the only one with problems. You know? Being white doesn't automatically make everything so fucking great."

"Whoa, calm down Girl. Okay. Point taken." He nodded at her grudgingly.

She hurried back toward Buster and he didn't try to stop her.

Buster's face lit up and he jumped to his feet when she returned. He stepped toward her, his chest like the prow of a ship coming into port. She smiled at him.

"We better go," she said.

The leader had the pipe and Buster's plastic baggie of pot. He held them out.

"Keep it," Buster said.

"Thanks, man. Take your pipe."

Buster pocketed his pipe.

"You can come back, man, anytime. And her, I guess. But

don't bring anybody else."

"Absolutely. I agree. The glass garden is not for everybody."

Lacy glanced at the quiet college boy. Now he wouldn't look at her. He had not even tried to kiss her. She wondered what he would think if he knew she'd had her first real kiss just an hour ago. Right here. In this place.

"Bye-bye," she said as if they were friends she'd met for ice cream.

Lacy and Buster forced their feet to walk nonchalantly all the way to the torn place in the fence. Buster crouched and went through first, then held the chain link back for her. Once on the other side, they broke into a run across the street to the car. Only after Buster had started it up and pulled away and driven around the corner did Lacy giggle. Then Buster laughed. They were triumphant, they had faced down bad guys and won, they had left with body and dignity intact. Lacy felt invincible. And it was all because of him.

"You were great," Lacy said. "The pot was a good idea."

"What did he do to you?"

"Nothing. He showed me these weird little deformed animals." She did not tell Buster that he went to UCLA. Or that when he spoke to her he was not scary at all.

"You are so brave."

"So are you."

He pulled the car over. He reached for her and they kissed. It was the most romantic moment of her life. Her stomach fluttered and lurched. She could barely breathe. Danger was such an amazing turn on.

"My house?" he asked.

"Nobody's home?"

"Working."

She nodded. She could not wait to be alone with him. She turned her cell phone off.

17.

Jonathan watched the surfers at El Porto beach through the windshield of his car. He felt in his pockets, but he didn't have any quarters for the parking meter. Just like always. His friends back in the day would kid him about it, always made a big show of giving him parking meter money. Where were those guys? He hadn't stayed in touch.

The sky over the ocean was hazy with smog or moisture or both. In this light, the sand was more gray than tan. He opened his door. The breeze was brisk and cool and smelled of salt and seagulls. He shivered, turned his face to the lackluster sun and closed his eyes. It was chilly. It didn't smell as he remembered, but the waves were music to him, the song of his youth. He recognized the building rhythm, the crescendo and crash, and then the murmur of the water retreating. He left his shoes in the car and walked across the beach toward the water. It didn't matter if he got a ticket.

A surfer with gray hair was coming out of the ocean, walking backwards in his flippers and carrying his board. He turned around, kicked off his flippers and peeled his wetsuit down halfway revealing a potbelly covered by graying hair.

All over Los Angeles there were people who didn't work. Right now, at two o'clock in the afternoon on a Tuesday, people were sitting in coffee shops, or at restaurants, or shopping, or exercising. Jessica said it wasn't like this in her hometown of

Hamilton, Ohio. In Hamilton, the mall, the grocery stores, the tennis courts were empty during the day except for the occasional stay-at-home mom with a stroller. Then, after school, you'd see kids in the soccer fields and at the swimming pool. And later, after work was over, you'd see men out walking the dog or playing with the kids in the front yard while the little woman cooked dinner. Jessica said the LA lifestyle was a more enlightened—or enlivened? He couldn't remember the word—way of living. She said people could explore and promote their own natural lifestyle, not conform to an unhealthy schedule just because it was the norm.

They'd had this conversation post sex one late weekday morning. They were lying in Jessica's bed at her apartment while Lacy was in school and Winnie was wherever, unaware he was cheating on her. Jonathan hated that word. He didn't cheat. He fell in love. He fell in love with his job at the game show. He fell more and more in love with his eight-year-old daughter, her giggle, her ringlets, her skinny little arms around his neck when he got home. He fell in love with Jessica. His mouth opened with the memory, that perfect corn-fed body, the way her eyes widened when she looked at him, as if every time was the first time. You. It's you. Those days. He was in love with himself.

His toes curled, digging under the warm top layer to the cooler, wetter sand below. The wind blew and he was cold. Time to head back. Tomorrow he would surf. It had been too long.

"Do I know you?" the silver surfer asked.

Jonathan prepared his TV smile.

"'Cause you're staring at me like you know me," the guy continued.

"Oh no, man, sorry, no, no, no. I wasn't looking at you. I mean I guess I was, but I wasn't looking, you know. I was just thinking. Sorry. I used to surf here three or four times a week."

The guy nodded. "Look over there," he said. "Just don't look at me."

"Sorry," Jonathan said again.

He turned around, his shoulders tightening in embarrassment. He took a couple of self-conscious steps back toward his car. There were houses in a line along the concrete boardwalk, with decks and balconies and sliding glass doors right there. They seemed so friendly. Inviting. Maybe this guy lived in one of these. Jonathan looked away. Now he didn't want to seem to be staring at the guy's house. He wasn't sure where to look.

He kicked through the sand to his car. He hoped he seemed laid-back, indifferent, lost in thought. If he had one of these houses, he could surf whenever he wanted to. Or he could sit out on the deck, drink a beer, and listen to the waves. If he got cold, he'd have a sweatshirt right inside. Even if he came home to one of these houses every day at five-thirty exactly, conforming to the norm, even so he could stand in his own living room and still be at the beach. He would ask Jessica about moving. He and Winnie had planned to live here when they could afford it. Winnie loved the beach, not as a swimmer or a surfer, but the sand and the wind and the attitude, she said. She loved the beach attitude. She wore that same one-piece red bathing suit all the time he knew her. Wait. That couldn't be right. In nine—no, ten—years she must've bought a new bathing suit. But maybe not. He only remembered her on the beach in that stretchy bit of red. How faded it got like a wagon left out in the yard. How she would step out of it at home and leave it on the floor inside out with a little scattering of sand. Sometimes it would stay there until the next time they went back to the beach. Princess Winnie. Not that it ever bothered him, the sand under his feet and in the corners of the shower. The salty tang of her skin under his tongue.

Jessica would like living here. She would look amazing in a bikini on the deck of that three-story yellow clapboard house right behind his car. He could surf in the morning, and then head into work totally chill, at peace, one with the ocean's qi. Jessica said it was restorative, or rejuvenating, or recuperating.

He got to his car and turned back toward the sea and saw the surfer dressed now in cheap chinos and a wrinkled button down. He pretended not to watch as the guy trudged across the sand with his battered surfboard and pushed it through the sunroof of some old, dented Japanese car. Jonathan got into his Porsche and relaxed in the warmth. It still smelled almost new. The leather seats were like a hug. He heard the guy's car struggle to start, finally catch and whine out of the parking lot. Jonathan shook his head, did a television laugh at himself. That guy had made him feel bad? That guy?

The wind blew a piece of trash across the sand. The beach was speckled with tar and waste. He couldn't move down here. Lacy's new school was very close to the Beverly Hills house and Jessica's yoga studio was only minutes away. Maybe when Lacy was in college and Jessica was making movies or whatever they would move to Malibu, someplace more private.

He looked at his watch and, as always, admired the weight and shine of it. The most expensive watch made, a wedding gift from Jessica. It was handsome, a thing of beauty that would be a thing of enjoyment—or whatever the phrase was—forever. The second hand moved in increments, not sweeping, but ticking off the seconds.

Even as he was admiring it, he knew he shouldn't be watching the second hand. He should never pay attention to the ticking, the slow slip slip from one second to the next. Stop it, he told himself. He tried to look away, but then the feeling came. It rushed into his chest and the back of his throat, that horrible,

desperate feeling of his life passing, moment by moment. With
every click of the second hand, he was aware of his existence,
his being, winding down. He heard his heart beating, throwing
away his precious allotment. His heartbeats were limited. There
went one. And another. And another. He felt each breath. He
wanted to catch his life in both hands, but there was nothing to
grab. He was dying a little with every second. It was a familiar
feeling, too familiar lately and he hated it. It was like when he
was a kid and would become aware of his tongue. In his mouth.
Behind his teeth. Taking up breathing room. Unable to think of
anything else. Recently, at night, in bed, he had taken to counting the beats of his heart, afraid to stop, as if his counting kept it
going. And one. And two. And three. And four. When would it
stop? When would it stop?

Jonathan opened his car door and gulped the air. He swung
his bare feet around to the pavement and bent his head to his
knees. He tried to avoid looking, but he caught sight of his feet.
His feet. These could not be his feet. Bony and translucent, the
veins prominent, the toenails gone yellow. His father's feet. His
grandfather's feet. Jessica had a framed saying in the den, "Nothing is worth more than this day." He wanted to make this day
special; he wanted to make every moment count, but how? How
could he make each moment of his life the best it could be? He
had to eat and shit and shower and drive in traffic and do his job.
He had to smile and please people and to do that he had to get
his teeth whitened and his hair frosted and spend an hour every
day at the gym. So was this it? Was this not wasting his life? Sitting in his car watching other people surf?

Oh, God! Oh, God! Tears came then, but a man's tears that
offered no real release, only further awkwardness and shame.

He forced himself to get back in the car, to start the engine,
to turn on the radio so he could concentrate on whatever the

announcer was saying. Instead it was music, classical, written by some dead guy who had left a mark on the world. No one would watch his game show years from now. No one would care that he had been alive. What was he doing here? What was he doing with it? He unfastened his watch and tossed it behind him, out of reach in the back seat. He would drive home right away, as quickly as he could. He needed Jessica.

18.

Winnie knew exactly where she was. Oren was taking her
through Inglewood, west toward the airport. Manchester Avenue was six lanes wide and flat, a straight line through the tra-
ditionally black neighborhood of older homes, small shops and
many churches. A lot of the stores were boarded up and out
of business. Even the 'for lease' signs looked old and forgotten. Three middle-aged men clustered in front of a liquor store
smoking cigarettes; one of them had a bottle in a brown paper
bag. Winnie saw two young, white hipsters going into a restaurant that advertised 'authentic soul food.' She could hear them
telling their friends later how cool it was, what brave pioneers
they were. A young black teenaged girl laughed with a friend.
Her bouncing, tightly curling hair reminded Winnie of Lacy.
She closed her eyes. At that moment, she knew Lacy was sitting in class absently playing with her hair, twisting one ringlet
around her finger as she had since she was a toddler. At home,
the dog would be sleeping on the sofa. Jonathan was annoyed
she never called, but he wasn't worried. She was not missed
yet; no one knew she had been abducted. Would she make the
evening news? Not tonight. Not until tomorrow at the earliest.
Daughter of famous movie star. Ex-wife of famous game show
host. Missing, presumed dead. Finally she would get her own
moment of fame.

Oren—she was glad to know his name—tapped the steering wheel. A steady one-two rhythm like a heartbeat. Where did he get these ideas about her? That she had servants. That she would lock Lacy in her room at night. Was there a tabloid that had made her out to be a witch? Jonathan Parker's horrid ex-wife. But no one cared about her anymore. Oren was definitely not anxious to call Jonathan for a ransom. He had something else in mind. Something worse, she was sure. His father had killed his mother. Beaten her to death. Buried her in a corn-field. She could expect the same. He was taking her somewhere, some remote place to kill her slowly. The knife. The gun used as a hammer. His feet in his white sneakers. His fists. Like father, like son. She heard Jonathan at her funeral, "The apple doesn't fall far from the bag—the branch—whatever." She pictured Jessica, Jonathan, and Lacy around the dinner table. She hated that image in her mind when Lacy went there just for a weekend. The thought that it would be the rest of Lacy's life made her sick. The three of them. Lacy's family. She imagined Christmas, Easter, Fourth of July, Lacy leaving for college, Lacy bringing her first boyfriend home. And when that boyfriend broke her heart, Winnie could not believe Jessica would comfort her, tell her he wasn't good enough for her anyway. Jonathan thought Jessica would be great with Lacy. He had said she would be a wonderful influence and could teach Lacy so many things.

"Like how to steal someone's husband?" Winnie had retorted.

"Very funny."

"I'm not joking."

The look on his face. His guilt made him hate her some-times; at that moment he despised her. If she were dead, if he didn't have to see her or talk to her on the phone, it would be a gift to him.

Winnie opened her eyes. They were passing the round and columned pseudo-Roman Forum on her left. The sign advertised Sunday services for the Faith Central Bible Church and also the comeback tour of a 1980's heavy metal band. A giant cemetery stretched off to her right. She had made no instructions about her funeral. The cemetery was pretty, a swath of deep green grass and leafy trees in the middle of the sinking urban scene. It was bordered on the west by Prairie Avenue. She had always loved the word prairie, the wide, open spaces, the long grasses moving in the breeze. She had never seen a prairie, never been to Nebraska or Kansas or any place where she could see empty land for miles and miles.

"I'd like to be buried there," she said.

"I'll tell Lacy," Oren replied.

Winnie recoiled as if he had hit her again. "I'll do whatever you say. Just leave her alone."

"You can't make deals with me."

He was crazy. He didn't know where Lacy was, he couldn't. They crossed under the 405 Freeway.

"We're almost there." He had his phone out giving him directions. He turned right abruptly, throwing her against the door.

"Sorry," he said. "This is it." He turned into the parking lot.

"Tip Top Coffee Shop," she read the neon sign aloud. The second "o" was only partially lit and the rest of the slanted 1960s building was equally neglected. But she could see customers inside, sitting at booths in the window. A handsome black man looked right at her as they drove in. She held up her bound wrists, but he had turned back to his eggs and potatoes or grilled cheese sandwich, whatever was on his plate much more interesting than her.

"What are we doing here?" she asked.

"This has nothing to do with you. I'm sorry you had to come along."

Oren drove through the parking lot and around behind the building. The back area was completely empty except for a young Latino man in an apron throwing garbage into two green dumpsters. He wiped his hands and went back through the kitchen door and closed it behind him. Oren looked at his watch.

"Are you late?"

"Tell me he didn't leave."

"We're meeting someone with a female iguana, aren't we?"

"You're pretty smart." Oren sighed. "He's a reptile dealer. The best. He doesn't have the female yet. He's going to get me a good one. From the jungle. A young adult and a clutch of eggs." He continued proudly, "I negotiated for the clutch. Won't cost me a penny more."

"How much money is in that envelope?"

"He wanted three thousand for her, and fifteen hundred expenses."

"Forty-five hundred dollars? He'll wait."

"I'm short three hundred."

Oren groaned and pressed his palms into his eyes. He had a redhead's hands, every wrinkle obvious in the white skin, with fiery little hairs and freckles. Winnie thought of his mother telling him not to bite his nails, slapping his hand out of his mouth. His mother, his dead mother. Maybe he didn't bite those nails until after she died. And what happened to his father?

"It's a lot of money." Winnie tried to reassure him. "Maybe he's inside."

Oren shook his head. He sighed again and let his shoulders drop, his chest sink, his hands fall open on his lap. Everything about him collapsed.

"I shouldn't have come." He looked used up, an old rag wrung out.

"He's got to be here." She soothed him as she eyed the back

door to the coffee shop. There were people in that kitchen, right through that door. If she screamed as she climbed out the car window, somebody would hear her, somebody would run out and see her. Slowly she inched her hands toward the button, leaned over on one hip preparing to leap.

"Thwock!"

Oren jumped. So did she. An overweight man in a safari jacket was knocking on Oren's window.

"Kidney!" Oren grinned as he rolled it down. "Thank God."

"Where the hell've you been?" The man asked Oren, but he was staring at her, taking in her tied hands, her sweaty face, the bruises on her bare legs. Oren tried to lean forward, keep him from seeing her, but it was too late.

"What you got there, Oren?"

"Nothing."

The man leaned in, pushed Oren out of the way. "Hey there. You're not nothing."

"Please. I'm Winnie Parker and he's kid—"

Oren clamped his hand over her mouth. She struggled, but it didn't matter. She was saved. The man had heard enough. Then he began to laugh, a slippery sharp laugh that turned in her gut like a knife.

"Heh, heh, heh. Pleased to meet you Winnie Parker. I'm Kidney." Then to Oren, "She looks a little old for you."

"It's not what you think." Oren said. "We're just talking."

Kidney laughed some more, but it sunk to a scratching low in his chest. Oren handed him the envelope of money. Kidney counted, and then gave a little tsk tsk.

"You're missing some."

"Just a little."

Kidney handed the envelope back to Oren and started to walk away. He was bluffing. Winnie could tell by the way he took tiny steps with his head cocked back waiting for Oren's plea.

"I can get it to you. I can. Kidney, please."

Kidney turned and did a little funny move, as if he was dancing, pulling an imaginary hat over his forehead. She had hoped he would save her. He was crazier than Oren. He came to the car and squatted down. He held onto the door through the open window and his fingernails were too long and dirty. The pinkie nail was the longest, for cleaning his ears or picking his nose.

"You owe me three hundred dollars. That's a lot of money."

"I'm good for it. You know that. You know me."

"Fact is, I hardly know you at all." Kidney stood up. He hitched up his pants and Winnie saw the crotch of his old man light washed jeans was spotted with pee or spilled food. "Get out of the car, Oren, so we can talk face to face."

Oren looked at Winnie.

"Don't let him push you around." Winnie whispered. "I mean it, you shouldn't have to pay the rest until he delivers her." She surprised him and herself. She was not his mother. She should have told him to punch Kidney, to get into a fistfight. Then the cops would come or the manager would run out. Someone normal who wouldn't laugh when he saw her. Oren gave her a little smile, calmly turned off the car, took his keys from the ignition, and got out. She saw the butt of the gun protruding from his jacket pocket. Surely anyone walking by would see it too. But nobody was walking by. There was no reason to be back here unless you were the busboy with the garbage and he had finished that job.

The busboy and that kitchen door. Oren and Kidney were talking on his side of the car. Oren was pleading with Kidney, holding out the envelope, begging him to take it. On her side, the kitchen door was closed but it had to be unlocked. It had to be. She counted to three and lunged for the door handle. The door opened and she half fell from the car. Her ankles were tied, but she had thought she could manage to stay standing. She struggled to her knees. She opened her mouth to scream just as Kidney grabbed her from behind and squeezed the air from her lungs. She could smell beer and sweat and his dirty clothes and hair. She thought she would vomit. She thought she would pass out.

"Where do you want her?" Kidney asked Oren. He spun her around like a child in her father's arms. Around and around and around.

"Stop," Oren said, "C'mon, Kidney. Stop."

Kidney chuckled and put Winnie down on her feet. She was so dizzy, and her feet so close together, she fell over. He pushed her prone and straddled her. She would have bitten an ankle, anything, but he wore scuffed and dirty cowboy boots.

"Who is this bitch?" he asked.

"She's my girlfriend's mother."

Winnie twisted to look at Oren. He was making this up. He was trying to get Kidney to leave her alone, but it was so ridiculous no one would believe him.

"Sure, she is." Kidney looked down at her. His face was bloated and sagging, but his arms had been like a vise around her ribs. The cuts on her stomach were bleeding again; Oren's white T-shirt stuck and pulled as she tried to get to her hands and knees.

Again Kidney pushed her flat with one foot. "Listen, Oren. You owe me three hundred bucks. I got a deal for you. Why don't I take her off your hands? We'll call it even."

19.

Buster had done this before and Lacy was glad. The top button of her jeans had been hard to undo. She sometimes had trouble with it herself, and Buster was only using one hand. She was also happy he was absolutely stone cold sober for this most momentous act of her life so far. He told her he'd been too nervous to even take a single toke with the guys in the glass garden.

"But you seemed so cool."

"Shaking and quaking on the inside."

His bedroom was familiar, the same Ikea furniture everyone had, done in boy colors of blue and brown. She smiled at his football-themed sheets.

"Mom," he said embarrassed.

"I still have ballerinas."

The bed was a single but they managed to fit. As long as he kept kissing her anything was possible. His hand stroked her stomach. She squirmed, but it was good. She hoped Buster would be her boyfriend. It would be great to have a boyfriend at school. They could sit together at lunch. They could walk down the hall holding hands. She could put "in a relationship" on her page. And she really, really liked him.

Buster's hand slipped under the elastic on her underpants and between her legs. She was damp down there and she knew that was normal. Her breath came faster. Her whole body tingled. She lifted her hips so he could wiggle off her jeans. Good thing she had worn decent underpants, a favorite pair decorated with flowers and a little lace. Buster took her hand and put it on his thing. She gasped. It was so much softer than she expected.

"Don't worry," Buster said. "You're not hurting me."

"It's like velvet."

"Glad you think so."

"Are they all like this?"

"Frankly, mine is the only one I've ever touched."

"Me too."

"I'm honored. Really." He looked into her eyes. "Touch. Explore. Discover. "

She giggled. "Like at the Science Museum."

"Exactly. My dick is your personal exhibit."

He laughed too. What a relief to be herself. With Buster she could say or do anything. With her older, mystery man she had to be Lacy Parker—wealthy, sophisticated, and abused young adult. She had not meant to lie to him. They had been on the phone for the first time. It was very late at night, after her mother was safely asleep. She turned out her bedside lamp so she could listen to him in the dark. He was looking at her picture online while they talked. He told her she was beautiful and obviously smart, not a combination he thought regularly went together.

"Beautiful? Really?"

"Absolutely."

She said no one told her she was beautiful and his response was so vehement and his outrage so comforting that she wanted it to continue. So she lied, just a little that night, about her father and especially about her mother. The divorce was true. Her famous father and the popular game show he hosted were true. Her mother's anger and unhappiness were probably true, but the way she took it all out on Lacy was not true.

"I'm a senior. I'm eighteen, but she won't let me go anywhere by myself. She makes the chauffeur follow me everywhere—even to school. I had a chance to play flute once with the Los Angeles Philharmonic and she wouldn't let me go. She doesn't want me doing anything better than her."

He had been gratifyingly incensed. "She's insane."

"She's so jealous of me."

"What does your father say?"

"He doesn't believe me."

"Asshole."

The next time she had upped the ante.

"My mother's boyfriend followed me around the house. He stalked me. He came in the bathroom when I was taking a shower. He told me he wanted to rape me. And when I told my mother, she got mad at me. She slapped me. She took away my clothes and made me wear this enormous ugly dress."

He had shouted into the phone. He had been desperate to save her. He would not let this continue. He'd come and get her, wherever she was, break down the door if necessary. Lacy had loved his passion, loved that she inspired it. No man had ever wanted to fight for her.

"Are you sure you want to do this?" Buster asked her. "We can just kiss."

His face was flushed and he was practically panting. He ran his hands over her naked body. He kissed her eyes and then her collarbones and then her tits. He circled her nipple with his tongue. She thought she might lose her mind, fall into this crazy sex place and never come out. His thing was hard, but soft at the same time. She looked down at it. A tiny drop of milky moisture came out the tip.

"I'm... I'm sure."

She was. She was sure. It was about time, she was sixteen years old. Losing her virginity was just another kind of piercing.

So cool when it was done. And it felt so good to be wanted, to see the desire on Buster's face that only she could answer. He needed her.

"What do I do?" she asked.

"I'll try to go slow, but I am a teenage boy. We are notoriously self-centered."

Her confusion must have shown on her face because he smiled. "I'm just talking," he said.

"You talk a lot."

"Not more than you."

She put her hands behind his head and pulled his lips to hers. When they talked she was not as brave. She needed his kiss, his tongue, his breath in the back of her throat. He lifted himself over her. She spread her legs. He tried to find the right entry. She had not thought that part would be so difficult. But every time he missed and ran the tip over her special spot, she gasped. It was so much different than her own furtive explorations at home. So much better. She reached down and guided him back over that spot. Was that okay with him? He moaned. She assumed that was a good thing. Anyway it was too wonderful to stop, she never wanted to stop. She knew an orgasm would come, she was not a child, but dancing along the edge of it was the best feeling she had ever experienced. A little bit was good, but more was a whole lot better. Don't stop. Never, never, never. Some small part of her worried she was becoming a sex maniac. Sex might be like heroin—one time and she was addicted.

"Oh no," Buster grunted and erupted in her pubic hair. His whole body went rigid and then shaky and then he collapsed on top of her. She pulled her hand away just in time. His semen squished between them, sour smelling and all globby. It couldn't be over. This wasn't it, was it? He was done and she was just beginning.

He rolled off her and closed his eyes. This was it then. He had had his fun and he would drive her back to school and they hadn't even really had sex. He said "oh no" which did not sound good. She had done something wrong by grabbing him, guiding him. Lacy began to cry.

"Oh oh oh oh oh. Don't cry."

It was just too much. Skipping school for the first time. The scary guy in the garden. Kissing Buster and now this. She wanted her mother. She wanted to be home on the couch with tomato soup and the TV, as if this were a fever from which she needed to recuperate. Buster stroked her hair and kissed her cheeks.

"You're even pretty when you cry."

"Really?"

"Most people get all puffy and red. You should see my sister. It's gross."

She smiled at him.

"I love your smile."

"You do?"

"Since eighth grade. Well, I was in eighth, you were in seventh and those juggling clowns came to assembly and everybody was booing and bored but you had a great big smile on your face."

"My mom just said she wants to be a birthday party clown."

"She'd be a good one."

"Mortifying."

"No, it's cool. Definitely a give back kind of thing."

It seemed so normal to be talking to Buster. Even though they were naked and her stomach was sticky and she needed to blow her nose. Buster. Buster and Lacy. It was nice.

"Did I—" she began and stopped.

"What?"

"Did I do something wrong? Is that why you said oh no?"

"No! It's all me. I was—you were perfect. Really. And you're technically I guess still a virgin, so if you want to save that for some other, more important guy, I mean, I understand. It—this was great, for me, but—"

She started to laugh. "Why do we both think we suck so much?"

"I just want it to be right for you."

She reached for him. "Can we try again?"

"As many times as you like. What I lack in staying power, I make up for in—"

"Please shut up."

20.

Oren blinked. He rubbed his eyes. Could this really be happening? He would get his iguana from the world's greatest reptile guy and he could go home alone. This would all be taken care of. Kidney had offered him the perfect solution.

"Oren!" She called to him. Her face was dirty.

"What are you going to do with her?"

Kidney looked at him and grinned. Winnie struggled under his boot.

"I like a woman who will fight," he said. "It's more fun. For awhile."

"And then what?" Oren wasn't sure what he wanted to hear.

Kidney gave his weird, growling laugh. "Maybe I'll take her to Paraguay with me. She's a little thing. I can put her in the suitcase like I did the snakes."

Winnie squirmed and bucked. Her voice was squeaky as if it was hard for her to breathe. "Oren, you can't do this. What is the matter with you? I thought you needed to teach me something. What about your plan? Haven't I been good? You can't give me to him. I'll give you the rest of the money. You know I will."

Kidney moved his boot to her head and pressed her face into the pavement. "Have to get her a muzzle. Shut her up." He took a handkerchief out of his pocket. It was obviously well used. "We can use this." He bent to stuff the grimy handkerchief into Winnie's mouth.

"Wait," Oren said. Then he wasn't sure what else to say. "Wait," he said again, and, "Someone might see us."

Not really. Not at all. The back of the restaurant was a blank wall of yellow bricks. The door to the kitchen was closed. An alley bordered the parking lot and across it was a high wooden fence. They were between the dumpster and the alley. If some-one drove around the side they would see him, and maybe the top of Kidney's head, but not Winnie lying on the ground. Win-nie. His girlfriend's mother. He had said it, but she didn't believe him. She didn't know he loved Lacy more than anything in the world. Even more than Cookie. He walked over to Winnie and waved Kidney away.

"Say goodbye," Kidney chuckled as he took a step back. "My turn now."

Oren squatted beside her. His head hurt. He was sore all over and he was so tired. Winnie's eyes were closed. Maybe she was sleeping. He wished he could sleep. He circled her wrist with his thumb and forefinger. She was tiny. The women in his family, his mother and sister, his aunt the one time he met her, were large with stomachs that jiggled and breasts that flopped and threatened to spill in every direction. Winnie was compact and all in one piece. Her hands were half the size of his. He could not give her to Kidney to be folded into a suitcase with a filthy handkerchief in her mouth. He could not let her be used and thrown away. Even if it would help him. Even if it would solve all his problems. He was so tired. He needed to get more sleep. He did not want to continue with his plan. But he had to, he had to, he had to.

Her wrist looked brown against his fingers. That olive color, so much different than his, so different than he expected. How odd that she was the mother of his beautiful, pale, long-limbed blond girl. "Huh," he grunted aloud. Maybe she wasn't really

Lacy's mother. Maybe Lacy was adopted. Or maybe this woman, this Winnie, was a kidnapper, a Jew or a gypsy, who had stolen that golden baby. It was not his fault she was so damn difficult. She was a trickster. A thief. A witch.

Oren stood up. Let him have her. Let him take her and fuck her and throw her out the window. "Wake up," he said.

Winnie's eyes opened immediately. "I'm not sleeping."

"Who are you?" he asked. "Did you steal your daughter? Take her from the hospital when she was born? Are you really her mother?"

"What are you talking about?"

"Maybe you aren't who you say you are."

She pushed herself up to sitting. There were bits of gravel on her cheek. "Of course I'm her mother. Of course I am."

She was crying, but silently. He had never known tears to fall without the woman wailing. She was such an oddball. The mother of his girlfriend.

"I want to believe you," he said.

"We have the same nose. I have a picture in my wallet. She's blond like her father and her grandmother."

"Liar, liar, pants on fire."

"Believe me."

He considered her wide mouth, her brown eyes. She blinked slowly.

"Do that again," he said. "Blink like that."

She did and he saw something in her face. Something familiar. He had to see it. The picture of Lacy he had downloaded. There was something in the eyebrows, or the chin. Something. The nose. Definitely the nose. Yes, Winnie was Lacy's mother. Daisy Juniper was Winnie's mother. Jonathan Parker the game show host was Winnie's ex-husband. Of course Lacy was blonde. It was just Winnie who had lost out, who was dark and small and like a little animal. An unfortunate mouse, he thought. Possibly a Jewish mouse, but that was not important to him. It was how she was. Who she was. Not what. Poor thing. So dark and dirty looking. No wonder she was so mean to Lacy. She was jealous.

"Times a'wastin', boy," Kidney chuckled.

He had listened to her beg for her life. He had listened to her pee. He had carried her to bed with his arms under her bare legs and been close enough to breathe in the flakes of her skin. As his fingers had tied the around her ankles, their sweat had blended. He could smell her on his fingers. There was so much more he had planned. He bent and whispered to her, "I want you to know me."

"I do know you," she said. "The way you talk. The way you move. The way your fingers close when you're angry."

"Not that," he said. He wanted her to understand. "That's barely anything."

She had not begun to see the real him, the good Oren. He liked people. All kinds of people. Anybody, any kind of person, could be his friend. He had a cheerful greeting for each and every co-worker in the morning. Everybody at Carpet Barn liked him.

She patted his shoes with her bound hands. "Oren. Don't give me away. Not to him. He'll hurt me. He'll kill me. Please. You're better than this."

She looked up at him and her eyelashes were wet and dark and her eyes were so terribly disappointed. In him. She dropped her head and he felt her reproach in his chest.

"You're better than this," she whispered it again. "Would you let someone treat Cookie this way?"

Kidney snorted as he walked over to them. "Over and out, Oren boy. I got lots to do today." He easily lifted Winnie off the ground and held her in both arms like a bride about to cross the threshold. She opened her mouth to scream, but Oren shook his head no, and she didn't. Her eyes were pleading with him. Like Cookie when he was hungry. Like any creature who needed taking care of. And Oren could do that. He was good at that.

"Put her down," Oren said.

"This means no female," Kidney said. "I don't get one, neither do you."

"I'm taking her with me."

Kidney laughed. "C'mon, boy. What're you gonna do with her?"

The way he said it was insulting. "Put her down. I want my money back."

Kidney slung Winnie over his shoulder, like some kind of big game, and started for his car. "I'll get you the best little lady iguana you ever saw."

Winnie was fighting now. She did not want to go with him. Oren could see she was desperate not to go with him. "Oren," she screamed. "Please."

But Kidney was a big man. He reminded Oren of his uncle, his father, all the men he had known. He stood there, afraid to move forward. "Stop," he said feebly.

Kidney swung around to laugh at him.

"The gun," Winnie shouted. "Use the gun."

Oren had forgotten his gun. He took it out and pointed it at Kidney.

Kidney's squinty little eyes opened. He stopped laughing. Then he shrugged. "Oh, right," he said, "like you're really gonna use that."

Oren took a step toward him. He began to smile as he saw Kidney's concern, his involuntary step back. "Put her down and give me my money."

"Jesus Christ. Have your old housewife."

Kidney dropped Winnie and she fell awkwardly onto her knees with a crack Oren could hear. He grimaced. More bruises. He had forgotten her ankles were tied and she couldn't catch herself on her feet.

"Now my money."

"No iguana for you."

"Give me back my money."

"I drove all the way down here, sat in there drinking god awful coffee waiting for you."

"I drove all the way down here too."

Kidney just gave a humpf and turned to go to his car.

"Wait!" Oren shouted.

Kidney kicked Winnie as he walked past her. She had been struggling to her feet and she fell again. He should not have kicked her. Oren launched himself at Kidney, leapt onto his back and wrapped his arms around his neck. He pounded Kidney's face with the fist not holding the gun.

Kidney roared and twisted and tried to peel Oren off his back. He pulled at the hand holding the gun.

"Hey," Kidney wheezed. "This gun ain't real!"

"What?" Winnie spoke from the ground.

"Give me back my money!"

Kidney twisted the gun out of Oren's hand as he shook him off. He threw the gun to the ground and stepped on it. It splintered into pieces. Winnie moaned.

"Don't," Oren whined. "Don't."

Kidney pushed Oren to the ground and kicked him once in the ribs. "You little twat."

Oren curled into a ball. He saw Winnie getting to her knees, trying to crawl with wrists and ankles bound. "Winnie!" he called to her. She couldn't leave him now. He had protected her from Kidney. He pushed himself up, all the way up, until he faced Kidney, who had his fists out, prepared for a fight.

"Dickwad," Oren said.

"What did you call me?"

"Dickwad," Oren said. It just came out of his mouth. He never called people names. He was going to apologize when he looked over and saw Winnie smile at him. A genuine smile filled with love and respect. He felt his chest expand. "I said give me my money."

"Fuck you." Kidney started for his car.

"I said—" Oren slipped the knife out of the pocket of his jeans and flicked it open. Once again he jumped onto Kidney's back. This time he held the knife against Kidney's throat. "Give me the envelope."

He pressed the knife into the wiggly flesh. He pressed hard enough to draw blood, a little prick, but Kidney howled as if he'd been skewered. Oren stretched and grew. He was six feet, eight feet, ten feet tall. No one could stop him and he loved the sound of his own voice. "Right now—Dickwad. Give me my money, right now."

A firmer touch with the knife, a little more blood.

"I was only kidding anyway." Kidney grunted. "Get off me."

Oren jumped down but held on to Kidney's belt buckle. Kidney took out the envelope and threw it to the ground.

"Don't ever call me again."

"Don't worry." Oren let him go.

Kidney ran the rest of the way to his car. Oren watched him start it up and the tires smoke as he sped out of the parking lot. He laughed as he walked back to Winnie.

"All this time, it wasn't a real gun?"

"Can't you say thank you?"

"For what?"

"I saved you," Oren said. He could not believe the frown

on her face. "I saved you from Kidney. Did you want to go with him?"

"No."

"I gave up the best female iguana he could find, for you."

Winnie sat on the ground with her knees up. She put her head on her knees and whispered, "Right. Thank you."

He figured she was embarrassed she had been so thoughtless and ungrateful. "That's okay," he said. He used his knife to cut the rope around her ankles. "We have to go. I have to get home."

Oren smiled as he helped Winnie to her feet and to his car. He felt better than he had all day. Kidney was a big man both in size and in the world of reptiles. Oren had stood up to him. Carefully he helped Winnie into the front seat. "We have much to discuss." That was the right way to say it.

She held out her hands, asking him to cut those ropes as well, but he shook his head. They had made a step in the right direction, but he was not a fool. They had a long drive back to Altadena.

21.

"Where are you?" Jonathan wailed as he threw open the front door. He let it bang the wall. He slipped on the marble floor as he ran toward the curving central staircase.

"Jess!"

Chakra whined from her kennel. If the dog was locked up, then Jess could not be home. But where was she? He spun in all directions. "Jessica!"

"Mr. Jonathan, what is it?" Lupe, the housekeeper, hurried out of the kitchen. "Everything okay?"

He realized what he looked like. He was barefoot. His hair was a mess and his nose still red from crying. He took a deep breath and closed the front door gently before turning back to Lupe. "Sure," he said. "Everything is hunky dunky. Is Jessica here?"

"She teaches an ashtanga class at noon. Then back-to-back hatha. She won't be home until almost five."

Lupe was wearing one of his show T-shirts. It read, "*Tie the Knot* Will Pull Your Heartstrings." It made him feel better to see the bright red lettering. He had come up with that slogan. It was a good one. He had thought of it all by himself.

"Oh. Right. You're so good at keeping her schedule straight."

Lupe shrugged as she went back to the kitchen. "It's on the refrigerator."

Chakra scratched and whined. If he let her out, she would

never go back into her kennel, but if he left her in there she would keep whining. She didn't do it for Jessica, but the moment he walked in the door she started. He missed Buddy, aloof and quiet. He took out his cell phone and called Winnie. She was supposed to call him at eleven. It was way past that now. He had many things to discuss with her. Her phone rang and rang. It was definitely turned on. Where was she? Then he heard someone answer.

"Hello."

"Uh... Winnie?" It didn't sound like her.

Giggling. He heard a kid's voice muffled in the background, "Say yes. Say yes!" And more giggling.

"Who is this?" Jonathan asked. "Is Winnie there?"

"I'm sorry." A fake deep voice. "The party to which you are calling is not in service."

"I'm trying to reach Winnie Parker. This is her phone." Jonathan was almost shouting. "Did you steal it? I will report you."

"She left it on my lawn." The kid sounded both young and belligerent.

"Your lawn?"

"I found it. In the grass. Chill-lax, man. I just found it."

"Hang up!" Jonathan heard the other kid. "He can trace it. Hang up!"

The phone went dead.

Jonathan tried to call back, but it went straight to voice mail. Whoever it was had either turned off the phone or was making long distance calls to Australia. They sounded like kids, but you never knew. Maybe it was a ring of cell phone thieves. They had ways of stealing your identity, your passwords and bank accounts. Winnie could be in serious trouble. He called his lawyer. When Harry got on the phone, Jonathan explained what had happened. Winnie was supposed to be in her car after a tennis lesson.

"I'm worried the kid stole it, you know, part of a ring of cell phone criminals," Jonathan said. "What should I do?"

"Do you pay her cell phone bills?" Harry asked.

"No."

"So no offense," Harry went on, "but your ex-wife is kind of flakey, right? She probably dropped it out of her bag at the tennis court and these kids picked it up. It's her problem."

"It's not like her." Winnie was many things, but flakey wasn't right. She was hard-baked, you could even say crusty—he thought that was the word—but not flakey.

"Call her at home. Leave her a message. You've done a good deed."

They talked a moment more about his contract for the movie, but Jonathan felt anxious. It had been a hard day. Nothing had been as good as he expected. He looked around his mansion. Lupe was singing in the kitchen, something low in Spanish. She had the radio on, but the announcer was talking and she was singing something else. He was still standing in the front hall. It seemed he spent a lot of time there. Jessica was always coming and going. He often held the front door for her and then stood there after he had shut it behind her. He started for the den, library, whatever Jessica called it. It was supposed to be his room, a man's room, in leather and forest green with hunting pictures on the walls. He liked it as well as anywhere else in the house.

"Excuse me, Mr. Parker." It was Lupe's daughter, Libby, in tiny shorts and a tiny tank top, carrying the vacuum cleaner. She was pretty and twenty-something, but she had two babies at home already. Of course, Winnie had Lacy when she was twenty-one. Libby went into his den to vacuum. He followed her.

"Didn't you do this yesterday?"

She laughed and shook her head as she plugged in the cord. The vacuum cleaner growled over the carpets, clattered on the hardwood. It took a staff to keep the house as clean as Jessica liked it.

He went back to the entryway. Lupe was still singing. He listened to Libby vacuuming. She was so young, and her husband had left her. Just as he had left Winnie.

That was it. He was going back to Winnie's house and check to make sure those hoodwinks who had stolen her phone hadn't figured out where she lived. They could be lying in wait for her. He would surprise them.

He ran his hands through his hair, fluffing the curls. He checked his reflection in the mirror over the mail table. First he would go upstairs and change his shorts. He wanted to be wearing jeans if he was going to confront a criminal. And maybe a different shirt.

He grinned as he went upstairs to the bedroom. No one could say Jonathan Parker, actor, host of the country's most popular game show, was not a courageous man.

22.

Oren's good feeling was long gone. It was taking forever to get home. Winnie would not stop crying. He thought they had come through something together, something bad and now it was better. He reminded her she was safe, he told her this would all be over soon, but she sniveled and snorted and every so often her breath would catch in her throat and she would sob and hiccup at the same time. He checked his watch. He was behind schedule. Traffic was bad on the surface streets, so he slipped back onto the freeway. Winnie slouched low in her seat. No one in the other cars was paying any attention to her. He had not told her all the important stuff, had not yet convinced her that she was a bad mother and should treat her daughter better. If she never stopped crying, he would never be able to talk to her. It had been a terrible day. Nothing had gone as planned. First Winnie and then Cookie. His poor friend. There were other places, legal places, to get a female, and he would start researching it, but Kidney had the best reputation. That bridge was burnt to a crisp. Because of Winnie. Because of the day.

"Why me?" he breathed.

The thought of going home to his hot house depressed him. Cookie would be waiting for him, bumping and scratching, wanting, wanting, wanting. He dreaded telling him he had failed. And with Winnie there, he could not get on the computer, he couldn't make lunch, he couldn't do anything. Not until this was done, his plan completed, Lacy beside him holding his hand.

"Not much longer." He looked at his watch again. "Not much longer." Like a mantra.

Winnie wanted to stop crying. She was relieved to be back in the car with Oren—the known psychopath better than the unknown—but it didn't really matter. Oren's hot house and his iguana. Sex and a suitcase with Kidney. She had become a commodity, a black and blue effigy of herself to be passed back and forth. It made no difference. She was done. She was gone. She swallowed her snot and gagged. Kidney had crushed her. Her spine rattled. Her brain felt loose. Together he and Oren had done serious damage and she would never be the same. She stared out the window at passing Los Angeles and didn't care anymore. No one would help her. No one ever had. Except Oren. Oren had fought for her, if only for the pleasure of killing her himself. Still, that was something she supposed.

"Thank you," she said. "Oren."

"That was in—tense."

His voice broke like a teenager's and she realized he had been scared.

"You were great," she said. "Tough."

"Thanks."

His little smile, the straightening of his shoulders, helped her. As long as he was happy, she would stay alive.

"What happened to your dad?" she asked.

"What happened to yours?"

"My father was a one night stand—my mother never really knew him."

"You're so dark. Your mother and Jonathan Parker and Lacy, they're all blond. You must be Jewish."

Winnie shook her head. "Is that what this is about? Some kind of hate crime?" How ironic that after all this he had kidnapped her because he thought she was Jewish. She would be killed for an identity she had always wished she had: the large family, the loud and loving parents, the clichés of a childhood with heritage and faith and ritual. She'd grown up with nothing. Later there were Daisy's psychics and aromatherapy, the sweat lodge retreats, raw food diets and crystal meditations.

"I have no idea." She didn't know why she was trying to explain it to him. "My father was basically a sperm donor. He disappeared when he found out my sixteen-year-old movie star mother was pregnant. I only met him once. When I was seven."

It was a furtive, shadowy meeting, in her school hallway. She had been called out of class. He had come to see her wearing a suit and tie. None of her mother's friends or boyfriends wore suits. In her memory, he was in black and white, holding a hat in his hands, like a character from an old movie. He had that Clark Gable hair, black and shiny, a face as smooth as celluloid, and eyes as dark as hers. She remembered the way his forehead creased as he searched her face. Then he nodded.

"Thank you," he said to the headmistress.

"Daddy?" Winnie asked.

"Looks that way," was all he said. He reached out as if to touch her, but pulled his hand back and left.

What could she tell Oren? What was she? Just a mother. That was all. A normal, everyday mom who made mistakes and sometimes got it right and loved her daughter fiercely. Just like everybody else. She woke up in the morning, went to the bathroom, ate food and wore clothes and worked and did exactly what other people do. She did it day after day. She did it. At this moment, the life she had led last week, even yesterday, seemed an incredible accomplishment. It was enough, more than enough. And that's what she would tell him. He had asked her who she was. I want to live, she would reply. I want to live. There was nothing else to claim. That was enough of a summation of her existence: that she wanted to survive.

Quietly she said to him, "We can't control who our parents are or what we are when we're born." She paused, and shifted in her seat to face him. "We only have power over who we become."

"No. You're not listening!"

He was angry suddenly.

"What?" she asked. "What did I say?"

"I'm doing it. I am taking care of her."

"Who?"

"Listen to me!"

Oren felt the frustration filling his lungs again, making him pant. And sweat. She was so stupid she was making him crazy.

"Winnie." He forced himself to calm down. "I need you to listen." He wanted her to understand. "I'm not doing this to you. I wanted to help someone else. I thought if I got you and talked to you—I thought you were different."

"Different than what?"

"Stop doing that!"

"What?"

He wanted to hit her, smack her with his right hand, knock her senseless, make her quiet, push her out of the car onto the road. But he took the ten deep breaths he had read about on the Calm Yourself website. He could calm himself. He looked over at her. He felt sorry for her. That was all.

"Watch out!" Winnie shouted.

He looked back at the road just in time to swerve around a stopped car and bump onto the shoulder. It had been very close. He crept back into his lane as the traffic moved up.

"Keep your eyes on the road."

"You were distracting me."

"You can just let me out right here."

"Very funny."

He heard her stomach growl. He looked at his watch. Hours had passed since she had arrived. He was hungry too. Maybe his head would stop hurting if he ate something.

She had stopped trying to jump out of the car. She had stopped trying to fight him since he saved her from Kidney. She was just crying because she was hungry and tired like him. She realized he was her friend. Maybe he could do a drive thru burger place or run in and get sandwiches somewhere. He glanced at her, but then he sighed. He could not take any chances. That was the one thing his father had taught him. Just when you think a girl is down, he had said, just when you think the fight has gone out of her—that's when she'll attack you. His father's words of wisdom. Oren wondered what other gems his father would have provided if he'd had the chance. If Jilly Bean had not been such a whore and Marcus had not gone to jail forever.

It was Jimmy who had turned him in. Jimmy had been fucking Oren's mother for years. He didn't believe it when Marcus announced to the carnies that Jill had run off with a guy from the last town.

"Who?" Jimmy wanted to know. "What'd he look like?"

"What do you care?" Marcus retorted. "Just a guy. Believe me, she wasn't picky."

But Jimmy had seen Oren throwing up and knew Fiona had moved in with another family. He snuck into the RV and all of Jill's things were still there, even her purse with her wallet and her favorite photo of herself. Then he broke into the trunk of the car and found Marcus' blood stained clothes in a plastic bag.

Fiona testified against Marcus in court, but the lawyers said Oren was too young. Marcus broke down at sentencing and cried that he was sorry, sorry, sorry. His skin had turned gray in prison and his muscles sagged and wobbled and the swagger had left him. Oren hated him for changing, hated that he begged for a lighter sentence, tried to say it was all because he loved his wife so much. It was embarrassing to have Jimmy laugh in the courtroom and his father do nothing. Be an asshole, Oren wanted to shout, but be a real asshole. He had shuffled when they took him away.

Fiona went to live with Jill's parents and Oren went to the carnival owner he called Uncle Nolan and he never saw Marcus or his sister again. He never wanted to. He was better than them. All of them. A child truly could be nothing like his parent. It was not so odd for Lacy to be the opposite of her mother. Children could be completely different. In fact, children usually were so much better than their parents.

His heart swelled for Winnie, the poor stupid mother. How sad she must be that Lacy is more beautiful and more talented. He gave her a smile. He noticed her cheek was bruised. He touched it with one finger and she flinched. For the life of him, he could not remember when or how it had happened.

"Is this sore?" he asked.

"You tell me."

She was so sad and angry about everything. He wanted her to feel good. He tried the thing that always worked for him.

"Tell me one thing you're good at."

"What?"

"Tell me. Please." He smiled at her. "Tell me what you're good at."

She was thinking. He could tell. They were almost home. He would hop back on the freeway here. It was early enough that the 110 East would be empty. There was still time.

"Tell me," he said to her. "Go on. Don't be shy." He was the teacher. He was in charge.

"I am really good at laundry."

"Like washing clothes?"

"Yes." She was almost whispering. "I am good at laundry."

"How can you be good at that?"

"My grandmother taught me. I do small loads," she said. "I use less detergent than the box says. I take the clothes out of the washer right away, the instant it's done spinning. Same with the dryer. A lot of things I only dry halfway, just to get the wrinkles out, then I hang them up for the rest. I have really big fat hangers so the shirts or even the sweaters don't get lines or bumps in the shoulders. I don't use those dryer things—you know, those little papery things you buy and throw in? No. Every fifth load I wipe out the dryer with a cloth and lavender oil. The odor is barely there, but good and clean. Lacy says she loves the way her clothes smell. All the kids at school tell her how good she smells."

Oren smiled. He liked thinking about the way Lacy smelled. He knew from her picture she smelled good.

"Good," Oren said to Winnie, "Always remember what you're good at. It's who you are." Her face had relaxed and he was proud of himself. "What else?" he asked.

"I don't mind cleaning the filter in the dryer. In fact, I like it. I know it's supposed to be old skin and bacteria and germs and stuff, but cleaning that lint screen is so satisfying, like starting fresh with a clean slate." She actually laughed. "And I am a champion folder. I fold clothes like nobody's business. No one ever taught me, I just figured it out. I love the way clean clothes feel. I run my hands over a T-shirt right out of the dryer and the warm cotton is as soft and comforting as my own bed at night. I have a special table where I do the folding. I smooth out every wrinkle and I tuck in the sleeves just so. It's a pleasure to open a drawer of properly folded clothing. To pull something out and put it on without worrying about it being wrinkled or stained. I am good at stains. I know all the tricks."

He tugged self-consciously at his not so white undershirt. She noticed and shook her head.

"Look at me," she said. "This tennis outfit wasn't exactly spotless when I put it on this morning. I've been falling down on the job lately." She paused. "The past few months it just hasn't seemed to matter much."

Winnie thought of the hamper at home full of dirty clothes. Things that should have been washed long ago. Lacy had been doing her own laundry for a while. Winnie took her work clothes to the cleaners. She washed a load of underwear when she needed it and threw it jumbled into her drawer. What was the matter with her? Dear God, she prayed, if I ever get home I will do the laundry perfectly again. I will never stop. But God would not save her for her laundry expertise. She wondered who would do those final loads for her after she was dead. Not Lacy, please, not Lacy. She wondered if the Salvation Army accepted dirty clothes, or if her laundry would just be thrown away. And what about the rest? At the back of her closet someone would find the shirt she had been wearing when she met Jonathan, out of date but preserved. They would wonder why the hell she had kept this shirt with this piece of paper pinned to it—a corner of the parking ticket she had gotten that day. The housekeeper would do Lacy's laundry at her father's house. Winnie hoped Lacy would miss the lavender. At a new school, on her father's side of town, no one would ever know that she had smelled so good, of love and special care. At her new school she would smell of Tide or however everybody else smelled.

"What about you?" she asked. "What are you good at?"

He shook his head.

"I know you're good at taking care of Cookie."

He shrugged.

"What else? What are your dreams? Your goals? Maybe you could have a store for iguanas. Right? Or a zoo. There must be things you want."

Suddenly she wanted so much it flooded her. It made her muscles tense and her hands strain against the ties. A sniff of Lacy's vanilla scent. A morning to make coffee. A future.

"You're so young," she said. "Let's stop this and start over. You can let me out here and I'll shake your hand and we'll call it a day. Oren? Let's just start over."

For a moment, his face cleared. He wanted it too. She could see it.

"We can do that," she said, "We really— "

His cell phone rang.

"I better take this," Oren said. "It's probably work."

He started to answer his phone, but then looked at her. "I can't," he said. "I can't talk to anyone without you screaming." He sighed. "This is hard. I didn't think it would be like this."

His phone stopped ringing. Whoever it was did not leave a message.

"Look," he said. "We're almost home."

He was exiting the freeway. She bowed her head. They were almost there.

23.

Mary Krueger was annoyed. Oren had been rude to her on the phone—and worse than that, he was lying. He had some girl over there. Obviously. The second time she called he didn't even answer. She didn't believe his story. Ha. If he was sick at home, then she was a fairy princess. Then she smiled. She might be— she just might be a fairy trapped in human form. She patted the plastic fairy figurine hanging from her mirror. The tiny bell jingled. The glitter-covered wings sparkled in the sunlight. The rainbow ribbon was fading.

"Time for a new ribbon, Miss Twinkle."

She zipped through a yellow light and around a corner. The tires of her little red car squealed. The white paper deli bag tipped toward her on the passenger seat.

"Shit!" She caught it just in time. Spill the soup and she would have no excuse for dropping by Oren's. As if she need- ed an excuse. They had been out on actual dates twice. Slept together three times. Well, made love. They had not done any sleeping, but that was coming. Twice he had gotten up and dressed and crept away; Cookie needed him. Once had been in the afternoon at his house. She liked his house although it could really use a woman's touch. Some pictures on the wall. A cactus in a pot. Some pink quartz crystals in a glass bowl on the coffee table to attract love and harmony. A blue glass mobile outside near the front door to ward off negative energy.

She could do a lot with that place.

But first she had to nip this other woman in the bud. He was home with another woman and that was definitely not okay.

She bounced the fairy on her palm three times. Jingle, jingle, jingle.

"Three miracles a day," she chanted. "Three miracles a day. Thank you, Miss Twinkle."

The first miracle was that her favorite pink blouse was not too dirty this morning. She had worn it once before and hung it up. Sometimes when she pulled things out of her closet, they were dirtier than she remembered, but her pink blouse had been almost perfect. A small spot from something she had eaten, but the ruffle mostly hid it.

The second miracle had been the boss taking the afternoon off. That meant she could leave and take an extra long lunch, maybe not come back at all. Things were slow at Carpet Barn. People were holding on to their old floor coverings. Didn't they know that something fresh and clean would brighten their entire lives? "And relatively inexpensively." She said that out loud. It sounded so official and correct.

Jingle, jingle, jingle. "Three miracles a day."

At the next light, she checked her face in the rearview mirror. Eye shadow, check. Mascara, check. Eyebrows, check. Mary had to paint her eyebrows on. She was practically hairless. The khaki colored hair on her head was wispy and fine. She looked bald after a shower. She had no hair on her arms to speak of and only needed to shave her legs every couple of weeks in the summer time. Her bush—more like a couple of twigs—was a source of great consternation to her. She envied those women who could shave their boyfriend's initials in their pubic hair. She would never manage even a lower case "o". But fashions had changed and now she shaved what little she had as if she wanted it that way. At least she had her "D-lightful, D-licious double D's" even if the bra straps cut into her shoulders and her back ached if she had to walk more than a couple of blocks. She sighed. Then she shook her head.

"Every day, in every way, I am better and better, happier and happier. Right, Miss Twinkle?"

But damnit, she was on the wrong street. They were all alike. It was right down here, wasn't it? She remembered the front door, solid wood with no window in it. Like the top of a coffin, Oren had said. And the garage door—just like every other.

"C'mon. Where is it?"

She should have looked up his address before she left the office. The personnel files were right behind her desk. She should have remembered from last time, but then she had been in the pre-sex haze, worrying too much about her breath, her deodorant, and when to tell him she loved him.

Was there a tree out front? He had pulled them into the garage. Maybe she would see his sexy black car. He kept it so clean; she had seen him wince at how dirty her car was. She stopped at a stop sign. A jogger with a long California blonde ponytail crossed in front of her. She wore tight yellow leggings with "juicy" written across her butt. Mary's plump hands squeezed the wheel. The soup smelled good. She was hungry. She had waited and waited for Pete to leave so she could duck out unnoticed. She had not ordered anything for herself. Maybe she would just go back to the office and eat the soup at her desk. If Oren really had a woman there, she would be the last person he'd want to see. She could really blow it if she showed up.

"I am likeable and capable and Miss Twinkle knows it. I know it. Oren likes me and I am just bringing him some soup."

Her stomach rumbled and whined. When this was all over she would reward herself with a package of her favorite cookies.

Her fuzzy sweatpants and her old sweatshirt, her couch and the TV beckoned her. She had that to look forward to.

"I am likeable and capable. Better and better, happier and happier."

She still had one miracle left. She did not want to waste it on finding his house. She would just systematically drive up and down every street in the neighborhood until she recognized it. It might take a while, but she would find it. She hoped he had a microwave for the soup.

24.

The garage door closed behind them.

Winnie did not want to be here. While she was out in the world, rescue had seemed possible, freedom only one thin car door away. She should have done more; she should have leapt from the car, grabbed the steering wheel and pulled them into a tree or a truck. And the gun wasn't even real. It was plastic.

Oren was a puzzle. He wanted something, not money and not sex, not torture with a tool box or dismemberment. Something else. She wasn't sure why, but he had chosen her—some article he had read or something he had seen somewhere online from long ago when she was with Jonathan.

He turned the car off. She glanced at the switch for the garage door.

He exhaled. "I'm so tired." And rubbed his eyes.

"Don't make me go back in there," she said. "Tell me whatever you need to say right here. I'll listen. I'll be quiet. It's too hot inside."

He dropped his hands and turned to her. "Really?"

"We can talk right here." She held out her hands for him to cut the rope. "I'll listen to every word."

He cut her free and put the knife back in his pocket. He seemed honestly pleased. "Great. This is great."

He relaxed back in his seat. She opened her door and leapt out of the car. Her feet were free. She could run. She hit the switch on the wall and the door began to open. She ran to it, fell to her knees and began to crawl out underneath. He grabbed her legs. She kicked herself loose. She wiggled away, got to her feet and started to run. She was out in the driveway when he grabbed her. She fought him. She screamed. Where was everybody? Not a door opened, not a single curtain moved. People had to be in these houses, a woman watching her afternoon talk shows, a man painting a bird house. Normal, suburban people.

"Help!" she shouted. "Help me!"

She kept screaming as Oren dragged her back to the garage. He pushed her against the wall and hit the switch with one hand. Someone must have heard her. Someone was calling the police right now.

She couldn't help it, she grinned. "Somebody heard me. I know it!"

Oren's face went that awful empty again. She watched it happen like a TV going black and silent in the middle of a program. His eyes filled with tears.

He reached out his hands. He's a child, she thought, he wants a hug. He realizes the game is over. She stepped forward, opened her arms, but he circled her neck with his hands. His hands were cool and for one brief second refreshing. She almost said thank you and then he began to squeeze. Tight. Tighter. As he squeezed he danced and jittered. She was pulled to her tiptoes—and then she could not breathe. She struggled. She clutched his hands and tried to pry them away. She needed air. Air! Her head would implode without air. She tried to catch his eye, to make him see it was her, but he kept his face to one side as if to listen to her die.

And then, abruptly, he let her go. She collapsed, gasping, clutching at her neck, mouth open wide, gulping air.

He took her arms and yanked her to her feet.

"Come with me."

"Oren, please," her voice like a rusty hinge.

She tried to pull her arm from his grasp. He took the knife from his pocket and cut her forearm. Calmly, without a word, he left a two-inch stripe of red. Winnie froze. She stared at the blood bubbling up into a stinging mountain range, then up into his face. His eyes were small and dead, his face slack, but his body rigid. He took her upper arm and pulled her up the steps, into the hot, terribly hot house.

"Please!" She couldn't help it. Back in the oven, this time she would fry.

He flicked the knife and gave her another tiny cut. She started to exclaim, but stopped herself. Cookie was scratching. Oren led Winnie away from the kitchen, down the hallway. He stopped in front of the only closed door, the last room in the house. He opened it and pushed her inside. She stumbled against a pile of cardboard boxes. The room was full of stuff, old fashioned footlockers and decorated trunks, bolts of fabric rolled and stacked in the corner. But what Winnie noticed first were the bars on the two corner windows.

She turned to Oren, afraid to speak, but pleading just the same. He came toward her with the knife. She retreated, backed up against a stack of boxes and could go no further. She turned her face away and gritted her teeth, ready for pain and blood, but he gave her a push and she tripped and grabbed a box to keep from falling. On the top of the box there were two big jars filled with amber liquid. She looked closer and saw eyes, arms, too many tiny feet. Pickled Siamese twins, their tiny faces turned to her, eyes open and sadly staring. She quickly looked at the other jar: a single baby with four legs and a tiny head protruding from its stomach. She spun. The rest of the room was just as bad. More jars and containers. A poster leaning up against the wall advertised " O'Keith's Carnival of Wonders" and "Lobster Boy and the Two-Headed Cow" with a drawing of a skinny boy draping a lobster claw arm around the cow's two necks. A collection of sideshow oddities.

She turned to him. Blood spilled off her arm onto the carpet. She saw him look at her cuts and frown. "Don't leave me in here."

"Don't touch anything," he went on. "It's my uncle's collection. It's very valuable."

"It's scary in here. Please, Oren?"

"I have things to do."

He left and locked her in. Locked. The door locked from the outside. The windows had bars. It was as if he was expecting a captive. Her. He had been expecting her.

"Oren," she called. "Please. I'll be good. I won't go anywhere. Let me out of here. Come on. I'm sorry."

She did not know if he was right outside or if he had walked away. Her hands were shaking. The vertebrae in her neck ached. She kicked the door once, but then she stopped. She did not want him to come back and cut her. She climbed over boxes to the windows. The small diamond shaped panes had been so popular once. There was no way to open the sliding panels, they were nailed shut and the bars outside were permanent. She looked at the boxes. Maybe one of them would have a weapon or something she could use, a souvenir baseball bat, or an ornamental sword. She moved a stack of folded canvas off a narrow leather case and opened it. She gasped. Inside was a withered leg and foot, the skin like jerky over the bones, the toenails long and yellow, cushioned on faded purple velvet. A handwritten card read, "The leg of Prince Orloff." She hoped she would never meet Uncle Nolan. Or maybe he was coming later, with his bag of tools, to add her to his freak show. Stop it, she told herself again. Please stop it.

Some of the boxes were too large and heavy to move. She crouched down behind a stack, thinking she could hide behind it and when he came in she could jump him, stick her fingers in his eyes, kick him again and again in the balls. She could do that, she knew how.

After Jonathan left her, Winnie had enrolled in a self-defense class. She needed to take care of herself and little Lacy. She needed the confidence. Plus punching and pounding and yelling and kicking sounded so good. It was a morning class of five women and one younger man, taught by Master Yamada, an older Japanese man with many degrees of black belt in karate. They listened carefully as he described in his thick accent the wounds and destruction they were inflicting on their invisible enemies.

"Two fingers out. Dig in eyes. Pull down and leave him blind."

Winnie had been going for seven months when she had a question. "Master Yamada?"

"Yes, Mrs. Parker?"

"What if my attacker has a gun?"

The others looked at her. No one had ever asked about guns.

"What if he shoots at us? What do we do?"

Master Yamada nodded sagely. "Spread legs," he instructed.

Winnie did as she was told.

"Bend over. More. Farther."

She bent over as far as she could.

"Now. Kiss your ass goodbye."

He laughed so hard his nose whistled. The rest of the class laughed with him. Winnie tried to laugh too, but instead she saw how stupid the class really was. Seventy-five dollars a month—for nothing. She made the motions and got through the rest of class, but she knew she would never be back.

As she walked to her car, Stone Curtis, the only male student, trotted over. "I'm glad you asked that."

"Not a very comforting answer."

"Bullets win every time."

Winnie opened her car door, but he kept standing there.

He smiled. "Do you want to have dinner sometime?"

She was completely surprised. He was way too young for her.

"I mean it," he said. "Friday night?"

He had that no color hair, a tarnished taupe that would never go gray, and his eyes were not green or brown but neither and both. He was stone-colored just as his name suggested. She had no idea why he was free to take self-defense classes at nine o'clock in the morning. Waiter, writer, independently wealthy. She had nothing to lose.

"Sure. I'd like that."

He seemed pleased. He was prepared for her address with a piece of paper and a pencil waiting in his pocket. As she drove toward home she smiled out at the morning. She had a date. Only nine months after Jonathan had officially and legally left her for his farm-raised contestant with the perfect mammary glands. Jonathan would be sorry if Winnie and Stone fell in love. He would hate it if she found someone else, someone younger, so quickly. It could happen. One date could turn into a lifetime. Winnie and Lacy and Stone. Stone was an odd name, but solid.

She was jittery with anticipation waiting for Friday, deciding what to wear. The afternoon of her date she volunteered to drop Lacy off at her dad's, just so she could wear her new blue dress and say nonchalantly to Jonathan that she had met someone.

"He's a little younger than I am," she said, "and kind of dreamy."

She loved the cloud that crossed Jonathan's face, the way his lips pressed flat.

Stone rang the doorbell right on time. Winnie opened the door, breathless, happy, and stifled an immediate sigh. He was so young. He had even spiked his hair for their date.

"You look very nice," he said, but she could tell he was expecting something different than her blue dress. She probably looked like his mother.

"You look nice too."

Stone shrugged. "I thought we'd go see the new James Bond film."

"Perfect." She would have to tell Jonathan they'd gone to a club. "Glass of wine?"

"No, thanks. I'll have a Coke at the movies."

"Sounds good."

In the car he cleared his throat and said carefully, "I like older women."

She didn't like the way he drove with one finger on the steering wheel while he looked at her and not the road. She also didn't like the way he laughed when she asked him to pay attention. And then he drove past the freeway entrance and took the longer route through Griffith Park. He said he preferred it.

The park was dark. The headlights of an oncoming car illuminated Stone's smooth face. He looked calm, determined.

"What do you do?" Winnie asked him. "Why do you have Tuesday and Thursday mornings free for karate?"

"I'm a pool guy," Stone said. "I work for my brother." He looked at her. "Yesterday I had to clean a pool after a suicide."

They came to the stop sign by the entrance to the old abandoned zoo. There were still cages up there, carved into the rocks, with broken bars and metal doors jammed open. Winnie had gone with five-year-old Lacy and she had climbed inside and pretended to be a jaguar, a monkey, something else, until a homeless man woke from under a pile of leaves and chased them both away.

At the turn to Burbank and the movie theaters, Stone went straight instead.

"Where are we going?" Her voice came out high and worried. She didn't know him. She her hand inside her purse on her phone, her fingers poised over the buttons.

"This is fun," he said. "You'll see."

The section of the park that ran along the 134 Freeway toward Forest Lawn Cemetery had always been a meeting place for men. Winnie drove that way occasionally when the freeway was crowded and she had seen men in pick-up trucks, men in small compact cars, and men standing back partially hidden in the trees. Once she had seen an older man, white haired and potbellied, walking out of the woods straightening his clothing. The men were different ages and ethnicities. She didn't know if money exchanged hands or why the police allowed it to continue.

Stone pulled over to the curb between two other cars.

"What are you doing?"

"Watch," he said.

He rolled down her window, the park side window. A man emerged from the shadows. He had a buzz cut, tiny eyes, and a dark plaid shirt. He leaned into the car and at first he was puzzled when he saw Winnie and her frightened face.

"You available?" Stone asked.

The guy shrugged.

"Can she watch?"

He nodded.

"Oh no," Winnie said. "No. Absolutely not."

The man was waiting. Stone was trying not to laugh.

"Come on, honey," Stone said. "You told me next time you wanted to watch."

"This isn't funny." She turned to the man outside. His flesh was mottled in the single street lamp's light. "We're not staying," Winnie told him. "This is his idea of a joke."

The man's doughy face turned angry. He began to reach into the car. Stone laughed and peeled away from the curb.

"Stone!" Winnie didn't know what else to say.

"Come on. My friends and I do it all the time."

Winnie looked at him and a shiver went through her. He was young and mean.

"That was not funny," she said.

"Fucking faggots," he replied.

He pulled a U-Turn and drove back the way they had come. They made the appropriate turn toward the movie theater and Winnie exhaled. Then Stone put his hand on her thigh, up high and rubbed the blue fabric with his finger. She picked up his hand and dropped it in his lap. He laughed. He put it back on her thigh, but before she objected, he removed it and laughed again. It was a child's game; he reached his hand out, then drew it back, then left it hovering over her thigh, but not touching her.

"Your mother is Daisy Juniper, isn't she?"

The light—that old familiar light—went on. She had wondered why Stone asked her out. Now she knew. She nodded.

"I can't believe your mother is Daisy Juniper."

"Sometimes I can't either."

"She's hot. Daisy Juniper. Really hot."

Winnie heard the wistful lust in Stone's voice. Just the thought of her mother reduced most adult men to teenagers; they erupted with instant zits and boners, inane teenage slang.

"What was it like?" he continued. "You know, growing up with her? Did you—"

Winnie answered the questions before he asked them. She had heard them so many times before. "She was sixteen when she had me. She's never been married. She has been committed twice, but for insanity not drugs. She did lose her first Oscar in a poker game. Those are not body doubles—she does all her own nudity."

"You don't look a thing like her." Stone shook his head.

"I really am her daughter."

He put his hands back on the wheel as he turned into the movie theater's parking garage. Winnie hoped he would go up, but Stone took the route down and circled into the depths. She hated parking garages, terrifying on the best of days.

"How long's it been?" he asked.

"Since what?"

"Since you've been laid."

Stone's cute face aged a hundred ugly years. The garage was empty of people but every parking space was taken. He kept driving down.

He frowned. "You're divorced. Older women need—"

She did not want to hear what he thought she needed. "You can take me home," she said. "Or you can stay and see your movie. I'll take a cab."

"I don't want to take you home."

"Then I'll take a cab."

They had come to the bottom of the garage. There was one space left. He pulled in. Winnie undid her seatbelt and started to get out of the car, but he put his hand on her arm. It was not a friendly or apologetic grip.

"Ha, ha," she said, looking down at his hand. "You forget I know karate."

One fluorescent light sputtered and hissed, blinked off and stammered on. The cinderblock wall looked wet in the harsh light.

"I have to go." Winnie spoke as if talking on the phone, or to a friend she had met on the street. "I'll see you in class."

He leaned toward her and nuzzled her shoulder, still gripping her arm. "I thought you would be fun," he said. "I thought I could count on you."

A young couple, laughing and holding hands, got off the elevator in the corner. The guy wore a sweater very much like Stone's. The girl wore tight jeans and a tiny tank top. She was talking animatedly and he was smiling as they searched for their car. Stone sat back and put both hands on the wheel.

"We'll miss the movie," he said.

Winnie jumped out of the car.

"What the hell?"

She ran up the ramp toward the upper levels. On the next parking level up there were cars arriving, more people around. She merged in with a cluster of people and went with them into the elevator. As the doors closed, she saw Stone drive past, tires squealing on the slick garage floor.

The elevator opened into the lobby of the movie theater. A long line snaked away from the ticket window. She took out her cell phone. There was no one else to call.

"Where are you?" Jonathan said. Not hello, not anything else.

"I'm at the big movie theater in Burbank."

"Where's your date?"

She began to cry.

"Are you all right? Winnie. Answer me."

"I'm scared. He scared me." She knew she sounded like a child, but Jonathan's voice was deep and parental.

"I'll come get you."

"Really?"

"Are you in a safe place?"

"I'm in the lobby."

"Stay there until you see me pull up out front. Don't go anywhere, not even the bathroom, alone."

"Don't tell Lacy."

"What do you think I am? Nuts?"

Winnie almost laughed. "Hurry," she whispered.

"It will take me thirty minutes. But you know what? We can keep talking. Keep talking to me. What movie were you going to see?"

"James Bond."

"You're kidding."

She heard his keys jingling. A door open and close. He kept talking to her, about Bond, about movies, about the time he met Sean Connery at a party. His voice was so well modulated and professional, even as he was starting his car and driving with one hand. Even as he was coming to rescue her.

When she and Jonathan were first sleeping together, he could make her cry with laughter by talking like a radio announcer in bed.

"Yes, that's right. Only $19.95 buys you all the cunnilingus a woman could want."

"Hurry," she said again. "Please."

Twenty-seven minutes later, Jonathan pulled up in his stupid Porsche and Winnie leapt into the passenger seat. He grinned at her, then frowned. "I meant to tell you earlier, you look really good."

She told him what happened and he laughed.

"Bad date," he said. "That's all it was. Good cocktail party story. Especially that visit to AIDS Alley."

"Is that what they call it?" Winnie stuck out her tongue. "Gross."

He patted her thigh and left his hand there, right where she remembered it. "I'm glad I was home."

"You're my knight in shining armor."

"Still?"

"Still." She put her hand on top of his.

At her house, their house, the house where they had lived together, he offered to come in, check around and make sure Stone wasn't lurking under the bed. Winnie accepted. She wanted him inside, back in their house. Once she got him there, as comfortable as an old pair of jeans, she was sure he would stay. He would have to. In the kitchen, she poured him his favorite vodka on the rocks and one for herself and looked into his eyes. This is it, she thought. My life resumes tonight.

"You know what?" he said. "I've got a guy who would be perfect for you."

"Oh really?" She knew he was kidding her, talking about himself. She kept her voice low so he had to lean in. "Do I know this guy?"

"Maybe. You might have met him a while ago."

"He was gone and now he's back?"

"No. I think he's always been in LA. But he was in a relationship, and now he's divorced."

Winnie frowned.

"You know Don Miller, right? Not very tall, but a handsome guy."

"You're kidding."

"I could call him. Give him your number. Or better yet, you call him."

He could have punched her; it would have been less painful. Jonathan setting her up on a date. Jonathan acting as her pimp.

She had been waiting for his kiss. He was looking in his cell phone for the number. The vodka bubbled in her stomach.

She should have known then, known for sure it was over. Instead, later, alone in bed, it was his look she kept thinking about, the way his eyes took her in. It was Jonathan driving up to rescue her. His laugh and his hand on her thigh. He still loved her. He did.

Winnie leaned against the wall in Oren's hot little house and wondered what Jonathan would do when he found out she was missing. She imagined his anguish when the police found her body. Through the door she heard Oren pacing. Then she heard his phone ring—a different ring—the same awful song that Lacy used on her phone with offensive lyrics, loud, strident, discordant, designed to be annoying. Oh Lacy. Lacy. She heard him answer, "Where have you been?"

He walked away from the door so she couldn't hear anything else. Oh, she thought, why did he use that terrible music? It made her sad, so, so sad to hear it. She slid down the wall and curled up on the carpet. She wanted to go home. Not to the home she had left that morning, but back in time to when Lacy was little and Jonathan still loved her. She wanted them both. She wanted Jonathan. Her Jonathan. The dry carpet odor filled her nostrils and scratched the back of her throat. The fibers dug into her cheek. Five years after their separation, three years after his marriage, in a room full of pickled freaks, she could admit she was still waiting for Jonathan to return. All this time, she had expected a late night phone call, the receiver filled with his tears and apologies. One day she knew he would knock on her door with his hands open at his sides and the familiar contrite hunch to his shoulders.

That would never happen now. He could not save her this

time. This heat, this white carpet, this collection of carnival freaks, the smell of rotting vegetables and lizard piss were it for her. Her life would end with this unhappy, insane boy. They would find his skin under her fingernails, his red hair on this white T-shirt. No trace left on her of the man she loved or the daughter she adored.

25.

Lacy didn't want to get out of the car. She did not want to leave Buster, ever.

"As promised, my lady," he said, "in time for orchestra."

They were across the street from school. End of the day. To Lacy, the white stucco building, the flagpole, even the kids spilling out the doors onto the sidewalk, looked picturesque and old fashioned. Simple, ordinary children leaving school for the afternoon to play and do homework and drink milk at dinner. She had moved so far beyond them now.

She looked at Buster. He looked in the rearview mirror. She looked down at her hands. He looked out the window. But when she looked at him again, he was looking at her.

"When are you done?" he asked.

His brown hair fell in his eyes. His lips were parted. Those lips and all the places they had been. Did he think she was a slut?

"What?"

"When are you done with orchestra?"

"Five-thirty."

"I'll pick you up."

"Really?" Her chest swelled, her arms felt as if they would float to the ceiling. "You don't have to do that."

He bit his lip—those lips—and frowned.

"No, no," Lacy continued in a rush. "I want you to, but, I mean—my mom can come."

"Call her. Tell her you're being borne home on the wings of love." Then he blushed. The "L" word—even in passing—was too much for either of them.

Lacy giggled and sighed at the same time and then had to cough. There was an excess of air in her lungs.

Buster leaned toward her, she leaned in, they bumped and then they kissed, a little goodbye kiss. She sniffed the smoky, slightly unwashed smell of him. She sucked it in, to keep it until five-thirty when she saw him again.

She floated down the corridor to her locker. She pulled her cell phone out of her back pocket and turned it on, wishing she had a girlfriend to call. Maybe she would see Marissa. Maybe Marissa had seen her with Buster. Instead, she ran into her history teacher.

"Feeling better?" Mrs. Lee asked. "We missed you in class today."

"Oh. Yes. Much better."

"Good. See you in class tomorrow. Better call someone for the homework."

Even Mrs. Lee could not deflate her. Homework. What a quaint idea. She grabbed her flute from her locker. Her phone vibrated. Four messages. The first was from her father. She deleted it without listening. The next message was from Oren, her online man. He sounded squeaky, bad, nervous about something. The next was from him as well. And the next. In the last message he was actually screaming at her. Who the hell did he think he was? Then she had a little pang that somehow he knew what she had been doing. She thought about Buster's bedroom and she flushed. He couldn't know. He couldn't know that she had fallen in love—that was it, wasn't it?—with Buster. Buster.

She called her mom first. Winnie's cell phone rang and rang but she didn't answer. It was obviously turned on. Lacy had told her a zillion times to get a ring she could actually hear. Poor thing, so out of it. Lacy felt benevolent and magnanimous and left dear old Mom a sweet message on the cell and then at home. Then she dialed Oren. Perhaps she could help him. She could do something nice for him before she told him not to call her anymore.

"Hey," she said into the phone. "What's the matter?"

"Where have you been?" The words were tight and small, each one said with an exhalation of breath.

"At school."

"You usually check your phone at lunch."

"I… I was busy."

"You don't sound right."

"Listen, I—"

"No!" He shouted into her ear. "Not now! Now is not the time!"

"What's going on?" Lacy asked. "Are you okay?"

His voice held no attraction for her anymore. He was twenty-five. He probably had wrinkles and a scratchy man face like her father's. Just that morning she had craved his phone calls. She trembled, her skin crawling like ripples on a horse's flank.

"I have to go to orchestra," she said.

"It's three-thirty," he said. "Time for you to be done."

"You know I have orchestra."

"I don't care." He was angry and she did not know why.

"What is going on?"

"Tell me again how much you hate your mother. Tell me again how badly she treats you. Tell me."

But Lacy did not want to hate anybody anymore. "Oh, c'mon, you know? I guess she's not so bad."

"WHAT?"

A kid walking past heard him screaming through the phone.

Lacy was mortified.

"I have to go," she said. "I'll send you an email."

"I thought you hated your mother."

He was panting—his breaths short and loud like the woman in the birth film in health class.

"Are you okay?" she asked.

"You lied to me."

His words came out in little explosions. It gave Lacy the creeps.

"I have your mother."

"What?"

"I took your mother today. I have her."

"My mother?" It didn't make sense. He took a picture of her? He knew her?

"I'm going to teach her a lesson. Teach her to take better care of you."

"Wait. Oren. What? Where is she? What are you talking about?"

Lacy was frozen in the hallway. She was in school and some guy she had never even met had taken her mother. But taken her where? What did he mean? Lacy had to lean against the wall. Her legs were shaking. She heard him taking deep breaths, breathing in and exhaling slowly.

"I did it for you," he said to her. He was almost whispering now. "I thought she was hurting you. I wanted to help you."

"Where are you? Where is she?" Maybe they were sitting at a coffee place somewhere. Maybe he had her in his car right outside the school. Maybe he was so angry because he had seen her with Buster.

"I'm at home. She's here with me. I called in sick. And now I'm not sure what to do. She's so mad at me. And I really wanted her to like me. She needs to realize I have your best interests at heart. I am just trying to take care of you."

"Mom is supposed to pick me up at school."

"She won't do that now."

"Is she okay?"

I'm sorry I'm bothering you. Go to orchestra. We'll talk afterwards. I can wait that long."

"No, Oren, please."

"Go on. Don't worry. When you're done, we can all talk about this together. I think you haven't been exactly honest with me. Actually, I know you're a lying bitch—you all are." He sighed. "If you call the police, I'll kill her." And he hung up.

Lacy remained where she was, with her phone at her ear, her locker door open, her flute in the other hand.

26.

For an instant, as he listened to Lacy's scared little voice, Oren had seen reality. He had kidnapped a woman, hurt her and almost sold her, all to impress a girl who had lied to him. A girl he had never met. A girl who was still in high school. Just as quickly that vision was gone. He was back to his purpose and his plan. Lacy loved him. If she had lied, it was because she wanted him to love her more. As if that were possible. His love for Lacy filled him, elevated him, prepared him to be the man he knew he could be.

Poor Lacy, he thought. He had frightened her and she would go to orchestra and worry. She would not perform well, and he was sorry about that. He had been angry with her, but now he realized this was another challenge he had to meet. He would talk to her, she would come clean about everything, they would start fresh and she would never lie to him again. And he was beginning to like Winnie. A little. She was so strange and moody, but she would be an okay mother-in-law one day. He knew now she was not as mean as Lacy said. He should have figured that out—Lacy couldn't be so sweet after being abused for eighteen years. It was just like Cookie. Discipline done with positive reinforcement, affection, a good diet. That's why Cookie was so gentle.

"Doesn't your iguana claw you or snap at you?" Rick at Reptile Land had asked.

"Never," Oren said. "We've worked that out. He understands it hurts me, so he doesn't do it. I give him a treat when he's careful. I stop playing with him when he's not."

"Do you smack him on the nose or anything?"

"Hitting an animal only makes it mean. Cookie is really socialized and friendly."

"You are the Iguana Man," Rick said. "Very impressive."

He was. He read books and websites about iguanas and watched videos. He was the longest sitting president the Iguana Keepers Club had ever had. Usually people did their one year term and were happy to give it up. Not him. At the monthly meetings he spent a lot of time answering questions. He was also the go-to guy for a lot of iguana caregivers through the club's website. His inbox was always filled with requests for advice and problem solving. Yes sir, he was the Iguana Man. He knew how to take care of someone. He had taken care of Winnie, she was resting in the back room, he had protected her from Kidney. And he would take care of Lacy. He was the Iguana Man, but even better, he was the love of Lacy's life.

He needed to finish discussing the problem with Winnie and make her promise to treat Lacy better. She did not seem like the type to hit her daughter, or lock her in her room, or not feed her, but she had to be cruel in other, less obvious ways. Lacy had told him she was a monster.

Oren sighed. In the beginning, it had all seemed so simple, so straightforward. He never meant to hurt her, but Winnie talked too much and she was so clumsy. She was always stumbling and knocking her head. The blood on her stomach made him sick. The bump on her head and the bruises on her legs and the scratches on her arms. He hadn't done any of that. She had done it to herself. She had. It wasn't his fault. No. No. No.

He punched the wall and dented the drywall. "Fuck!"

Another thing to fix. Blood on the rug. Cookie scratching. Oren dropped his head and swung it back and forth. It was all Lacy's fault. It really was. Lacy had done this to him. Lacy had made him do everything. He did it for her. That bitch. That lying bitch. He was panting. His heart was a freight train in his chest. The sweat poured. He put his head between his knees, but the pounding was worse. He ran to the bathroom and splashed cold water on his face. Water would clean it up. Water. More water. In some grimy corner of his brain he knew he had hurt Winnie, that a lot of her clumsiness was because of him, but he shook that thought away. Cookie scratched and scratched and scratched at the swinging door. Uncle Nolan had made it quite clear that anything Oren damaged would have to be repaired. The door was beyond repair. It would have to be replaced when he moved out. If he moved out. He dried his face. He breathed into the soft terry cloth. He was not going anywhere. This was home for him and Cookie. He hung the towel neatly. He stuck his left ring finger in his mouth. It was his least favorite, but he chewed at the nail, catching the tiny bit that was left and tugging on it with his teeth. There was a little spark of pain in the cuticle and he tasted blood. He kept nibbling and gnawing. Think, he told himself. He had to go to work the next day. If he missed work again he could be fired—sick or not. Every muscle tensed. He chomped down hard and tears started.

Stop it, he told himself. Oren, get a hold of yourself. He took ten, he took twenty deep breaths. His heart slowed; he felt better. It would be fine. Now that Lacy knew Winnie was with him, she would want them all to sit down together. Oren pictured himself the mediator, helping Winnie and Lacy get along. How grateful they would be.

He went down the hall to Winnie's door. He hoped she was sleeping. If she took a nap, maybe she would not be so cranky.

He leaned his head against the door. It was quiet in there. He was such a fuck up. He had believed every word that stupid lying high school bitch had said. He closed his eyes. He was counting to ten. And ten again. And again.

Winnie had heard Oren shouting, but not what he was saying. She had no idea whether he was speaking to an accomplice or a friend. It didn't matter. She thought she heard the word "mother" and knew he used it as a curse word.

Maybe she was a terrible mother. Maybe Oren was right. Before the divorce, she was over protective, she hovered, never let Lacy out of her sight. After the divorce, she had been distracted. Once she forgot to pick Lacy up from a birthday party, more than once she had forgotten some important item at the grocery store. On the other hand, Winnie went on all the field trips in elementary school. She and Lacy baked cookies for every holiday and sewed elaborate Halloween costumes. They slept in a tent in the living room so Lacy could get used to it before the school campout. They went to the movies and drew pictures together and searched for fairies in the grass. Things had changed, it was true. Lately, all they did was fight. When was the last time she and Lacy had sat down to dinner together? Lacy took a plate of food, usually something reheated in the microwave, into her room while Winnie ate a bowl of cereal and read the newspaper. It hurt to admit it, but she knew the only legacy she would pass on to Lacy was an old-fashioned recipe for applesauce cake and some laundry tips. Lacy's freshest memories would be of sullen drives to school and slamming doors. Maybe Lacy would be better off with her father. At least she still felt close to Jonathan. Even though he only saw her on the weekends, he was a good dad. He called her and they really talked. He had left Winnie, but he was with Lacy every week no matter what. The only visits he missed were the three weeks he was on his honeymoon in Bora Bora.

Was there really a place called Bora Bora or was it just a euphemism for ecstatic sex?

"Oren?" she called. "Oren?" His phone call had finished. She knew he was right outside her door. She could feel him out there. She put her forehead against the door and spoke to him. She kept her voice soft, urging him to come closer.

"Maybe you're right about me. Maybe I'm not a good mother, but I wanted to be. All I ever wanted was a family, a real family. I wanted a house and a dog and a child who colored at the kitchen table while I cooked. I wanted to be different than my mother. She ignored me, sent me to my grandmother, left me with the housekeeper whenever she met a new guy. She was like your mom: she needed a man. She was—still is—more interested in men, any man, than me." She paused. "Oren? Are you listening? Are you there?" He didn't answer, but she continued anyway. "I'm not any different than you. I'm not. Yes, okay, I've always had plenty of money—but there are so many kinds of hunger."

She put her hand against the door. She imagined his palm was pressed against hers with only the wood between.

"If I've done something to make you angry, I'm sorry. If I'm not who you want me to be, well—I'm not who I want to be either."

"Who is?" Oren whispered.

She was startled by his voice only an inch away. "You're there."

"I'm here."

"What happened after your dad went to jail? What happened to you?"

Oren rolled his forehead back and forth against the door. It felt good. The rumble of the wood drowned out the throb in his brain. "I told you, I lived with Uncle Nolan."

"Was that okay? Didn't you miss your sister?"

"I guess. A little." He had cried at night, trying to be silent huddled under the pillow and all the blankets. His uncle had opened the door once, looked at him and gone away again. "I had Cookie. He was with me and I was lucky, I stayed with the carnival," he told Winnie. "Uncle Nolan was the boss and I didn't have to work at the hot dog stand anymore. I took tickets at the Haunted House."

"Uncle Nolan sounds nice."

"He took me to my first reptile convention. They were advertising a two-headed snake. My uncle wanted to buy it and have it stuffed for his collection of oddities and deformities. It had never been in a circus or carnival, but he didn't seem to care. He said, 'Its very existence is a goddamn circus.'"

"That's funny," Winnie said. "Did he buy it?"

"It's in there somewhere."

Uncle Nolan had bought the two-headed snake when it was very much alive in its glass terrarium. It was not deformed but a perfect "Y," a long single snake body that branched into two perfect heads. Were there two hearts? Two stomachs? Oren had asked the snake man.

"How the fuck would I know?" Then the snake owner smiled. There were bits of red jelly in his teeth, crumbs of pastry in a Hansel and Gretel trail down his T-shirt. "Interesting question, kid. You're pretty smart, huh? You should be a herpetologist."

"What's that?"

"Someone who studies reptiles."

"Cool." Oren nodded.

The snake man punched Uncle Nolan in the arm. "Kid wants to be a herper. You should be proud."

Oren had wandered up and down the aisles in the Anaheim

Convention Center while his uncle haggled with the snake owner. At fourteen, Oren's face had erupted with pimple clusters and he was constantly flushed and sweaty, as if the Southern California sun was blistering him from the inside. He was aware of himself, of every joint and freckle, even the follicles on his head, and he felt wrong, stretched, and twisted. Some half-awake mornings he did not recognize his own feet: red hair had sprouted on his toes.

But the reptiles were oblivious and the reptile lovers were so strange looking themselves. They were all either shaved, pierced, and tattooed, or overweight and unwashed. Oren felt invisible among them. He felt like one of them. No one knew how he had ruined everything. No one cared.

"You idiot!" Oren's sister's face was bright red and swollen the last time she spoke to him. "Why didn't you stop him?"

"I couldn't," Oren began. "I... you know what he's like."

"You knew she was in there."

"I couldn't stop him," he insisted, but the truth was something different. He wanted his mother to get caught; he wanted his father to catch her.

"And now he's dead. They're both dead."

"He'll be back."

"He'll die in jail."

She balled up her fist and nailed him one in the cheek. He knew it was coming and he stood still to take it. The pain was good. His father told him it would make him strong and he was weak. He waited for her to hit him again. Turn the other cheek. "It's not my fault," Oren whispered. He tapped on the wooden door. "Winnie. Before, when I told you about my father. I could have stopped him. I knew what she was doing." It felt so good to confess, he could not stop. "I saw her go in there with that boy. I knew my father would find her. I hated her. I hated him. I hate myself."

"Oh no," Winnie whispered. "It's not your fault, Oren. You were a child. They are responsible."

He had not told Marcus what he knew, what he had seen his mother doing. He had not mentioned it the first time or the second, or the twenty-second. Only finally, when his mother seemed to be doing it every night, only then had he told Fiona what he knew and she had threatened to poke his eyes out if he said anything to Dad.

"I should have stopped him." His lips fluttered against the door.

"You couldn't stop him. You said yourself, he was a frightening man."

"I killed her. I killed her myself."

Winnie could not bear the pain this boy was feeling. He was troubled, he was sick, but it wasn't his fault. He started tapping on the door, a fast stutter with one finger. He was getting agitated, she could tell. She didn't want that.

"It's not too late for you," Winnie said. "You can prove them wrong. All those teachers, your sister, anyone. They can see you do something amazing and wonderful."

"Selling carpet."

"I'm sure you're good at it. You can fall in love, get married, have children you take care of. You're so young. Look at all you've done already. Look at Cookie. Cookie is healthy, thriving. Cookie is an amazing accomplishment."

The tapping slowed, and finally stopped. His fingers were right on the other side of hers.

She continued. "You can go back to school. You can open a pet shop or a reptile store. You can do so many things. I know you and I know you're capable of so many things."

"Do you talk to your daughter this way?"

"Not enough." And she knew it was true. "She's a remarkable, brave, sweet young woman and I almost never say that to her."

"You should." He whispered to her, but she heard him as clearly as if he was shouting.

"You're right, Oren. You're right. I promise, I promise if you let me go, I'll do better. I will. I'll be a better mother. I'll listen to her and I'll think before I yell and I'll tell her all the time how wonderful she is."

Oren put his hands on his cheeks. "Really?"

"I promise." Her voice was strong through the door.

"Oh, Winnie," he said. "Oh, oh, oh."

He grinned. He had done it. His plan had worked. His stomach lifted into his chest as if he was going down the big hill on the roller coaster. Was this joy? Was this true happiness? It felt so much like fear; he couldn't breathe, his eyes were dry and wide, his hands were shaking. This must be it, he thought, he was happy.

"Really?" he asked again.

"Yes," Winnie said from right inside. "I promise."

He put his hand on the doorknob. He would open the door and they would hug and then together they could wait for Lacy. He would make sandwiches.

But then there was a knock on his front door.

A sharp quick knock and he heard a spiky, high voice from outside, "Helloooo?"

"Shit." Oren grimaced. He did not need this now. It was Mary from work. She was a pain in the ass. Hadn't calling him been enough? She was cute, but she was always after him. Always calling, always wondering where he was and what he was doing.

"Oren?" She was shouting so the whole neighborhood

could hear her. Her stupid squeaky voice. "Are you okay? It's me. Oren?"

He had to answer her. She would not go away until she saw him. He cracked open the front door and she instantly started talking.

"Well, well, I guess you really are sick. You look awful. You look all sweaty and weird."

He leaned against the doorjamb, the locked screen between them. She was dressed for work, black pants and a pink and fluffy shirt he liked. It was too small or something. He liked the way the buttons gapped.

"I just need to sleep," he said.

"I brought you some soup." She held up a white deli bag. "Chicken noodle."

He nodded.

"Aren't you going to let me in?"

He liked her strawberry blonde hair and her little blue eyes. She had a face like a pug dog, all smushed up together. He could see up her nostrils and her mouth was usually open and wet. She was plump and he liked that too, the feel of her on top of him, the flesh against his bones, the way he could put a finger between the rolls of fat around her middle. It was warm. Soft.

"I'm contagious," he said to her.

Her eyes narrowed, almost disappeared in her plump face. Her lips contracted and wrinkled as if a drawstring had been pulled tight. "Let me in. Is that woman still here?"

She rattled the handle on the screen. That was what he did not like about her. She was bossy. All the women in his life were bossy. Even Winnie told him what to do and she had no right. Only Lacy had asked his advice. He slammed his fist against the doorjamb. Lacy! Now it was her turn to learn a lesson.

"Oren. Answer me."

He bent his head. One of her marshmallow hands held the doorknob. The other clutched the bag. "What?"

"I asked you a question."

"No," he said. "I have to go. I'll see you tomorrow."

"Oren." She shook her head. Her blue eye shadow sparkled in the afternoon sunlight.

"I'm sick. I have to go."

He was closing the door when Winnie started banging on her door and yelling. Oren was shocked. They had come so far. They were so close. Why did she want to get out now?

"Help me! Help! He's locked me in. Help me!"

Mary tapped her fat little foot. "Who the hell is that?"

"Nobody. Nothing." Winnie kept yelling. He would go back there and kill her. That's what he would do.

"Open this door, right now."

"Go away."

Winnie was screaming. "Please! Help! This is not a joke! Help me!"

"What have you done?" Mary's words were clipped and precise, disapproving, like a schoolteacher or worse, a mother.

"I said go!"

Oren tried to shut the door, but Mary was strong. She ripped the screen door open and with the other fat hand pushed back the front door. She nudged him aside with her substantial hip, deli bag trembling in her furious fist, and started walking to the hallway.

"It's a friend," Oren told Mary. "She's just fooling around."

He reached for her, but she shook her shoulder out of his grasp. There was nothing for it. He grabbed both her arms, but she outweighed him and pulled herself free.

"Oren Baines, I am going to see that woman. You can't stop me."

But he had to. He launched himself and wrapped both arms around her ham hock thighs. She fell forward onto the floor hard with a woof and a fart. The soup flew from her hand and hit the wall. It spilled through the bag onto the goddamn white carpet. Oren had had enough. He kicked her in the stomach.

"Shut up!" he screamed at Winnie, at both of them, at Cookie scratching, still scratching, scratching. "Shut up!"

Mary, fucking Mary, was fucking everything up.

"Oren?" She rolled over on her back and looked up at him. "What is going on with you? Are you okay?"

Her little mouth was in a pout. Her cheeks were pink. He liked her. He really did. When it was over he would do something nice for her and she would be sad he had found someone else, but she would understand. He took his deep breaths.

"Please," he said to her. "Just go home."

Winnie shouted, "Please! Are you there?"

He ignored her and offered Mary a hand to help her up, but she yanked him to the floor and scrambled up on top of him.

"You're insane," she croaked at him. "Who is that woman?"

"Get off me. Get off!"

She refused to listen. She kept crawling, crawling like a scorpion up his body. Her fingernails scratched his neck. He punched the side of her head. She grunted and kept coming. She lifted her head to yell at him and he punched her throat, up under her chin. There was a snap and she stopped clawing. He lifted a leg and kneed her in the gut. A little spit up came out of her mouth and he pushed her off, desperate to keep her saliva from touching him. She rolled to her back. She was scratching at her throat. Her eyes were as wide and blue as he had ever seen them.

"Mary?" he said.

Her mouth opened but she would not speak. He saw the

throw up in her mouth; he could smell it mixed with the spilled chicken soup. She coughed and sputtered and then her eyes fluttered closed and she was quiet.

Sleeping, he told himself. She is sleeping. Or maybe she had bumped her head. She just needed to rest. Like Winnie, she would rest. He couldn't lift her, but the carpet was soft and he dragged her back to the room with the bed. He had been so smart to put Winnie in the collection room—almost as if he knew this would happen—he would need this room with the bed. He was smart. He was doing fine. As he lugged Mary past Winnie's door, she called to him.

"Oren? What's going on?"

He did not reply.

"Who's there? Oren? Is that you?"

At least she was asking for him.

Mary did not stir as he pulled her into the bedroom. He tried to lift her, but he could not get her up on the bed. In her sleep she was even heavier than usual. She did not smell clean. Maybe she had peed her pants a little when she fell. He didn't want to, but he had to leave her on the floor. He covered her with the blanket, tucking it in around her arms and hips. When she woke up she would know he had tried to make her comfortable.

He sat back on his heels and looked at her. He liked her, but he loved Lacy. He was sorry it had happened, sorry for Mary, but she would find someone else. Her face was a funny color. She needed to rest.

Winnie tried to listen through the wood. She heard a body being dragged along the thick, plush carpet. It made a gentle woosh, like a brush going through her hair, a sound only she could hear.

"Oren?" she called to him. "Oren!"

No answer. She shivered, frozen where she stood. Perhaps

the girl had hurt him. Maybe she was another criminal, in on it with him and angry at the way he had done things. Now there would be a new person in charge. Not Kidney, but someone else. Women were most cruel to other women.

"Please be okay," Winnie prayed.

She heard the other bedroom door close and she knew no one was coming to save her. Not that girl and not Oren. She backed away from the door and went to the window. There was a tiny crack of air along one seam. She pressed her face against the wood and gasped at the cool air coming in. She had never before realized how wonderful a breeze could be. An orange tree was blooming nearby and she actually smiled breathing in the sweet fragrance. It was early in the season for orange blossoms, but there had been rain and the tree in her yard was budding too. She wanted to see it bloom. She wanted to live that long. The air helped her to breathe, to think. The street was quiet now, but a neighbor had to come home eventually. She would break the glass and call to him. For now, she would wait. She would be quiet and not let Oren hurt her again. She kept her face against the crack and breathed.

The door to the room flew open. Oren's hair was a mess, his face flushed.

"Winnie. Winnie, can you help me?"

"What?

He took her by the hand and pulled her out into the hall. The carpet was dark with what looked like chicken soup. There were carrots and noodles and bits of celery soaking into the white fibers.

"What do I do?" He was frantic.

"Club soda—do you have club soda?" She had no idea if club soda would help, but maybe.

"Ginger ale?" he asked.

"No. Water then. Bring me water and dishwashing soap. Don't worry. We'll get it up."

He ran to the kitchen. She was on her hands and knees picking up shreds of chicken before she realized what she was doing. Helping a kidnapper clean his carpet. She sat back. Oren came running with a dishtowel, the roll of paper towels, soap, and a cereal bowl of water.

"Okay," she said and shook her head. She had missed her chance to run for the front door.

"My uncle is going to kill me." He sounded like a kid who had broken his mother's favorite vase.

"This is your uncle's house?"

"He lives in Arizona now. I rent it."

"And you put in the carpet."

"He got a discount, but my uncle paid."

"It's good—definitely stain resistant. Look." The soup was coming up, the brownish color changing to plain wet. "If you let me out of here, I'll buy all my carpeting at Carpet Barn. I'll carpet my entire house."

He exhaled. His hands were trembling. His fingernails were bitten down to nothing. Each fingertip was irritated, swollen around what was left of the nail. Like red dough puffing around the edges of a cookie cutter.

"Who's in the bedroom?" Winnie tried to keep her voice casual. "What happened?"

"A girl I know. She's not my girlfriend. Just from work. She came by. She wouldn't leave. She fell."

"You mean, like I fell?"

"Exactly." He looked relieved. "Hey, and you're fine."

Winnie smiled at him. He did not even know he had hurt them. He could not see how terrible he was. Something was missing in his brain. It was a chemical thing or a gene or a chromosome that was wrong. It was growing up in a carnival with a violent dad and a nonexistent mother. He was hopelessly damaged. He was just a boy and he would never be right.

When Winnie was nine, she and her mother had spent the weekend at the island home of a famous director. Winnie had been forced to play with his daughter. The girl had blue eyes and dimples. She had long legs and wore frilly girlish clothes. She was everything Winnie was not.

"Come outside on the patio," the girl said proudly. "Watch what I can do."

Winnie expected a one-handed cartwheel, something she had been attempting for weeks, but the girl squatted on the hot, flat cement next to an anthill. For a moment she and Winnie watched the ants going about their business, scurrying in and out. The girl whispered as if the ants could hear her.

"Okay. Watch."

With her thumb, she crushed the back half of ant after ant, leaving their front legs to scramble. They could no longer get anywhere, but they did not die. They tried to crawl, to stay in line, to continue on their journey.

"Look how they try to get away. Look how they stay alive. You do it."

Winnie had refused and the girl had laughed at her. When Winnie went out on the patio after dinner that night, the ants were still there. Some were even still alive, still trying to crawl away. Winnie ran to her mother. The girl told her father that Winnie had pinched her. Daisy was furious and sent Winnie to her grandmother for a long, long time.

But Oren wasn't cruel. He wouldn't smash her legs so he could watch her try to crawl away. She ran her hand over the nicks on her arm, felt the fresh scabs. He didn't mean to be violent. He bit his lip as he scrubbed the carpet. He looked so worried. He needed a hospital, not a jail cell. That's what she would tell the police when she was saved. He's sick, she would say. He needs help.

Oren finished and handed the cloth to Winnie. The carpet was wet, but it would be fine. He smiled at Winnie as she wrung the cloth out into the little bowl. It was wonderful of her to help him and she was right, the carpet would not stain. They had solved the problem together. They would get along very nicely when they were family, when he was her son-in-law as good as a son.

"Thank you," he said.

Something had changed in her face. She smiled back at him with an energy he had not seen before. He grinned at her. Carefully, he picked up the bowl of dirty water.

"Get the soap and the rag," he said to her. "Follow me."

Gingerly he carried the bowl down the hall, with Winnie walking right behind him. They were a team. They had cleaned the carpet. He had saved her from Kidney. She was coming around. Yes, she had yelled for Mary, but he could not blame her for wanting to come out of that room. He never went in there. Not even to dust like he was supposed to. As they reached the living room he turned to her, "I'm sorry that room is scary. You know, some of those things aren't even real."

Winnie stopped by the front door. "I'm going now," she said. "It's been an interesting day. Let's get together soon."

She confused him. At first he wanted to just say goodbye. Watching her go would be a relief. But why was she leaving? She opened the front door. The screen door was crooked; Mary had pulled it off the hinge or something. Damn her.

"No," he said.

"Thank you so much," Winnie smiled at him. "See you soon."

She had one hand on the doorjamb. She used the other hand

to give him a little wave. She was waving at him? He dropped the bowl and slammed the door shut. He had to, he had to, and he caught her hand. She howled. She could not get it free. He held the door closed. She would have to ask him.

"What do you want?" he said and he meant so much more than opening the door, or her hand or to leave. He wanted her to be happy, he wanted to give her everything she wanted so she would stay. "What?" He had to yell to be heard over her shriek-ing. "Tell me."

"Open the door," she cried.

He opened the door, she pulled her hand free and he yanked her back and knocked the door shut. She balled up her other hand and hit him in the face. It surprised him and it hurt and before she could do it again, he grabbed both her hands and squeezed.

She screamed. "My hand!"

"I thought we were friends."

"Let go!"

"Be quiet," he said. "You promised me—"

"Let go of my hand!" She stopped screaming. "Please."

Her hand, the one that got stuck in the door, was darkening, purple and black rolling in like spilled grape juice across a table-cloth. It made him angry to see it. She was so damn stupid. He squeezed a little harder. "Now we have to clean up more mess."

He tried to push her to the floor. She stumbled, but remained standing.

He gestured to the spilled bowl of dirty water and vegeta-bles. "Now clean that up!"

She faced him. "Why should I?"

She was his helper. She was his friend. He could smell the soup and the dishwashing soap and something else from the hallway, something disgusting like piss and shit mixed with ammonia. Like the port o' potties at the carnival. Winnie's face was red and angry and ugly. He held her purple hand in his sweaty palm. Lacy would not be happy when she saw her mother. But it was not his fault. Winnie had done this to herself. Lacy would have to understand.

Oren closed his eyes. He tried to call up the image he had of all of them around the dinner table. Of the three of them smiling and laughing together. He forced his breath to slow, the picture to come. Lacy had her hand on his. Lacy's eyes were shining. He offered her a glass of wine and she refused. Then she blushed, shyly, and leaned forward so her breath moved the candlelight. "I'm pregnant," she whispered to them both. "I'm going to have a baby."

He opened his eyes. He had Mary in the back room. He had Winnie in front of him. There was dirt on the carpet. But soon it would not matter. Soon, they would all be together. In his mind's picture, he added Mary and a new boyfriend for her at the table. They would be a happy family. He tried to smile at Winnie.

"It's okay," he said. "We're getting to know each other. Don't worry. We'll all be together soon."

27.

Lacy drifted toward the music room. She was late for orchestra. But was there something else she should be doing? She held her phone in one hand and her flute in the other. Then she stopped. She had left her locker open. She had not even closed the door. She turned around and headed back down the hall to her locker.

Two girls walked toward her. They stared at her so strangely. Lacy blushed. Could they tell she was not a virgin anymore?

An image of Buster spun into her mind, and the scary gang guys, and a little deformed glass dog. Buster's bed and room. The smell of his pillow. His finger inside her.

One of the girls put a hand on her arm.

"Are you okay?"

"What?"

"Maybe you should go to the office."

"Why?"

The girls exchanged a glance. There was something really wrong with her; Lacy could see it on their faces.

"Come on," one girl said.

"We'll take you," the other one said.

Lacy recognized them. Younger girls, ninth graders. They were best friends, always together.

They each took an arm and pulled her toward the office. She was afraid to go. She had lost her virginity and now she was sick or something because of it and everyone would know. She wanted Buster to come pick her up right away, but he had lost his cell phone. The office would call her mother—and Winnie would be so disappointed in her. When Buster came later to get her and she was gone, he would be so sad. He would think she didn't like him anymore.

Please don't call my mother, she thought. I can't let them call her.

"I'm late."

She pulled her arms free, turned and ran to orchestra.

28.

"I want to go home." Winnie whispered, but every damaged bone and muscle, every nerve, even her blood was screaming, "I want to go home."

It was all she wanted. Home. With the damn dog, the dirt, her daughter. Oh God, Lacy. Lacy. Lacy. She closed her eyes and leaned her face against Oren's chest, just above the scoop neck of his undershirt. His skin was damp and cool. His sparse red hairs tickled her cheek. If only his body would listen—not his mind, but his body—he would respond. His heart would hear hers crying and reach to it.

"I'll take you with me," she said.

She could take him home with her. They would stand together at her kitchen window and stare out at the hazy Los Angeles sky and the ugly telephone wires. Together they would go to the foot of the stairs and yell at Lacy to get up for school. He could hear them argue about vegetables and cigarettes and homework. She would teach him to fold the laundry—just so— and together they would open Lacy's bottom drawer to put the clean clothes away and together they would sigh at the chaos inside. He could be with her at home. She found his hand and held it. When Lacy was a baby, her fingers curled around Winnie's pinkie and her grip was so strong. She nodded against Oren's chest. She wanted to bury her face in her daughter's pillow and breathe in her smell, the vanilla oil and the watermelon shampoo and even the smoke, but also the baby girl she had been. Still there. Still there.

"Oren," Winnie said, her voice muffled against his chest. "I lied to you."

"What a surprise."

"I was scared, I'm sorry. But listen, listen, I have to go home. My daughter, she's not all grown up. She's young. She needs me."

Oren took a deep breath. He didn't mind her sweaty cheek against his skin or even holding her hand. His other hand gently patted her back. He was so glad she was telling him the truth. It was the beginning. Now she would confess all the terrible things she had done to Lacy, the abuse, the punishments. He had her promise, now he would hear the truth.

"Tell me," he breathed.

"She doesn't live far away. She lives with me." Winnie stepped away from him to look into his face. "I'm her mother. She's just a girl."

"Not so young," Oren disagreed.

"She's a child."

"She's eighteen."

Winnie shook her head. "I never said that. Lacy is only sixteen. A baby. So much younger than you."

But instead of being moved, Oren frowned and all his features went dark. His eyes grew smaller, his lips disappeared. Anger rolled in like a cold front across his freckles.

Winnie backed further away. "I'm sorry I lied to you. I was scared you'd hurt her."

"Hurt her?"

"You were probably very grown up at sixteen." She desperately tried to soothe him. "Capable. Independent. She's not. She's young for her age. Maybe she's not as smart as you—"

"How old is she? Tell me the goddamn truth."

"I swear to you she is only sixteen. She won't be seventeen until April. She's in tenth grade."

"I thought her birthday was in August. I thought she was a Leo."

"Why did you think that?"

It seemed he didn't know as much about her as he had implied. He was so confused. Winnie wondered if he had kidnapped the wrong mother. Poor kid. He turned away from her. She saw his hands clench into fists and relax, clench and relax. He was taking deep breaths. He was trying to control himself and she wanted to touch him, to tell him she recognized his effort and appreciated it. He was hardly any older than Lacy. Just a boy in over his head. "Oren?"

He turned and exhaled. "I can do that," he said slowly and even proudly. "If all you want is to go home, I can give you that. You'll be home tomorrow." He looked at his watch. "Maybe later tonight."

He gave her a strained little smile. She closed her eyes. She could not bear it. If he was lying to her, she did not want to see it in his eyes. If he was not lying, she did not want to see that either. Kindness as painful as another injury.

"Come on." He patted her shoulder awkwardly. "Forty-five minutes more and everything will be cleared up. Everything."

Fucking bitch! Oren screamed to himself. She had told him she was eighteen. She had told him her mother was cruel. She had told him nothing but lies. Bitch, bitch, bitch. Even her birthday was wrong. He told her he had always been attracted to Leos and she'd said her birthday was in August. His dreams evaporated like sweat in the breeze—the cold, shocking breeze of truth. Fuck her. She was too young for him. He called up his picture and saw them sitting around her mother's dining room table. He and Winnie were drinking wine while Lacy was drinking soda pop. The only thing she leaned forward to whisper was, "I got an A on my history test." He could take her out for an ice cream cone. That's what he could do for her. A balloon and an ice cream cone. Maybe a ride on the goddamn merry-go-round.

He should just open the door and let Winnie go home. Or he could take her back to the car place. Her car was probably done by now. He could take her out someplace nice for lunch and apologize. She was fine. She looked bad, but it was hot in the house, people always got sweaty when they came over. She tried to smile at him. She swayed on her feet and he reached out and caught her arm to steady her. Fuck! He had nothing to apologize for! It was Lacy! Lacy. She had to get her butt over here to his house and apologize to both of them.

He took out his cell phone. He dialed. She was in orchestra, of course. Her cell phone was off. He sent her a text. "Hey, Baby." Baby was sarcastic, but she was probably too young to get it. "Come over to my place. Do you know how to drive?" He could not help the anger. He took a deep breath. "Call me for directions."

It was obvious Winnie did not know what Lacy had been saying about her. Poor Winnie. She was good and nice. She wanted to go home and help that bitch of a daughter. If she only knew. Wait until she found out. Wait until Lacy showed up and Winnie learned what a lying sack of shit her daughter really was. He stepped forward and pulled her to him again. Her forehead was slick against his chest. It made everything hotter to have her against him, but he was sad when she stepped away.

"I told you what I want more than anything in the world." She smiled at him. "I was honest with you. Tell me, what do you want? What is this all about?"

Nothing. That was what all this was about. But she did not need to know that yet. He could be honest in another way. "I want you to like me."

"I do," she said, "I do like you." Then her eyes closed and she started to go backwards. He had to catch her to keep her from falling.

"I'm sick," she whispered.

"What's wrong?"

She slid out of his grasp and melted to the floor until she was crouched there. She bent forward and held her stomach.

"What is it? What?"

"It's my hand," she said. "Can I have some ice?"

"Yes. Yes." That was easy. That he could do. Her little hand. She had left her hand in the doorjamb and he had to close the door. She should have known better. "Ice," he said as he pushed into the kitchen.

Cookie looked at him and bobbed his head. It was almost frantic, the bobbing, up and down, up and down.

"Not now," Oren said.

Cookie bobbed and turned away from him.

"Please. Not now." He could not stand it if Cookie was mad at him. It would be just too much. He tapped Cookie's tail. Cookie swished it out of reach. "C'mon."

Cookie's tail went back and forth. Pissed off, Oren could tell, and jealous. Usually when Oren was home all day, he spent a lot of it with Cookie. He tried to stroke Cookie's head, but Cookie turned and snapped. Oren pulled his fingers back just in time.

A wind began in his ears. The room seemed to be spinning, everything spinning inside him and outside.

"Stop it! He shouted to Cookie, to himself, to the room. "Stop it."

He put his head between his knees. The room slowed and his breathing returned to normal. He stood up and felt the rush of the blood dropping to his belly. He was getting better. He could control himself. Ice. He was there for ice and Cookie could just go fuck himself.

"Fuck you," he snarled. His throat closed. He had never sworn at his friend before.

He filled a clean dishtowel with ice cubes and pushed the door open. Winnie was not there. His stomach lurched. Just when he thought he could trust her. He opened his mouth to shout her name and then he saw her. She was sitting on the floor just behind the door with her back against the dining room wall. She had not gone out the garage door, or back to the front door. She was relaxing against the wall. She was waiting for him.

"Ice," he said to her.

Winnie opened her eyes and looked at Oren. Her kidnapper. She had to remind herself he was a kidnapper. He had gotten ice wrapped in a dishtowel for her. She reached for it with her good hand. He knelt beside her.

"That looks bad." He sounded concerned.

Her hand was swollen and red where it wasn't darkly bruised. The knuckles seemed out of order somehow, crooked. It throbbed and to look at it made her sick to her stomach. The ice felt good, a little shocking, but good, good, good. She smiled at Oren gratefully. "Thanks."

He sat down beside her.

"What happens now?" she asked.

"We wait."

"For what?"

"I'm expecting a call. And then we'll get this all straightened out."

The ice numbed her hand; her stomachache subsided. She took a deep breath and exhaled, forcing her shoulders to relax and her toes to uncurl. If she rested her head against the wall carefully she could avoid the bump on the back. Then her head didn't hurt either. She was grateful for the absence of pain.

Most of the time we don't notice it, Winnie thought. Usually people are unaware of feeling fine. But then something hurts or something is broken and out of joint and it is all we can think of. Bad tooth. Headache. Broken heart. The pain adjusts everything we see and do, the colors are muted, the air thicker and it is more work to breathe and move. People curl around a hurt—she could always tell when someone was in pain. The rejected, jilted girl at the bus stop, head down, chest collapsed. The athlete at the end of his run pretending his bad knee wouldn't end his career. The unemployed woman at the grocery store counting her change. All of them with their shoulders hunched over as if waiting for the next blow.

And then it leaves. Through drugs or time or healing or change of circumstance we wake up one morning and the pain is gone. Winnie remembered the exact day, the very moment, when she realized her heart was mended. It was thirty-nine and a half months after Jonathan had left her, one o'clock in the afternoon, and she realized she had not thought of him once that day. She had taken Lacy to school, done some errands, eaten a tomato and cheese sandwich, and not until she was throwing in a load of laundry did she remember that her heart was broken. But it wasn't anymore; the ache in her chest was gone. She could think of Jonathan and Jessica together without wanting to double over. She did not feel like singing and dancing, she was not particularly happy, and her problems were still her problems, but she was not in pain. And that was enough.

Now it was enough to sit here with Oren and have nothing hurt. She knew she was in trouble, bones were broken in her hand and she probably had a concussion, but for this single pain free moment she could think clearly. He was beginning to trust her. He had left her alone as he went for ice. Something was not working with his plan and he was confused, worried. He seemed angry about something, someone who had let him down. That other woman had shown up unexpectedly and now she was passed out in the back, most likely tied to the bed as she had been. If Winnie could get to her, she might be an ally. They would be two against one. Oren, poor kid, was over his head, out of control. Yes, poor kid. Just a kid. She would help him—as soon as she got out of here and some place safe—she would find him help.

She eyed the bump in his pocket that was his cell phone. Unlikely she could take that from him. She would not attempt to get out the front door again; she had tried that too many times. But maybe the garage door again. The button to open it was just inside. She imagined the little girl who had lived here once long ago going out to play, calling to her mother, "I'm going bike rid- ing." The mother would want her home for dinner, but she would be happy to see her go too. Go away but never leave, the dilemma of motherhood. The girl would run out that door, flip the switch and the big door would lift. She would leap onto her bike and pedal away, her T-shirt flapping in her version of freedom.

Cookie was scratching again. Winnie watched Oren turn angrily to the kitchen door, then force himself to calm down. Cookie was the thing he cared about most. Cookie had to be her way out of here.

"Cookie," she said. "How did you learn about taking care of Cookie?"

Oren's face relaxed. "I've read books, I've talked to experts. I go to the reptile shows."

"Other people have iguanas?"

"I'm president of the Iguana Keepers Club. We have about sixty-five members. Monthly meetings."

"Wow. You're the president." It was working. Whatever was worrying him was drifting away.

"I know the most," he said proudly. "I'm the guy they come to. People don't realize how much work it is to take care of an iguana. It is not an easy job, oh no. Did you know, for instance, you must never feed them iceberg lettuce? Never. Almost no nutrients and to an iguana it's like crack cocaine. It's that addictive. Honestly, they'll stop eating anything else, get malnourished and die."

"Wish I found iceberg lettuce addictive—instead of chocolate." Winnie tried to laugh. "What's his favorite food?"

"Kale." But then Oren sighed. "Right now he's not eating much. He's not happy."

"He's lonely."

"Exactly. He needs his girlfriend."

"Everybody needs somebody."

Oren smiled, a genuine sweet smile, and nodded. "You are exactly right."

Winnie struggled to turn to him. It made her dizzy and nauseated, but she smiled back at him. "Let's go buy his girlfriend. Right now. You have the money."

He nodded. He was buying it, going for it.

"Think how happy Cookie will be. You could start breeding iguanas. You could probably make a lot of money, right? How many babies do they have?"

His face slipped and slid from open to shut. "Money. This is not about money."

"I know that. I was just thinking—"

"Don't think," he said. "I will do the thinking."

He stood up and turned his back to her. He stared up at the ceiling, cottage cheese flecked with sparkled. He looked down at the white carpet. Up at the ceiling, down at the carpet. Up and down, up and down. Rocking his head. Fists clenching and opening. Trotting a little in place. Winnie knew enough to tuck in her feet and stay quiet.

29.

Lacy took her chair behind the three other flutists. Once she had been a soloist, on her way to first chair, but not any more. At the beginning of the school year she decided it wasn't cute or interesting to be a music nerd and had stopped trying. She was last chair now.

Shit. She had forgotten her music. She had gone to her locker and gotten her flute and her cell phone had rung. She had answered her phone. Lacy stood up. Her neighbor's music fluttered to the ground.

"Watch it."

Ms. Ingram was on the dais with her baton raised. She scowled at Lacy. "What now?"

"I—"

Ms. Ingram had been one of Lacy's favorite teachers since seventh grade. She was nice and funny and pretty, even though she wore stretch pants with elastic waists and long sweater vests. She had short dark hair and brown eyes and her skin was olive toned like Winnie's. Something about Ms. Ingram reminded Lacy of her mother.

"I—" she said again.

"Are you sick?" Ms. Ingram's voice was soft with concern. "What is it?"

Lacy knew she had disappointed her. Ms. Ingram had worked hard with her, told her she was talented and she would help her get into college, and Lacy had blown it. Ms. Ingram had heard her making fun of orchestra in the hall. She knew Lacy had stopped practicing and ignored her flute, the one thing she had always loved. Now Ms. Ingram didn't like her anymore.

"I'm sorry," she said to Ms. Ingram. "I'm so sorry."

Ms. Ingram came off the platform. She was walking up to Lacy, right through the orchestra, pushing music stands and students aside. Her eyes looked liquid, like melted chocolate that Lacy could fall into.

"I know," Lacy said, "and I'm sorry. So terribly sorry."

"Catch her!" Ms. Ingram shouted.

Catch what? Lacy had time to puzzle and then the ceiling slipped sideways and she fainted.

30.

Jonathan woke on his bed. The house was quiet. He stretched and smiled; he loved napping. His stomach growled. He hoped the leftover Chinese food was still there, that Jessica hadn't thrown it away. She hated the white boxes in the fridge. She couldn't stand anything disorganized, or used, or messy. Not like Winnie.

"Oh, shit," he said aloud.

He sat up and looked at his watch. It was too late to go back to the house; rush hour cross-town traffic was murder. Well. She was the one who had lost her cell phone and his lawyer was right, it wasn't his problem. He stood and stretched again. Lupe and her daughter had probably left so he could eat his Kung Pao Chicken right out of the box and put his feet up until Jessica got back.

He hadn't meant to fall asleep. He had seen Jessica's beige slippery nightgown lying across the bed and lain down beside it for just a moment. He intended to go to Winnie's and confront the cell phone thieves, but Jessica's nightie felt so good against his cheek and it smelled of her and the sex they'd had that morning. He felt a little guilty for going to Winnie's and holding the nightgown made him feel better, like playing—paying?—tribute to Jessica. He would go, but first he would caress her silky nightgown and think about how beautiful she was. His penis pushed against his jeans. This is what Jessica did to him. It was all her fault. He closed his eyes. He reached down inside his pants. It reminded him of early mornings before high school, the rough cotton of his underwear against the back of his hand, the soft skin under his fingertips. Like a high school boy, it would not take long and then he would just lie there for a moment and then he would go.

But he fell asleep and now it was too late. He thought again about the voice on her phone and decided it was a child, a young teen at most, not a member of a cutthroat band of thieves. Winnie was fine. He knew it. They were still connected, he was still tuned in—if anything happened to her, he would know. He got up and went to the bathroom. The size of it never stopped impressing him. Two sinks. Two toilets. Two showers and a tub. All in beige marble. Jessica loved beige. She had all kinds of words for it, taupe and eggshell, cream and fawn and mushroom. She said it was classy. He supposed she was right.

His cell phone rang. He flushed the toilet and went to get his phone from the pocket of his discarded shorts. "Jonathan Parker."

"Mr. Parker. This is Mrs. Campbell, principal of Lacy's school. Your daughter has fainted."

Jonathan staggered. Not Lacy. Drugs? Pregnancy? "Why? What happened?"

"We're not sure. The paramedics have been called."

"I'll be right there."

"We can't seem to locate her mother."

"She lost her cell phone. I'm in Beverly Hills, but I'll get there as soon as I can."

He knew he should have gone over there. He knew it. Not for Winnie, but for Lacy. He had been tuned in, but he wasn't listening. That was just what Jessica always said: the messages come, but we're not home to receive them.

31.

Oren was beginning to really like Winnie's skin—so dark and smooth next to his freckles. Her face was pretty too, even sweaty and pale from feeling bad. He liked her big brown eyes. She got up from the floor stiffly, like an old lady for some reason, but he still thought she was a nice looking mom.

"Let's go," she said again. "Get Cookie that girl."

It was great that she seemed to like iguanas so much. He had been instrumental in other conversions to "Herp Fan," as new members were called in the club. But it was too late to go. Lacy would call soon. Maybe tomorrow they could all three go together. Oh right, he remembered, and then we can take Lacy to the petting zoo.

He picked up a lank of Winnie's dark hair. "Your daughter doesn't look like you."

"No," Winnie answered. "She's tall and blonde and beautiful."

"You're pretty."

"Not like Lacy. She takes after my mother, the movie star, except for her hair. It's incredibly curly. I love it. She hates it. She has ringlets like Shirley Temple."

Another lie. Lie after lie. She didn't even have straight hair. "Is she really blonde? Not from a bottle?"

"A true blonde."

"She must strut that stuff around, right? Showing off to the boys at school?"

"No. God no. She thinks guys don't like her. She has no idea how beautiful she is. Plus, as I said, she's young for her age. I mean, other girls have babies at sixteen; I don't think Lacy has ever been kissed."

Another lie from the bitch. There were men, supposedly, pursuing her all the time. She had told him she was experienced. She had said she was eighteen and had not been a virgin for two years.

"Are we going to the reptile store?" Winnie asked.

"Do you know your daughter is a big, fat liar?"

Winnie turned to him and a flash of pain erupted behind her eyes. "What are you talking about?"

He shook his head. He looked at the ground. His hands curled into fists. Winnie stepped away from him. Now the pain filled her head, then her back and then her hand. The ice wasn't working anymore. He put a finger in his mouth, gnawing at the nail. His other hand opened and closed. She shuffled farther away from him. What did he mean saying Lacy was a liar?

And all at once, like a piercing high note in the middle of the cacophony, it was clear to her. Lacy. He was doing this with Lacy. No. For Lacy. No. Because of Lacy. She had seen the laptop in his room. The screen he had quickly hidden when she entered, the momentary glimpse of a girl with white blonde hair. She had heard Lacy's ring tone on his phone. He had to wait until five-thirty to call. He had to wait until she was out of orchestra. No. No. No.

"Lacy!" she burst. "Is this about Lacy? Is that why I'm here?"

He nodded.

"Tell me right now what's going on." She stamped her foot and waves of pain undulated through her. "You tell me right now or I swear to God I will kill you."

He closed his eyes. When he opened them, he was crying. "Okay. Okay, I'll tell you. Your daughter. Lacy. I'm in love with her. I am. I know her. We met online. We are both, we were both in love. I thought we—well, I love her."

"You've met her?"

"Not in person. Not yet. But I thought—I mean, she said—"

"When did this happen?"

"We've been talking for six weeks. She told me terrible things about you."

Winnie reeled as if he had punched her. "Is she in love with you?"

"We haven't said it. Not yet. I wanted it to be in person. I wanted it to be special." He smiled at her. "Isn't it special? The first time?"

"This isn't happening."

"It will all be straightened out soon. We'll talk. She's coming over here."

"NO!" Winnie screamed. She didn't care what he did to her, but he could not touch Lacy.

"We can sort everything out."

"She is not coming here."

"Yes, she is!" Now he was on his feet and shouting. His face had gone white, the freckles standing out like brown paint spatters. "She has to come!"

"If you touch her—"

"She is a lying bitch! She lied lied lied lied—"

Winnie had to stop him. She rushed at him and swung the dishtowel full of half melted ice cubes at his face. She hit him in the temple with a slap. He roared and grabbed the towel and pulled her to him. She went at him with both hands, pounding on his face and neck and chest, whatever she could reach. She ignored her throbbing hand and kept at him. She kicked and kneed him. She remembered her martial arts and tried for his eyes with her forefingers. He grabbed her hands and squeezed. She gasped with the pain and her stomach lurched. She struggled to stay upright. He shook her and then pushed her violently into the kitchen door. Her sore head hit the wood and she stumbled through the swinging door and fell on the cedar chips covering the kitchen floor. He was coming after her. She scrambled to her feet and jumped up to sit on the kitchen counter. He tried to grab her. She kicked both legs straight out and hit him in the gut. He flew back against the refrigerator. She jumped down and ran to the door. It was stuck, it wouldn't push out. She had to pull it in. She struggled to get her fingers in the crack, to pull the door open. But she had forgotten about Cookie.

Cookie rammed into the back of her knees. His horrible mouth snapped and his serrated teeth tore into her calf. She screamed, the loudest scream of a day filled with screams. Pain seared through her as if every vein were on fire. She shook her leg wildly, desperately trying to tear it out of his mouth. The blood made Cookie crazy. His tail thrashed. His long nails scraped against the linoleum.

Blood was gushing onto the floor. Her tennis shoe was filling. Flaps of her flesh hung from Cookie's mouth. Her leg no longer looked like hers, but an image from a horror film. Her other leg gave way and she sank to the ground. Cookie released his jaw, but he was not done. He clawed his way up her thigh, his open mouth dripping blood – her blood. Winnie reached for Oren. She tried to grab his leg. He backed away from her, fascination and horror on his face. She tried to crab sideways to get out from under the enormous iguana. She rocked from side to side. Cookie was on top of her. He was bigger, longer than she was. His claws sunk and tore into her stomach. His tongue stretched out and flicked at her. He pulled himself toward her breasts. The fabric of her shirt ripped away.

"Oren!" she screeched.

"What?" He blinked at her.

"Help me." He turned his head away from her. "Listen," she continued desperately. "You can have me. Leave Lacy and take me. I'll stay with you. Forever."

She was fading away, she was disappearing into a white hot flame of pain. There was something else she needed to tell Oren, something important, some description about how the world was supposed to be. But the kitchen was spinning too fast; it was too hot and too bright. She could not remember what she had to say. Cookie's toenails were too sharp. She was burning from a million little stars. His sizzling breath on her face smelled of rotten vegetables and cedar, of the reptile house at the zoo, moist and fetid. Something hard pressed against her leg. Cookie was too heavy, she could not push him away. She covered her face. Cookie would not stop. He rubbed and pumped against her bleeding belly. She felt his dick trying to get in and his tongue on the back of her hands.

"That's enough!" Oren shoved Cookie with his foot so he fell off her onto his side. "Enough!"

Oren lifted her to her feet as Cookie righted himself and lunged again. Oren stamped and shouted and Cookie stopped. There was a pulse in her leg, but no pain, just a throb she could feel in her chest, like the bass turned up too high in the car next to her at a stoplight. Far away, beneath her somewhere, she saw Cookie waiting. Mouth opening and closing. Legs pumping up and down. His organ protruding.

Winnie leaned her head on Oren's bony shoulder. Cookie thrust himself at her. Oren pushed Cookie away again, but Cookie charged, trying to get around his master to the bloody female. Oren kicked him. Too hard, even Winnie could see that.

Cookie slid back across the linoleum with a weird, squealing cry. When he spun back toward them, his nose was bleeding worse than before. Oren got the door open. He and Winnie went through it together, she had her arms around him, and he held her tightly as he closed the door in Cookie's face.

32.

Buster saw the paramedics pull up at school. He was stoned, sitting on the wall across from the school, waiting for Lacy. He felt amazing. He had loved her for so long. Maybe because he was high he knew the ambulance was for her. He jogged across the street and followed the guys into the school. They looked at him.

"It's my girlfriend," he said.

They just nodded and let him come along. The principal was waiting.

"She's in the music room. Down that hall."

"I'll show them where it is," Buster said.

He felt calm and purposeful. The reflective strips on the paramedics' jackets were beautiful. He ran down the hall with the stretcher clattering behind him. The wide, open hallways were wonderful to run in. It smelled like school, but kind of fresh, without the bodies or the lunch bags.

"In here."

He held open the door for them. The kids were gathered around Lacy. She lay on her back. Ms. Ingram held her hand. Principal Campbell huffed and puffed in behind them. The students cleared for the paramedics. One of the guys shone a light in Lacy's eyes. The other checked her pulse.

"It's my mother," Lacy said. "I'm fine. Ms. Ingram. Tell them."

Ms. Ingram nodded. She touched one of the guys on the

shoulder and made him look at her. "She says her mother has been kidnapped."

"Whoa," said Buster. "No shit."

"Buster?" Lacy called to him.

"I'm here, Sunshine."

She reached for him and that made him feel great. The students stepped back to let him through. He held her hand.

"Your mom was kidnapped?"

"She got a call on her cell phone," Ms. Ingram said. The paramedics were unconvinced. "Her grandmother is Daisy Juniper. Her dad is Jonathan Parker."

The paramedics exchanged raised eyebrows then a nod. Buster nodded with them. His girlfriend was famous.

"We'll call right away," one of them said.

"Wait," Lacy said. "No. He said he'd kill her if I called the police."

"They all say that," the paramedic said. "Don't worry. The cops are good at this."

One of the paramedics spoke into the weird little walkie-talkie on his shoulder. Buster definitely wanted one of those. What the guy said was unintelligible to Buster, but obviously a call to the cops. He grinned. He had the coolest girlfriend in the world—the whole fucking world.

33.

Oren carried Winnie to the couch and laid her down.

"I'm sorry," she said. There was blood on his carpet. A lot of blood on his perfect carpet. She did not want him to be angry. "Sorry, sorry, sorry."

"It's okay."

She needed to get up. She needed to call Lacy and tell her not to come. "Wait," she said to him. "Give me your phone."

She would clean up the blood if he would give her the phone. She tried to sit up. She couldn't. She had to lie down and close her eyes. Just for a moment. She had to rest. She heard him go away. She heard a door open. Now is the time, she thought as if rehearsing lines in a play. The character says, now is the time. Now is the time and the actress gets up and walks the five steps to the front door. Now is the time, but Winnie could not get up. She would never get the part. No one wanted an actress who could only lie down. It hurt to shake her head. It hurt to move. She would never be an actress now or a real estate tycoon or even a birthday party clown. She would never be anything, but that was okay. It was all absolutely fine if she could just call Lacy. Her leg was wet. It did not seem right. When she got rid of that, when her leg was dry again, when she had spoken to Lacy, she could go to sleep.

Oren closed a door. He was coming back. She had missed her chance, but she knew there had never really been any chance.

She lay still on the couch. Maybe he would call Lacy and tell her not to come.

"Oren," she said. "I'll stay with you. I'll cook and clean and take care of you. I'll be your friend. Just let Lacy go. Forget about her. It's okay. I'll never see her again. I'll stay with you, if you'll leave her alone." She was crying. "Please. Just call her and tell her not to come."

She knew he didn't like tears, but she couldn't help it. She would stay with Oren and Lacy could go far away. She could go to Daisy's in New York. Daisy's apartment building was like a fortress. Lacy would be safe there.

"Shhhh," Oren said. "Lacy will be here soon."

"I don't want her to come."

"I won't hurt her."

A shooting pain made her scream. She tried to shake Cookie from her leg, but it just hurt worse. Oh! Cookie wasn't even there. She felt him, but he wasn't there.

"I wouldn't shake it like that," Oren said. And then, "It looks pretty bad."

She opened her eyes. He was frowning. The side of his face was red where she had hit him with the ice.

"I'm sorry."

Cookie scratched at the door. "Cookie! Stop it!"

Cookie clawed faster, harder, like a dog digging.

"One day he'll get out of there," Winnie whispered. "He'll get me."

"He won't. I won't let him."

"Promise me you won't hurt Lacy."

Oren nodded. It was the best she would get. "You're still bleeding." He lifted her leg and put it back down on top of a towel. Her leg began to twitch.

"Don't," he said. "Don't do that."

The twitch spread all over her body. She was trembling, shaking, and she couldn't stop.

"Winnie," he said. "Winnie, come on."

It meant so much when a lover called her by name. It always had. She yearned for the moment when a man said her name late at night, rolled over and breathed it into her hair. It was a gift, as if she was given back to herself, as if he was saying you, only you are the one I want.

"Don't cry," he said. "It's not that bad. Now that I've cleaned it up, I can see it'll be fine." His hands were gentle. The water was warm, but cool at the same time. "This is going to sting."

A liquid gurgled from a bottle. Then the pressure of a towel. And then the pain. She shrieked and he put his hand over her mouth to keep her quiet. He had put hot needles into her leg, all the way up to her stomach. Her back arched.

"Hold still," he said. "If you can."

He took his hand off her mouth. He was kneeling beside her. The fire subsided, but her leg was now in agony. She tried to breathe slowly and quietly. He concentrated on bandaging her. He took his knife out of his pocket and opened it. She half hoped he would kill her, kill the pain. He cut the gauze and the tape. Then he set the knife down on the coffee table. She thought it was sweat on his cheeks and then she saw it was tears.

Winnie reached for him, put her hand on his smooth arm, his young skin.

"We're all frightened," she whispered. "Everyone is scared to death. The world is such a scary place. So many people hate us. We don't even know them, and they hate us just for living. And now we've gotten in over our heads, haven't we? One thing came along and then another and another and we were swept up, we had to go with it, and suddenly it was out of control."

She was trying to make him understand. He wiped his eyes

and nodded.

"It seemed like such a good idea." He looked so sad. "A perfect plan."

"Tell me."

"I met Lacy online. I saw her picture, I read about her. We started emailing back and forth. Then texting. Then I asked for her number and I called her. She said she was eighteen. I swear I didn't know she was so young. She said you kept her locked in her room; only let her out for school. She said you let the dog bite her and you had a chauffeur that almost raped her and you did nothing about it. She said you wouldn't let her see her father. She said you made her wear shirts that itch and uncomfortable baggy pants and would not let her shower."

How unhappy did Lacy have to be to make up all these things? What life was Lacy missing? "Oh God." A prayer as much as an exclamation.

"I wanted to save her. I thought she would love me if I—if I—"

"If you killed me?"

"No. If I taught you a lesson. If I made you be nice to her. She and I would get married and you would learn—eventually—to appreciate what I had done."

She put her hand on his head. Her fingers tucked a curl of his clown-colored hair behind his tiny ear and stroked his cheek. "Don't be scared."

He closed his eyes. The tears did not stop.

"I'm not scared anymore," she reassured him. "Really, I'm not."

He bowed his head, touched his forehead to her thigh. She smoothed back his hair and wiped his tears from is cheek. Cookie scratched at the door. Winnie tried to stay focused.

"Lacy can't come here," she said. "She's too young. This will hurt her, damage her forever. We made a deal. I'll stay here. I'll give you whatever you like. Please," she whispered. "Tell her not to come."

She was so sure she was dying. Her body was a mass of pain, it could not last long. She would miss her darling girl. She missed her now, almost more than she could bear. Lacy's constant singing, the way she giggled, the curls on the back of her neck. Winnie groaned. She could not come here. Winnie had to stay alive long enough to make sure Oren told her not to come. Lacy had her life ahead of her. She was smart and she would survive this. Her father would help her and he would get her a good therapist. If only Winnie could make her one more sandwich. It seemed so important to make Lacy one more peanut butter and honey sandwich.

"I don't feel well," Winnie said and it was true. "I'm going to be sick."

He had a bowl there with a little soapy, bloody water. The same bowl she had used to clean the carpet. He got it to her just in time. She turned her head and vomited. There was nothing much to come up. She retched and dry heaved and he held her hair back from her face.

"Sorry. Thank you." He was sweet to help her.

Cookie scratched. He wouldn't stop. Scratching. Lusting.

"Cookie!" Oren shouted. "Cookie, for fucks sake!" He shook his head, took a deep breath, and turned to her leg. "You're still bleeding."

"If I bleed to death," she said. "Then it definitely wouldn't be your fault."

He stood up. He picked up his knife from the coffee table. She closed her eyes. She did not want the knife to be the last thing she saw.

"You're a good mom," Oren said quietly, "I can tell. You

worry about everything, the little things. You would never let anyone hurt your daughter. You love her. You like animals too. You take care of them. You give them the food they like and you pet them and talk to them. You don't think they smell. You bake pies and make dinner at night and help Lacy with her homework. You love your daughter. You smile at her even when she can't see you. You touch her all the time, whenever you can, when you walk past her, or when you give her something to eat. She doesn't even notice you, but you're always there.

"You smell good," he continued. "You are good at keeping things clean, staying organized, making the bed. You never forget a birthday or a class project or what she wants to be for Halloween. You buy the good candy. You make her eat healthy food, not just fast food. You want her to go to bed early and get plenty of sleep and get up and go to school and pay attention and do well. "

"No mother is that perfect all the time."

"I should have known how good you are when I picked you up. I should have seen that and let you go right away." He sighed. "Why me? Why do the bad things always happen to me?"

Winnie gave a little laugh. "I think, this time, the bad thing is actually happening to me."

Cookie clawed at the door. It sounded like he was coming through the wood. She reached for Oren involuntarily. When she touched his thigh he tensed. Then he relaxed and put his hand over hers.

Outside, they heard an ice cream truck. The annoying repetitive tinkling song, the first four measures of "You Are My Sunshine," grew louder and louder as the truck came closer. Outside there were children. Fathers getting home from work. Mothers offering dollar bills for ice cream just to keep them quiet until dinner, and bath, and bed. A child's voice called to a friend again and again. The singsong blended with the bells on the truck. She and Oren looked at each other. Then he turned back to the closed Venetian blinds. Listening.

"Want a popsicle?" she asked. "Sure is a hot day."

Oren almost smiled, but looked toward the kitchen. Cookie's scratching was becoming a soundtrack, their soundtrack. He stood up. He opened the front door, made sure the screen was unlocked.

"You can go," he said.

"What are you going to do?"

"Who cares?"

"Wait."

"Go. Isn't that what you want?"

If she started to leave, he decided, he would kill her. He would stab her in the back as she headed out the door. He would not stand one more betrayal. He would kill her if she tried to leave.

"Go on," he said again.

Part of him wanted her to try it. Part of him, the bigger part, was begging silently for her to stay. He waited. She shook her head.

"I can't go now," she said in the smallest voice. "Not until you tell Lacy not to come."

As if on cue, his cell phone rang with Lacy's special, heavy metal ringtone. He looked at Winnie. Silently she pleaded with him. Unfortunately, he had to finish what he started.

"Well?" he said into the phone. "Are you coming over?"

"I want to speak to my mother," Lacy replied.

Her voice sounded weak, tremulous. Good, Oren thought, she knew she was in trouble.

"Lacy! Stay away!" Winnie summoned her strength to shout. "Stay away!"

"You heard her," Oren said to Lacy. "Obviously she's fine, for now, as long as you get your ass over here. Better than fine, your mother is a very honest woman."

Lacy was quiet. She did not have anything to say to that. He heard papers rustling.

"Where are you?"

"School. I'm still at school."

"Can you get over here?"

"My—my friend can take me."

"Do you even know how to drive?" She did not reply. "What about that night you told me about? Remember? You broke out of your room, snuck past the guards, and took your mother's Mercedes?"

He stamped his foot, ran his hand through his hair. He had not meant to get into this now. When she arrived there would be time enough to clear up all the lies, to get everything out into the open.

"Oren, I'm sorry," Lacy whispered.

That surprised him. "Really?"

"Please don't hurt my mother."

"She's the good girl here."

There was a pause and some more rustling of papers. Then Lacy's voice, tiny, scared. "What's your address?"

His heart went out to her. She was still the beautiful girl he loved. She realized her mistakes and she wanted to make amends. He gave her the address and told her it would take about thirty minutes. He did not want to hang up, but he had to, so she could find her friend with the car.

"I can't wait to see you," he said. "To meet you face to face."

When he set his cell phone down he saw that Winnie was crying. "Don't worry." He squatted down beside her. "It's going to be great. You and I will talk to her."

The terrible day did not seem so bad. His plan had worked after all. Lacy was coming to his house. He had wanted her here for so long. This is what his plan was about. This was everything he wanted. He was not stupid; he was not an idiot. He had made it happen. She was coming and his anger liquefied and drained away. She had lied because she was young and she wanted to impress him. She was young, but not so young. He could wait for her. Plenty of high school students got married. He smiled at Winnie.

"I'll be nice to her. You'll see. I will."

"Like you were to that other girl?"

"What other girl?" He had no idea what she was talking about. It had been years since he had a girlfriend. More than years, it seemed there had never been another girl in his life. Only Lacy.

Winnie's eyes fluttered and shut. Her face was pale gray and shiny as if oiled. She looked like a vampire.

"Winnie," he said. "Winnie, sit up."

She didn't move so he took her wrists and pulled her to sitting. She grimaced and complained with a groan.

"You don't look good. You need to sit up, feel better. You can go home soon. I'll drive you both home. We'll have dinner together." His fantasy come true. Still she did not move or open her eyes. "I'll bring you some water."

When he got to the kitchen, Cookie was waiting for him. His head bobbed up and down. His tongue flicked in and out. His tail whipped across the floor. His dewlap was puffed up and extended. He was really, really angry.

"Not now, Cookie."

Oren stepped across him to get a glass and water and Cookie lunged. Oren jumped out of the way just in time.

"Cut it out." He would not let Cookie ruin his happiness

that Lacy was coming. "I'll give you a good scratch later."

But when he stepped back toward the sink, Cookie snapped at him again. Oren gave up and turned to the refrigerator. He had a Coke in there somewhere. It would probably be better anyway—give her some energy.

Winnie heard Oren talking to his pet. All she really wanted to do was lie back down and go to sleep, but she knew Lacy was coming. She had to last that long. More than that, she had to figure this out for Lacy. The front door was still open and the screen unlatched. The air coming in was cool and dry. She took deep breaths and struggled to her feet. Her bitten leg hurt like hell, but it supported her. The worst of it was the wet squish of blood in her shoe. Maybe she could get outside and wait on the front step in the cool afternoon air. If she could get outside, she could keep Lacy from coming in.

Then she saw Oren's cell phone on the coffee table. He had left it there. She would call Lacy and tell her not to come. She would call Jonathan and tell him to come get his daughter, take her far away. She held the phone in her hand and her brain clicked back into gear. What? Jonathan? Dial 9-1-1. She almost laughed—happy to be thinking again. But the kitchen door swooshed open and Oren was returning. She stuffed the phone down the back of her tennis panties and sat down.

"Here." He handed her the soda.

"Thank you." She popped it open and drank it. It was cold and bubbly and absolutely delicious. She felt the phone press into the small of her back, a plan, an idea. The pain swelled and receded like waves against the shore. It was there, but she could stand it.

"Oren," she said. "Don't you have someone tied up, passed out, hurt in the back room?"

His eyes went wide as he remembered. "Oh. Mary."

"And there's blood all over the carpet. The new carpet. And Lacy is squeamish."

"Shit. Fuck."

He looked around. A trail of Winnie's blood led from the kitchen door, across the white carpet to the couch. The blood had soaked the towel he put under her and dripped into a sea anemone-shaped puddle on the floor.

"It wasn't me. It was Cookie. I bandaged you. Helped you. The carpet is not my fault."

He picked up the bowl of bloody water and vomit. It was obvious he did not know what to do with it.

"Dump it in the toilet." Winnie used her mom voice. "It will flush away."

He hesitated.

"Go," she said. "Lacy will be here soon."

He practically ran to the bathroom. Winnie took the phone from behind her. She flipped it open, but then she couldn't see the numbers. They swam, blurred, melted in front of her. Then he was back. She closed the phone and hid it under her good hand, pressed down into the awful couch.

"Now," she said.

"Now what?"

"Don't you think you should deal with Mary? Isn't that her name? The girl in the back? The girl who fell?"

"Well, but—" He did not want to go back there. Winnie knew it.

"Lacy will not be happy if another woman comes out of that room."

"She is not my girlfriend."

"It doesn't matter. It looks bad."

"Okay, okay, okay."

Cookie was scratching again. Faster, louder, worse than ever.

"Cookie, shut up!" Oren shouted.

Winnie knew how flustered he was. The girl of his dreams was coming. Lacy was the reason he had ruined his entire life. What if she was not what he wanted? What if she didn't like him?

"You should wash your face. Put a shirt on."

"Cookie!"

"Can you calm Cookie down? You don't want Lacy to be scared of him. You want them to like each other, right? Can't you give him something?"

Oren turned left and right. She had given him too many instructions. Mary. Blood. His face. His shirt. And Cookie. Cookie scratched and scratched. He dropped his head between his knees, and then swung it up. His face was red and wild. "COOKIE!"

He slammed the front door shut and whirled around. He strode to the kitchen door.

"No, Oren. Don't."

He looked over his shoulder at her, at her leg, and at the blood all over his uncle's carpet. He was cold now in his hot house. The late afternoon light turned dark and brittle. His heart flopped in his chest. He could not breathe or see or think. All his happiness was gone and it was Cookie's fault.

He pushed open the kitchen door with both hands. "SHUT UP!"

Cookie hissed.

"FUCK YOU!" He kicked his friend hard in the ribs. There was a scrape as Cookie slid back across the floor, his long nails clawing the linoleum. "KEEP AWAY FROM THIS DOOR." Oren kicked him again, in the belly, and again. Cookie gave a woof and then began to squeal. It was the stupid thing's own fault. Cookie had brought this on himself. With every kick

Oren's heart accelerated.

"Don't hurt him," came Winnie's thin, tired voice from the living room.

Oren nodded as he kicked Cookie again. Winnie was beginning to understand. Only Winnie knew how to help him. He had opened the front door and she had stayed with him. He had gone into the kitchen and she stayed on the couch. Oren wanted her to make him a grilled cheese sandwich for dinner. Kick. Kick. Kick.

Winnie carefully opened the cell phone. She dialed. 9. 1. 1. He had not locked the front door again when he closed it and this time the screen was ajar. When she got out of here, when Lacy was safe, she would make everyone see the Oren she had seen.

"Help," she said into the phone. "I've been kidnapped."

Oren rushed in, grabbed the cell phone from her and threw it against the wall. It broke. He leaned over her and almost fell.

"I trusted you."

"I was only calling the doctor. I need a doctor."

"I take care of you!"

She saw his agony, his glazed eyes and trembling hands. Something had happened.

"Oren," she said, "What did you do?"

His mouth fell open. He dropped his head. His arms crossed around his ribs, his hands grabbing on tight to his shoulders. He seemed to catch himself, trying to literally hold himself together. He held his breath as if he wanted to get rid of the hiccups.

"What is it?" she asked again.

"I hurt Cookie."

"Come here."

He lurched toward her and fell onto his knees. She put her good hand in his hair. He looked up, took her hand and held it to his face. He stared into her eyes. She sighed. He was a beautiful boy, as familiar to her as her own past. He made her think of Jonathan when she had met him. A man and a child rolled into one.

"Stupid iguana," he pouted.

"It's not your fault."

"Did I say it was?" And suddenly he was that other self. He stood and stepped away from her. The color crept back into his face. He looked at his watch. "Get up."   "Why?"

"I can't believe you broke my phone."

"You threw it."

"Get the fuck up!" He thumped on her shoulder.

She sat up slowly. She did not know if her call had even gone through or had lasted long enough for them to trace her. Gingerly she put her feet on the floor. She was dizzy, but she tried not to show it. She didn't want him to put her in that back room again. "I don't know if I can walk."

Oren took the knife out of his pocket and opened it. She could see her reflection in the blade.

"What is that for, Oren? You don't need that anymore."

A car came down the street and stopped in front of the house. Oren leaned over her to look out the blinds. Winnie twisted around to look too. She caught her breath. It was Lacy in some old brown car, driven by a boy. He seemed familiar, but she wasn't sure. Lacy was getting out of the car, frowning at the house. The boy got out on his side. Winnie banged on the window and shouted.

"No, Lacy! Go home! Don't come in here! Lacy, no!"

Lacy heard her. She hesitated outside. She looked back over her shoulder, down the street as if help would come. Winnie knew there was no help.

"Run away!"

Lacy took a step back toward the boy's car.

Oren smacked Winnie hard on the side of the head and she fell back onto the couch. He would not have her ruin this for him. Lacy was here, almost here, almost inside. He was not stupid. His plan had worked.

He leapt to the front door and opened it.

"Lacy!" he called. She was still looking down the street. "Lacy!"

She turned toward him. She was taller than he imagined and her hair was lighter than in the picture. The sun was behind her and she glowed, she radiated, a spirit, a sprite, his angel. She had been sent to him. She was his. He reached a hand toward her. She would not move. She was frozen in that perfect moment where they saw each other fully for the first time.

He heard sirens and he had time to wonder why before he saw police cars coming toward him from all directions. They squealed to a stop in front of his house. Three of them. Four. Half a dozen. How did they know? He could not believe Lacy had called them. It must have been that boy who was driving.

He slammed the front door shut and locked it. Winnie was looking out the window. She saw the police. Lacy was being hustled back into a police car. The boy was being pulled back too.

Oren grabbed Winnie by the arm and yanked her to her feet. She gasped from the pain in her leg. He had to think. He pressed the flat side of the knife blade against his cheek. The metal was so cool it made his skin tingle.

"We have to convince them," he said to Winnie. "They don't understand."

"No," she said. "No one understands."

"Except you."

She nodded and he loved her then. He really did.

"Help me," he said. "How do I show them who I am?"

"Let me talk to them."

She shuffled toward the front door, but Oren knew he could not let her open it. A man's voice came over a loudspeaker. "Oren Baines. Let her go."

He could not stay in the house any longer. They would be coming in after him. He needed time to convince them he had just been following a plan. None of it was his fault. He was not stupid. He had followed a plan. He had expected them to put his name in the paper, practically give him a medal for single-handedly turning a horrible witch into a loving, considerate parent. It was not his fault that Lacy had lied to him. It was not his fault. He dragged Winnie with him toward the kitchen. He could go out the back door. They could hide and get his car later. Winnie began to struggle.

"No, no," she said. "Not in there. Not Cookie. I can't."

"We have to."

Someone in a helmet and a vest and dark mirrored glasses was pounding on his front door. The kitchen was the only safe place. He pushed open the swinging door, but Winnie's legs buckled. She collapsed in the doorway. Oren caught her before her head hit the ground. Immediately Cookie started for her. The beating Oren had given him had only made him angrier. Oren pushed him away. He kept coming back. He would never give up. Oren looked down at Winnie cradled in his arms, her face so pale and slick with sweat. One strand of her dark hair crossed her face. He pulled it free. Cookie snapped and chomped. Winnie opened her eyes and smiled at Oren.

"You're a good boy," she said. "As soon as this is over, I want you to come home with me."

They were hitting the front door with something. They would break it and then he would have to pay for that too. He started to cry. This was all too hard. Cookie would never leave her alone; after having a taste of her he would always want more. Winnie would never be safe. And Oren realized he would not be happy without her. He wanted to go home with Winnie. He needed it. With or without Lacy. It was Winnie he loved. He looked from Cookie to Winnie. Her eyes were closed and her breathing scratchy. Her leg was bleeding through the bandage. Cookie started for her.

"No, Cookie. No."

He pulled Winnie to safety, left her lying on the living room floor, and then went back to the kitchen. There was no decision left to make. He was not afraid. This was just Oren doing what had to be done. He straddled his oldest, only friend and drove the knife deep through the thick, scaly skin into the flesh beneath. Cookie writhed, but he did not fight as much as seven feet, 165 pounds was able. His final gift to Oren was a quick surrender.

The door broke open. Oren was afraid for Winnie. They would trample her. He hurried out to stand guard, knife in hand, iguana guts and blood spattered all over his white undershirt.

The SWAT team rushed into the house. They saw Winnie's blood covered body and Oren standing over her with the knife and opened fire. He was dead before she got her eyes open.

34.

A tropical bird hovered outside her window. It was irides-
cent green in the sun. The feathers shone and shimmied like
sequins on a costume. It had a bright yellow beak and it
looked right at her, turning its head this way and that, staring
at her from one beady eye and then the other. The bird was
going to speak, actually speak, and she was ready. Winnie had
waited all her life for this moment when something incredible would happen only to her. She had known all along this
day would eventually come. She had waited and she was
ready. She tried to lift one hand to wave, but she was mired
in the bed, weighted with cement blocks around her wrists
and ankles.

Oren, no, she thought. He did not want her to escape. He
wanted her to stay right there, to sink into the mattress and
disappear. Slowly, slowly, even her bones would disintegrate
until they became piles of dust on the blue and white ticking,
something to be brushed away. I won't go, she tried to say to
him, I'm not leaving you.

The bird was getting impatient. Winnie forced herself to
concentrate. Tell me, bird. Tell me.

The mysteries of life were about to be answered.

"I can see so far when I fly." The bird's voice was deep and
masculine. "Everything I see is beautiful." It swooped away.

"Oren," she said aloud. "Did you hear that?"

"Are you awake?"

She turned her head. Jonathan sat beside her. Jonathan.

"Oh," she said. "What are you doing here?"

"Jesus, Winifred. I was scared to death."

And then she knew everything. Remembered everything. Too much. She closed her eyes again. She was in the hospital. Her head hurt and they had put uncomfortable bandages on her stomach and her left hand and wrist were in a cast. Her leg throbbed from Cookie's bite and she ached from the stitches the doctors had used there and elsewhere to repair the damage from his teeth and claws.

But Cookie was dead. Oren had killed him. For her. He had killed his best friend for her. And Lacy.

"Where's Lacy? Jonathan, is Lacy all right? Where is she?"

"Yes. Shh. She'll be right back. She went to get something to eat."

Food did not sound good. Winnie swallowed and tried not to think of the bowl of bloody water that Oren had held for her. The way he gathered her hair as she vomited. Was he there? In the hallway, waiting for Jonathan to leave? She thought she saw him dart across the open doorway. She heard him calling to her. He couldn't stay for long. Her breath caught, she reached for him. Wait. Wait.

"Oren," she said. "Oren?"

"You'll be glad to know they got him. He's dead."

She knew it before Jonathan finished his sentence. Her stomach clenched and cramped around the truth. She knew Oren was gone like she knew the curls of his hair, the paleness of his skin, his freckles like constellations, his fingernails bitten to small scabby crescents. His hand on her back as she leaned against him. Tears in his small, green eyes. His little boy face inches from hers, so close she could have licked the sweat from his upper lip. He brought her aspirin. He didn't give her to the reptile man. What had she done for him?

"You're amazing," Jonathan grinned, "The cops say you did an incredible job staying alive. Especially after he killed that other woman."

The girl in the back room. But she had only fallen. Oren had not killed her. Winnie squeezed her eyes shut. She heard the organ music. She smelled the hot sugar in the cotton candy machine. She knew he was at the hot dog truck. Welcome! Welcome one and all!

"I'm sorry," she said. "I'm sorry."

She could have saved him. She could not have saved him. But he had saved her.

"No apology necessary."

Not Jonathan. Not him.

"Don't cry. You're safe now. You're going to be fine."

She hadn't realized she was crying. She sneezed. Jonathan handed her the box of tissues. Gray, industrial curtains covered the hospital room's only window. How would that magical bird ever find her?

"Jonathan."

"Yes?"

He leaned closer. She caught the strong scent of his expensive aftershave and underneath it, faintly, of meat. She had to turn her head away. He was like a limb that had been amputated a long time ago and someone had dug it up and handed it to her to hold. She recognized it, the moles and the hairs and even the smell, but it had become alien and repulsive.

"Open the curtains? Please?"

Jonathan walked around the bed and pulled the curtains

back. The California sky was so blue and cloudless, it hurt her chest to look at it.

"Your mother sent those flowers." Jonathan nodded toward an enormous, exotic bouquet. It took up half the room, but Winnie had not noticed it before. "She can't come, she's doing a play." Jonathan shook his head. "Daisy," he said with a sigh. "She wants me to tell you all the press you're getting could start you on a real career."

"Press?"

"There's a swarm outside the hospital. My agent has been fielding all your calls. Lots of calls. They want you on talk shows; somebody wants you to write a book; one of those TV cop dramas wants you to do a walk on; a journalist wants to write your life story. Everybody wants you."

He waited for her to thank him. She closed her eyes again.

"You're smart," he continued, "Still attractive. Victim, survivor, this true life crime stuff sells. You can strike while the iron is on."

"Hot," she said. "While the iron is hot."

Winnie knew he was right. Now was the time. Now was really the time. Her mother, Jonathan, her friends and coworkers would all be so impressed.

Jonathan spoke proudly, "You could really be someone."

He sounded like her mother. He sounded like himself. He sounded like everyone she had ever known. Except Oren. I am someone, she thought, I always was.

Lacy came running into the room and threw her arms around Winnie, climbing right onto the bed beside her.

"Mommy!"

"Don't hurt her," Jonathan warned.

"I'm okay."

"I'm so sorry. I'm so sorry."

Lacy's curls tickled her nose and Lacy's arms pressed on her sore neck and head. Winnie took a deep breath of vanilla oil and watermelon shampoo, cigarette smoke and baby girl all mixed up together. The same old blue sky, the same old ex-husband, the same old young beautiful wonderful daughter babbling about how scared she had been, how brave her mother was, how her new boyfriend had been a hero. Winnie held on tight.

ACKNOWLEDGMENTS

I would like to thank Sabine Phillips, Executive Director of the Reptile and Amphibian Rescue Network, for answering all my questions and letting me spend so much time with her four beautiful rescued iguanas. Thank you to my wonderful editors, Elizabeth Clementson and Robert Lasner, for their invaluable guidance. For hanging in there with me, many thanks to my agent, Terra Chalberg. For reading and listening, thank you to Diane Arieff, Heather Dundas, Seth Greenland, Denise Hamilton, Sally Harrison-Pepper, David Ivanick, Dinah Lenney, Kerry Madden, Donna Rifkind, Leslie Schwartz, Lienna Silver, and Ellen Slezak. Thank you to the United States Fish & Wildlife Service and The Humane Society for all they do. And to Tod, Benjamin, and Thea, who are so good at my care and feeding: you make it all worthwhile.